# SUSAN PALWICK
# *The Fate of Mice*

TACHYON PUBLICATIONS | SAN FRANCISCO

The Fate of Mice
Copyright © 2007 by Susan Palwick

Cover design: Ann Monn
Interior design & typography: John D. Berry
The typeface is Mercury.

Tachyon Publications
1459 18th Street #139
San Francisco, CA 94107
(415) 285-5615
www.tachyonpublications.com

Series Editor: Jacob Weisman

ISBN 10: 1-892391-42-2
ISBN 13: 978-1-892391-42-1

Printed in the United States of America
by Worzalla

First Edition: 2007

9 8 7 6 5 4 3 2 1

# THE FATE OF MICE

"Chilling and finely tuned . . . Palwick avoids pat solutions, offering instead a deeply felt, deeply moving tale."
*Publishers Weekly*

"Rewarding...Palwick's characterization of Emma is superb, as truthful as that of Scout in *To Kill a Mockingbird*. Emma's compelling voice carries this book into the world of first-class storytelling."
*Seattle Times*

"Simple, strong, and very powerful...a true page-turner.... A book so achingly true you want to thank the author. A book like this, a story that can captivate us and raise our awareness, tells truths that need to be told."
*Raleigh News & Observer*

"It is a deeply moving book. Palwick's withering understatements of pain are laced with a regret for the lost magic of childhood – even a ruined childhood."
GEOFF RYMAN, AUTHOR OF *Was* and *Air*

"*Flying in Place* is compelling, wrapping deep-empathy insights in lyric poetry to show us the monster behind the mask."
ANDREW VACHSS, AUTHOR OF *Dead and Gone*

"Palwick combines sharp political commentary with pleasing flights of fancy with deep psychological insight – and all in prose clear as water. Delicately balanced between hope and heartbreak, these are stories you'll remember."

KAREN JOY FOWLER, AUTHOR OF *The Jane Austen Book Club*

"This is a collection of magnificent, heart-breaking stories. Susan Palwick sees the world with a fearless clarity and tells a truth so sharp it makes you weep. Be warned: long after you close the book, these stories will haunt you. They'll stay with you, changing who you are and how you see the world around you."

PAT MURPHY, AUTHOR OF *The City, Not Long After*

"*The Fate of Mice* shines light on our dark secrets with compassion, wit, and very fine writing."

SHEILA WILLIAMS, EDITOR OF *Asimov's Science Fiction Magazine*

"These stories are brilliant and thought-provoking, as well as packing an unexpectedly intense emotional punch."

Jo Walton, author of *Tooth and Claw* and *Farthing*

"Graced with exceptionally intimate understanding of its characters, Palwick's beautifully crafted tale of exiles struggling to come to terms with a deeply troubled earth is exquisite."

*Booklist*, STARRED REVIEW

"A triumphant testament to the transcendent power of love and tribute to what being a stranger in a strange land truly means, Palwick's long-awaited second novel (after 1992's *Flying in Place*) succeeds as a heart-wrenching romance, a sharp meditation on refugees and displaced persons and a tragicomedy of cultural differences."

*Publishers Weekly*, STARRED REVIEW

"...a unique story of a family's love and the power of forgiveness to transcend the boundary between life and death...highly recommended."
*Library Journal*, STARRED REVIEW

"...terrifying intimacy... American ironies...lingering mystery, and raw, authentic emotions."
*Locus*

PRAISE FOR *Flying in Place*:

"One of the best and most moving novels by a new author I have read in years."
ALLISON LURIE, PULITZER PRIZE–WINNING AUTHOR OF
*Foreign Affairs*

"Packs a huge emotional wallop...*Flying in Place* is a brave and honest work, an impressive and important debut."
*San Francisco Examiner*

"*Flying in Place* is a bittersweet novel of a dead sister who returns to give our narrator the tools she need to break her family out of the poisonous pattern that is consuming them all...beautifully handled...a wonderful debut for a writer who has proved she can write well in long forms as well as short ones – may it be the first of many novels from Palwick, each one better than the ones before."
ORSON SCOTT CARD, AUTHOR OF *Ender's Game*

"The moving and compelling writing is sustained as the revelations unfold."
*Library Journal*

"Unflinching clarity and great dramatic power ... Susan Palwick, a young writer who has hitherto attracted some notice for her stories, poems, and essays, is with *Flying in Place* a novelist of moment."
*Newsday*

# CONTENTS

*for my father*

# Lessons in Mortality

PAUL DI FILIPPO

You're going to die. We all are. Maybe today, in the middle of reading (writing) this sentence. (Okay, I guess I made it through!) Maybe a hundred years from now. But unless and until some uber-technological "Rapture of the Nerds" rewrites the fatal certainties of the entirety of human existence up till now (and I'm not counting on any such rescue, although I haven't entirely dismissed eventual resurrection during the Big Crunch via the Omega Point), your passing from this mortal coil – my passing, the passing of all whom we love – is guaranteed.

Given this dire knowledge, the one sure prophecy granted to mankind, how then do we live our lives? How do we extract meaning from our limited days, experience pleasure and perhaps even joy while beneath the shadow of the Grim Reaper? Is such positivity even possible? Perhaps we should all just throw in the towel, adopt a nihilistic, despairing outlook on life, and trudge along glumly toward the grave.

Susan Palwick is someone who has pondered long, hard, and fruitfully on such matters, perhaps the central existential quandary of this human universe, employing a keen, unblinking, rational and yet empathetic gaze. And she has returned from her sojourn in the charnel grounds bearing answers, answers that do not minimize either the suffering or the triumphs of human existence.

Answers cloaked, as the best answers often are, in stories, myths, fables: the stories to be found in this fine collection, multivalent and captivating narratives whose own reasons for being transcend any mere preaching.

Palwick has two excellent, award-winning novels to her credit: *Flying in Place* (1992) and *The Necessary Beggar* (2005). This third volume represents a welcome addition to her small but hard-won canon. She is plainly not one of those writers who feels compelled to issue a book (or more) a year. The very sparseness of her output inclines us to regard her infrequent appearances as essential and weighty and valuable, and reading *The Fate of Mice* merely confirms this surface impression.

Each story herein occupies a different region in the great country of fantastical literature, exhibiting Palwick's extensive range and ambition. We meet with pure fantasy, horror, and science fiction, as well as subtle blendings of the three genres. In addition, we encounter a mimetic masterpiece, an example of excellent naturalism that would not be out of place in the pages of *The New Yorker*. But no matter what the form or venue, all of Palwick's work deals with the tender, aching dilemma addressed above.

How does one live boldly in the face of looming personal extinction?

The story that lends its title to this collection shows Palwick's ingenuity in framing this issue – and the universality of her concerns – by its very choice of protagonist: an intelligent talking mouse named Rodney. Raised above his bestial heritage of blissful unselfconsciousness by the interventions of science, he finds himself adrift about how to proceed with his new, larger, more problematical life, until he summons his courage and makes a break with fatalism. He's helped in this courageous course by a human, emphasizing another one of Palwick's lessons, that none of us are in this fix alone.

In subsequent stories, Palwick continues to find brilliant new emblems for her thesis.

Aligning itself with work by the great Carol Emshwiller, "Gestella" concerns a female werewolf (with an accelerated aging problem that dramatizes the issue of mortality even more keenly) whose doomed failure to consider her own best interests represents a cautionary parable about abandoning one's responsibilities in favor of societal pressure.

"The Old World" is a utopia, that rarest of science-fictional outings these days, one that would feel like a collaboration between Cory Doctorow and Ted Chiang, were it not utterly Palwickian. Here, Palwick humorously inverts her usual scenario, asking: how can one maintain glumness in a near-perfect world? The result illuminates the quandary from a totally novel direction.

Palwick can work on big scales, as in "The Old World," or on deliciously intimate levels, such as in "Jo's Hair," which chronicles the life of an inanimate hairpiece that enjoys all the experiences denied to its society-bound originator, before the severed halves achieve a unity at death.

The fate of a "mere" cat encapsulates a huge life lesson for the teen protagonist of "Going After Bobo," a tale which inhabits its contemporary Reno, Nevada landscape with the clarity of the best mainstream writing.

Like Lucius Shepard collaborating with Robert Sheckley, Palwick conjures up a zombie meditation on life and death in "Beautiful Stuff," wherein the dead are wiser than the living.

Another miniaturist wonder, "Elephant" is the record of a woman who wills herself pregnant, in the face of her own doubts about the life she's living. Bradbury might well have written something similar.

"Ever After" takes the Cinderella myth and grants it a horrific twist, sending its fairy godmother and young charge down a darkling road of independence from all seats of power. (It should be mentioned at this juncture that Palwick's strong feminist concerns usefully salt and season the universality of her approach.)

Replaying the old myth of the woman abducted from a fairy realm into human bondage, "Stormdusk" adds a twist that completely unbalances the old equations.

In a postapocalyptic setting where human freaks strive for the basic rights of life, Palwick constructs a love story worthy of Sturgeon, titled "Sorrel's Heart."

And finally, Palwick engineers a miraculous Vonnegut-like assault against the shared ills of all flesh with "GI Jesus," a bracingly heretical — yet ultimately deeply religious — story that conflates a mortally ill woman, the image of a lost soldier, and an icon of Jesus lodged in a most unlikely place, all against the perfectly-realized backdrop of Innocence, Indiana.

Taken as a whole, then, the varied stories in this volume offer a map of the labyrinth that is our lives. Not outward to a hypothetical exit, toward some impossible other world of infinite freedom (there is nothing beyond the labyrinth), but inward, to confront the Minotaur of Death, embrace him, and dance.

# THE FATE OF MICE

# The Fate of Mice

I remember galloping, the wind in my mane and the road hard against my hooves. Dr. Krantor says this is a false memory, that there is no possible genetic linkage between mice and horses, and I tell him that if scientists are going to equip IQ-enhanced mice with electronic vocal cords and teach them to talk, they should at least pay attention to what the mice tell them. "Mice," Dr. Krantor tells me acidly, "did not evolve from horses," and I ask him if he believes in reincarnation, and he glares at me and tells me that he's a behavioral psychologist, not a theologian, and I point out that it's pretty much the same thing. "You've got too much free time," he snaps at me. "Keep this up and I'll make you run the maze again today." I tell him that I don't mind the maze. The maze is fine. At least I know what I'm doing there: finding cheese as quickly as possible, which is what I'd do anyhow, anytime anyone gave me the chance. But what am I doing galloping?

"You aren't doing anything galloping," he tells me. "You've never galloped in your life. You're a mouse." I ask him how a mouse can remember being a horse, and he says, "It's not a memory. Maybe it's a dream. Maybe you got the idea from something you heard or saw somewhere. On TV." There's a small TV in the lab, so Dr. Krantor can watch the news, but it's not even positioned so that I can see it easily. And I ask him how watching something on TV would make me know what it *felt* like to be a horse, and he says I *don't* know what it feels like to be a horse, I have no idea what a horse feels like, I'm just making it up.

3

But I remember that road, winding ahead in moonlight, the harness pulling against my chest, the sound of wheels behind me. I remember the three other horses in harness with me, our warm breath steaming in the frosty air. And then I remember standing in a courtyard somewhere, and someone bringing water and hay. We stood there for a long time, the four of us, in our harness. I remember that, but that's all I remember. What happened next?

Dr. Krantor came grumbling into the lab this morning, Pippa in tow. "You have to behave yourself," he says sternly, and deposits her in a corner.

"Mommy was going to take me to the *zoo*," she says. When I stand on my hind legs to peer through the side of the cage, I can see her pigtails flouncing. "It's *Saturday*."

"Yes, I know that, but your mother decided she had other plans, and I have to work today."

"She did *not* have other plans. She and Michael were going to take me to the *zoo*. You just hate Michael, Daddy!"

"Here," he says, handing her a piece of graph paper and some colored pens. "You can draw a picture. You can draw a picture of the zoo."

"You could have gotten a *babysitter*," Pippa yells at him, her chubby little fists clenched against her polka-dot dress. "You're *cheap*. A babysitter'd take me to the *zoo!*"

"I'll take you myself, Pippa." Dr. Krantor is whining now. "In a few hours. I just have a few hours of work to do, okay?"

"*Huh*," she says. "And I bet you won't let me watch TV, either! Well, *I'm* gonna talk to Rodney!"

Pippa calls me Rodney because she says it's prettier than rodent, which is what Dr. Krantor calls me: The Rodent, as if in my one small body I contain the entire order of small, gnawing mammals having a single pair of upper incisors with a chisel-shaped edge. Perhaps he intends this as an honor, although to me it feels more like a burden.

I am only a small white mouse, unworthy to represent all the other rodents in the world, all the rats and rabbits and squirrels, and now I have this added weight, the mystery Dr. Krantor will not acknowledge, the burden of hooves and mane.

"Rodney," Pippa says, "Daddy's scared I'll like Michael better than him. If you had a baby girl mouse and you got a divorce and your daughter's Mommy had a boyfriend, would *you* be jealous?"

"Mice neither marry nor are given in marriage," I tell her. In point of fact, mice are non-monogamous, and in stressful situations have been known to eat their young, but this may be more than Pippa needs to know.

Pippa scowls. "If your daughter's Mommy had a boyfriend, would you keep her from seeing your daughter *at all*?"

"Sweetheart," Dr. Krantor says, striding over to our corner of the lab and bending down, "Michael's not a nice person."

"Yes he *is*."

"No, he's not."

"Yes he is! You're just saying that because he has a picture of a naked lady on his arm! But I see naked ladies in the shower after I go swimming with Mommy! Michael doesn't always ride his motorcycle, Daddy! He promised to take me to the zoo in his *truck*!"

"Oh, Pippa," he says, and bends down and hugs her. "I'm just trying to protect you. I know you don't understand now. You will someday, I promise."

"I don't *want* to be protected," Pippa says, stabbing the paper with Dr. Krantor's red pen. "I want to go to the zoo with Mommy and Michael!"

"I know you do, sweetheart. I know. Draw a picture and talk to the rodent, okay? I'll take you to the zoo just as soon as I finish here."

Pippa, pouting, mumbles her assent and begins to draw. Dr. Krantor, who frequently vents his frustrations when he is alone in the lab, has told me about Pippa's mother, who used to be addicted to cocaine. Supposedly she is drug-free now. Supposedly she is now fit to have joint custody of her daughter. But Michael, with his motorcycle and his naked lady, looks too much like a drug dealer to Dr. Krantor. "If anything happened to Pippa while she was with them," he has told me, "I'd never forgive myself."

Pippa shows me her picture: a stick-figure, wearing pigtails and a polka-dot dress, sitting in a cage. "Here's my picture of the zoo," she says. "Rodney, do you ever wish you could go wherever you wanted?"

"Yes," I say. Dr. Krantor has warned me that the world is full of owls and snakes and cats and mousetraps, innumerable kinds of death. Dr. Krantor says that I should be happy to live in a cage, with food and water always available; Dr. Krantor says I should be proud of my contribution to science. I've told him that I'd be delighted to trade places with him — far be it from me to deny Dr. Krantor his share of luxury and prestige — but he always declines. He has responsibilities in his own world, he tells me. He has to take care of his daughter. Pippa seems to think that he takes care of her in much the same way he takes care of me.

"I'm *bored*," she says now, pouting. "Rodney, tell me a story."

"Sweetheart," says Dr. Krantor, "the rodent doesn't know any stories. He's just a mouse. Only people tell stories."

"But Rodney can *talk*. Rodney, do you know any stories? Tell me a story, Rodney."

"Once upon a time," I tell her — now where did that odd phrase come from? — "there was a mouse who remembered being a horse."

"Oh, *goody!*" Pippa claps her hands. "Cinderella! I love that one!"

My whiskers quiver in triumph. "You do? There's a story about a mouse who was a horse? Really?"

"Of course! Everybody knows Cinderella."

I don't. "How does it end, Pippa?"

"Oh, it's a happy ending. The poor girl marries the prince."

I remember nothing about poor girls, or about princes, either, and I can't say I care. "But what about the horse who was a mouse, Pippa?"

She frowns, wrinkling her nose. She looks a lot like her father when she frowns. "I don't know. It turns back into a mouse, I think. It's not important."

"It's important to me, Pippa."

"Okay," she says, and dutifully trudges across the lab to Dr. Krantor. "Daddy, in Cinderella, what happens to the mouse that turned into a horse when it turns back into a mouse?"

I hear breaking glassware, followed by Dr. Krantor's footsteps, and then he is standing above my cage and looking down at me. His face is oddly pale. "I don't know, Pippa. I don't think anyone knows. It probably got eaten by an owl or a cat or a snake. Or caught in a trap."

"Or equipped with IQ boosters and a vocal synthesizer and stuck in a lab," I tell him.

"It's just a story," Dr. Krantor says, but he's frowning. "It's an impossible story. It's a story about magic, not about science. Pippa, sweetheart, are you ready to go to the zoo now?"

"Now look," he tells me the next day, "it didn't happen. It *never* happened. Stories are about things that haven't happened. Somebody must have told you the story of Cinderella — "

"Who?" I demand. "Who would have told me? The only people I've ever talked to are you and Pippa — "

"You saw it on TV or something, I don't know. It's a common story. You could have heard it anywhere. Now look, rodent, you're a very suggestible little animal and you're suffering from false memory syndrome. That's very common too, believe me."

I feel my fur bristling. Very suggestible little animal, indeed!

But I don't know how I can remember a story I've never heard, a story that people knew before I remembered it. And soon I start to have other memories. I remember gnawing the ropes holding a lion to a stone table; I remember frightening an elephant; I remember being blind, and running with two blind companions. I remember wearing human clothing and being in love with a bird named Margalo. Each memory is as vivid and particular as the one about being a horse. Each memory feels utterly real.

I quickly learn that Dr. Krantor doesn't want to hear about any of this. The only thing he's interested in is how quickly I can master successively more complicated mazes. So I talk to Pippa instead, when she comes to visit the lab. Pippa knows some of the stories: the poem about the three blind mice, the belief that elephants are afraid of mice. She doesn't know the others, but she finds out. She asks her mother and her friends, her teachers, the school librarian, and then she reports back to me while Dr. Krantor is on the other side of the lab, tinkering with his computers and mazes.

All of my memories are from human stories. There are also a witch and a wardrobe in the story about the lion; the mouse who is in love with the bird is named Stuart. Pippa asks her mother to read her these stories, and reports that she likes them very much, although the story with the bird in it is the only one where the mouse is really important. And while that story, according to Pippa, ends with Stuart looking for his friend Margalo, the story never says whether or not he ever finds her. The fate of mice seems to be of little importance in human stories, even when the mouse is the hero.

I begin to develop a theory. Dr. Krantor believes that language makes me very good at running mazes, that with language comes the ability to remember the past and anticipate the future, to plan and strategize. To humor him, I talk to myself while I run the mazes; I pause at intersections and ask myself theatrical questions, soliloquizing about the delicious cheese to be found at the end of the ordeal, recounting fond anecdotes of cheeses past. Dr. Krantor loves this. He is writing a paper about how much better I am at the mazes than previous mice, who had IQ boosting but no vocal synthesizers, who were not able to turn their quests for cheese into narrative. Dr. Krantor's theory is that language brings a quantum leap in the ability to solve problems.

But my theory, which I do not share with Dr. Krantor, is that human language has dragged me into the human world, into human tales about mice. I am trapped in a maze of story, and I do not know how to reach the end of it, nor what is waiting for me there. I do not know if there is cheese at the end of the maze, or an elephant, or a lion on a stone table. And I do not know how to find out.

And then I have another memory. It comes to me one day as I am running the maze.

In this memory I am a mouse named Algernon. I am an extremely smart mouse, a genius mouse; I am even smarter than I am now. I love this memory, and I run even faster than usual, my whiskers quivering. Someone has told a story about a mouse like me! There is a story about a very smart mouse, a story where a very smart mouse is important!

Pippa comes to the lab after school that day, scowling and dragging a backpack of homework with her, and when Dr. Krantor is working on his computer across the room, I tell her about Algernon. She has never heard of Algernon, but she promises to question her sources and report back to me.

The next day, when she comes to the lab, she tells me that the school librarian has heard of the Algernon story, but says that Pippa isn't old enough to read it yet. "She wouldn't tell me why," Pippa says. "Maybe the mouse in the story is naked?"

"Mice are always naked," I tell her. "Or else we're never naked, because we always have our fur, or maybe we're only naked when we're born, because we're furless then. Anyway, we don't wear clothing, so that can't be the reason."

"Stuart wears clothing."

"But the three blind mice don't." My personal opinion is that Stuart's a sell-out who capitulated to human demands to wear clothing only so that he could be the hero in the story. It didn't work, of course; the humans couldn't be bothered to give him a happy ending, or any ending at all, whether he wore clothing or not. His bowing and scraping did him no good.

I suspect that Algernon is non-monogamous, or perhaps that he eats his young, and that this is why the librarian considers the story unsuitable for Pippa. But of course I don't tell her this, because then her father might forbid her to speak to me altogether. I must maintain my appearance of harmlessness.

Am I a sell-out too? I don't allow myself to examine that question too closely.

Instead I tell Pippa, "Why don't you ask your mother to find the story and read it to you?" Since Pippa's mother doesn't mind letting her see naked women in the shower, she may not share the librarian's qualms about whatever misconduct Algernon commits in the story. It makes perfect sense to me that a very smart mouse would do things of which humans would not entirely approve.

"Okay," Pippa says. "The story's called 'Flowers for Algernon,' so it must have a happy ending. Mommy gets flowers from Michael on her birthday."

"Oh, that's lovely!" I tell Pippa. I've never seen humans eating flowers — Pippa favors chocolate and once gave me a piece, which I considered an entirely inadequate substitute for seeds and stems — but my opinion of people rises slightly when I learn this. I'm very optimistic about this story.

The next day, Pippa tells me cheerfully that her mother found a copy of the story, but is reading it herself before she reads it to Pippa, just in case the librarian had a good reason for saying that Pippa shouldn't read it. This frustrates me, but I have no choice but to accept it. "I told her that you'd had a good dream about it," Pippa says happily. "She was glad."

The next day, Pippa does not come, and Dr. Krantor makes me run the maze until my whiskers are limp with exhaustion. The day after that, Pippa returns. She tells me, frowning, that her mother has finished reading the story, but agrees with the school librarian that Pippa shouldn't read it. "But I told her she had to: I told her it wasn't fair not to let me know what happens to Algernon." Her voice drops to a whisper now. "I told her she was being like Daddy, trying to keep me from knowing stuff. And that made her face go all funny, and she said, okay, she'll start reading it to me tonight."

"Thank you," I tell Pippa. I'm truly touched by her persistence on my behalf, but also a little alarmed: What in the world could have shocked both a staid school librarian and Pippa's unconventional mother?

It takes me a while to find out. Pippa doesn't come back to the lab for a week. Dr. Krantor is frantic, and as usual when he's worried, he talks to me. He paces back and forth in front of my cage. He rants. "She says it's because she has too much homework, but she can do her homework here! She says it's because her mother's taking her to the zoo after school, but how can that be true if she has all that homework? She says it's because she and her mother and Michael have to plan a trip. A trip! Her mother's brainwashing her, I know it! Michael's brainwashing both of them! I'm going to lose Pippa! They'll flee the country and take her with them! He's probably a Colombian druglord!"

"Just calm down," I tell Dr. Krantor, although I'm worried too. The string of excuses is clearly fake. I wonder if Pippa's absence has anything to do with Algernon, but of course I can't talk about that, because Dr. Krantor doesn't approve of my interest in human stories.

"Don't tell me to calm down, rodent! What would you know about it? You don't have children!"

And whose fault is that? I think sourly. Often have I asked for a companion, a female mouse, but Dr. Krantor believes that a mate would distract me from his mazes, from the quest for cheese.

He storms back to his computer, muttering, and I pace inside my cage the same way Dr. Krantor paced in front of it. What in the world is wrong with Pippa? What in the world happened to Algernon? Was he eaten by a cat, or caught in a trap? Right now I would welcome even the mazes, since they would be a distraction, but Dr. Krantor is working on something else. At last, sick of pacing, I run on my exercise wheel until I am too exhausted to think.

Finally Pippa returns. She is quieter than she was. She avoids me. She sits at the table next to Dr. Krantor's computer, all the way across the lab, and does her homework. When I stand up on my hind legs, I can see her, clutching her pencil, the tip of her tongue sticking out in concentration. And I see Dr. Krantor frowning at her. He knows she is acting oddly, too. He stands up and looks down at her workbook. "Pippa, sweetheart, why are you working so hard on that? That's easy. You already know it. Why don't you go say hello to the rodent? He missed you. We both missed you, you know."

"I have to finish my homework," she says sullenly.

"Pippa," Dr. Krantor says, frowning even more now, "your homework is done. That page is all filled out. Pippa, darling, what's the matter?"

"Nothing! Leave me alone! I don't want to be here! I want to go home!"

I'm afraid that she's going to start crying, but instead, Dr. Krantor does. He stands behind her, bawling, his fists clenched. "It's Michael, isn't it! You love Michael more than you love me! Your mother's brainwashed you! Where are they taking you, Pippa? Where are you going on this trip? Whatever your mother's said about me is a lie!"

I stare. Dr. Krantor has never had an outburst like this. Pippa, twisted around in her chair, stares too. "Daddy," she says, "it has nothing to do with you. It's not about *you!*"

He snuffles furiously and swipes at his face with a paper towel. "Well then," he says, "why don't you tell me what it's about?"

"It's about Algernon!" she says, and now she's crying, too.

I'm very afraid. Something even worse than a trap or a cat must have happened to Algernon.

It's Dr. Krantor's turn to stare. "Algernon? Who's Algernon? Your mother has a new boyfriend named Algernon? What happened to Michael? Or she has *two* boyfriends now, Michael *and* Algernon? Pippa, this is terrible! I have to get you out of there!"

"Algernon the *mouse*, Daddy!"

Dr. Krantor squints at her. "What?"

And the whole story comes out. Pippa breaks down and tells him everything, hiccupping, as I cower in my cage. Pippa's upset, and it's my fault. Dr. Krantor's going to be furious at me. He won't let me have any more cheese. He'll take away my exercise wheel. "That's why I've been staying away," Pippa says. "Because of Algernon. Because of what happens to Algernon. Daddy – "

"It's just a story," Dr. Krantor says. It's what I expect him to say. But then he says something I don't expect. "Pippa, you have to tell the rodent – "

"His name's Rodney, Daddy!"

"You have to tell Rodney what happened, all right? Because he's been waiting to find out, and he can hear us talking, and not knowing will make him worry more. It's just a story, Pippa. Nothing like that has happened to my mice, the ones here in the lab. I promise. Come on. I'll help you."

Astonished, I watch Dr. Krantor carry Pippa across the lab to my cage. "Pippa," he says when he gets here, "Rodney's missed you. Say hello to Rodney. Do you want to hold him?"

She snuffles and nods, shyly, and Dr. Krantor says, "Rodney, if Pippa holds you, you won't run away, right?"

"No," I say, even more astonished than I was before. Pippa's never been allowed to hold me before, because Dr. Krantor's afraid that she might drop me, and I represent a huge investment of research dollars. But now Dr. Krantor opens the top of the cage and lifts me out by my tail, the way he does when he's going to put me in the maze; but instead he puts me in Pippa's cupped palms, which are very warm. She peers down at me. Her breath is warm too, against my fur, and I see tears still shining in the corners of her eyes. "See?" Dr. Krantor tells her. "Rodney's a very healthy mouse. He's fine, Pippa. There's nothing wrong with him, even though he's smart."

I don't understand this, and nobody's answering the main question. "What happens to Algernon?" I ask.

"He dies," Pippa says in a tiny voice.

"Oh," I say. Well, I'd deduced as much. "A cat gets him, or a mouse-trap?" And Pippa's face starts to crumple as she strokes my back, and I hear Dr. Krantor sigh.

"Rodney," he says, "In the story 'Flowers for Algernon,' the mouse

Algernon has been IQ boosted, the way you are. Only the story was written before that was really possible. Anyway, in the story, the mouse dies as a result of the experiment."

"He dies because he's smart," Pippa says mournfully. "Except he gets stupid first. The experiment wears off, and he gets stupid again, and then he dies! The flowers are for his grave!"

"Right," Dr. Krantor says. "Now listen to me, you two. It's *just a story*. None of my mice have died prematurely as a result of the IQ boosting, and the IQ boosting hasn't worn off on any of them. All my mice stay smart, and they don't die any sooner than they would anyway. If anything, they live longer than non-enhanced mice. Okay? Does everybody feel better now?"

"But how did they die?" I ask, alarmed. "How could they die if they were here in their cages, where there aren't any owls or cats or snakes or mousetraps?"

Dr. Krantor shakes his head. "They just died, Rodney. They died of old age. All mice die, sometime. But they had good lives. I take care of my animals."

"What?" I say stupidly. All mice die? "I'm going to die? Even if there aren't any cats?"

"Not anytime soon," Dr. Krantor says. "Everything dies. Didn't you know that?" A drop of water splashes on me, and Dr. Krantor says, "Pippa, sweetheart, you don't have to cry. Rodney's fine. He's a healthy little mouse. Pippa, dear, if you're going to drown him, you'd better put him back in his cage."

And he helps her put me back in my cage, and he says he's going to take her out for ice cream, and he'll bring back some special cheese for me, and I won't even have to run a maze to get it, and they'll be back in a little while. All of these words buzz over me in a blur, as I huddle in my cage trying to make sense of what I've just learned.

I'm going to die.

I'm going to die. All mice die. That's why the stories about mice never say what happened to them, because everyone knows. The mice died. The mouse who became a horse died, and the mice who freed the lion died, and Stuart Little died. I curl into a ball in a corner of my cage and think about this, and then I uncurl and run very hard on my exercise wheel, so I won't have to think about it.

You have taught me language, and my profit on it is, I know how to fear.

Where did that line come from? I don't know, and it's not even really true. I feared things before I knew that I must die; I feared cats and snakes and mousetraps. But fear was always a reason to avoid things, and now I fear something I cannot avoid. I run on the exercise wheel, trying to flee the thing I have learned I cannot escape.

Dr. Krantor and Pippa come back. He has brought me a lovely piece of cheese, an aged cheddar far richer than what I usually find at the end of the maze. He and Pippa sit and watch me nibble at it, and then he says, "Are you all right, Rodney? Do you feel better now?"

"No," I tell him. "You aren't really protecting me by keeping me in this cage, are you? You can't protect me. I'm going to die anyway. You aren't keeping me safe from death; you're denying me life." I think of my memories, the joy of galloping down the road, of chewing through rope, of loving a bird. "You're depriving me of experience. Dr. Krantor, please let me go."

"Let you go?" he says. "Rodney, don't be ridiculous! There are still cats and snakes and mousetraps out there. You'll live much longer this way. And you represent a huge investment of research dollars. I can't let you go."

"I'm not an investment," I snap at him. "I'm a creature! Let me go!"

Dr. Krantor shakes his head. "Rodney, I can't do that. I really can't. I'm sorry. I'll buy you a new exercise wheel, okay? And a bigger cage? There are all kinds of fancy cages with tunnels and things. We can make you a cage ten times bigger than this one. Pippa, you can help design Rodney's new cage. We'll go to the pet store and buy all the parts. It will be fun."

"I don't want a new exercise wheel," I tell him. "I don't want a new cage. I want to be free! Pippa, he says he can't let me go, but remember when he said you couldn't go to the zoo? It's the same thing."

"It's not the same thing at all," Dr. Krantor says. His voice isn't friendly anymore. "Rodney, I'm getting very annoyed with you. Pippa, don't you have more homework to do?"

"No," she says. "I already did my homework. The page is all filled out."

"Well then," Dr. Krantor says. "We'll go to the pet store — "

"I don't want you to go to the pet store! I want you to let me go! Pippa — "

"Stop trying to brainwash her!" Dr. Krantor bellows at me.

I can feel my tail flicking in fury. "You're the one brainwashing her!"

"Stop it," Pippa says. She's put her thumb in her mouth, muffling her words, and she looks like she's going to cry again. "Stop it! I hate it when you fight!"

We stop. I feel miserable. I wonder how Dr. Krantor feels. Pippa goes back to the table where her homework is, and Dr. Krantor goes back to his computer, and I nibble disconsolately on the excellent cheddar. No one says anything. After a while, Dr. Krantor comes back over to my cage and asks wearily, "All right, Rodney. Ready for the maze?"

"Are you out of your mind? I'm not going to run any more mazes! Why should I? What's in it for me?"

"Cheese!"

"I've had enough cheese today." I'm being ungracious, I know. I should thank him for the excellent cheddar. But I'm too angry to mind my manners.

"It's for my research, Rodney!"

"I don't *care* about your research, you imbecile!"

Dr. Krantor curses; Pippa, at her table, has covered her ears. Dr. Krantor reaches into my cage. He lifts me by the tail, none too gently, and plunks me down at the beginning of the maze. "Go," he says.

"Go groom yourself!"

He stomps away. I sit in the maze and clean my whiskers, fastidiously, and then I curl into a ball and take a nap.

I wake to feel myself being lifted into the air again. Dr. Krantor puts me back in my cage, even more roughly than he took me out, and says, "All right, Rodney. Look, this has all been a terrible mess, and I'm very sorry, but if you aren't willing to work tomorrow, we're going to have a problem."

"Going to?" I say.

Dr. Krantor rubs his eyes. "Rodney. Don't do this. You're expendable."

"I am? Even though I represent a tremendous investment of research dollars? Well then, you should have no problem letting me go."

He glares down at me. "Don't do this. Please don't do this. There are things I can do to make you compliant. Drugs. Electric shocks. I don't want to do any of that, and I know you don't want me to either. I want to keep a good working relationship here, all right, Rodney? Please?"

"You're threatening to torture me?" Outrage makes my voice even squeakier than usual. "Great working relationship! Hey, Pippa, did you hear that? Did you hear what your father just said?"

"Pippa isn't here, Rodney. Her mother came to pick her up while you were asleep. They were going to a birthday party. Rodney: Will you run the maze tomorrow, or will I have to resort to other methods?"

I'm frightened now. Dr. Krantor's voice is calm, reasonable. He's very matter-of-fact about the prospect of torturing me, and Pippa isn't here as a witness. He's probably bluffing. Coercion would probably compromise his data. But I don't know that for sure.

"Rodney?" he says.

"I'll think about it," I tell him. I have to buy myself time. Now I know why Stuart bowed and scraped. People are so much bigger than we are.

"Good enough," he says, his voice gentler, and reaches into the cage to give me another piece of the excellent cheddar. "Have a good night, Rodney." And then he leaves.

I stay awake all night, fretting. I try to find some way to escape from my cage, but I can't. I wonder if I could escape from the maze; I've never tried, but surely Dr. Krantor has made the mazes secure, also. I don't know what to do.

I dread the morning.

But in the morning, when Dr. Krantor usually arrives, I hear three sets of footsteps in the hallway outside, and two voices: Dr. Krantor's and a woman's.

"Why do you have to take her on this trip in the middle of the school year?" Dr. Krantor says. "And why do you have to talk to me about it now?"

"I already told you, Jack! Michael's family reunion in Ireland is in a month, so if we go we have to go then, and I need you to sign this letter saying that you know I'm not kidnapping her. I don't want any trouble."

Dr. Krantor grumbles something, and the lab door opens. Dr. Krantor and the woman – Pippa's mother! – come inside, still arguing. Pippa comes inside too. Pippa's mother walks to the computer; Pippa races to my cage.

"How *do* I know you aren't kidnapping her?" Dr. Krantor says. "Pippa, there's more of the new cheese over here, if you want to give Rodney a nice breakfast."

"Pippa," I whisper, "he threatened to torture me! Pippa – "

"Shhhhh," she whispers back, and opens my cage, and reaches into one of her pockets. "Don't make any noise, Rodney."

She's holding a mouse. A white mouse, just like me. Pippa puts the new mouse in the cage and we stare at each other in surprise, nose to nose, whiskers twitching, but then I feel Pippa grasp the base of my tail. She lifts me, and I watch the new mouse receding, and then she puts me in her pocket. I hear the cage close, and then we're walking across the room.

"All right, Jack, here's the itinerary, see? Here on this map? Jack, look at the map, would you? I'll tell you every single place we're going; it's not like we're spiriting her away without telling you."

"But how do I know you'll really go there? You could take her to, to, Spain or the South Pole or – "

"Michael doesn't have a family reunion in Spain or the South Pole. Jack, be reasonable."

"I'm bored," Pippa says loudly. "I'm going outside."

"Stay right by the front door, sweetheart!" That's Dr. Krantor, of course.

"I will," she says, and then I hear the lab door open and we're out, we're in the hallway, and then we go through another door and I smell fresh air and Pippa lifts me out of her pocket. She sits down on a step and holds me up to her face. "Mommy and I went to the pet store last night, Rodney, and we got another mouse who looks just like you. He was in the cage of mice that people buy to feed to their snakes. Being here is better for him. Daddy won't feed him to a snake."

"But your father will torture the other mouse," I say, "or worse. When he realizes it's just an ordinary mouse he'll be very angry. Pippa, he'll punish you."

"No, he won't," she says cheerfully, "or Mommy and Michael will say he isn't taking good care of me." She puts me down on the warm cement step. I feel wind and smell flowers and grass. "You're free, Rodney. You can have your very own adventures. You don't have to go back to that stupid maze."

"How will I find you?" As much as I yearned for freedom before, I'm terrified. There really are cats and snakes and mousetraps out here, and I've never had to face them. How will I know what to do? "Pippa, you have to meet me so I can tell you my stories, or no one will know what happens to me. I'll be just like all those other mice, the ones whose stories just stop when they stop being useful to the main characters. Pippa – "

But there are footsteps now from inside, forceful footsteps coming closer, and Dr. Krantor's voice. His voice sounds dangerous. "Pippa?

Pippa, what did you do to the rodent? It won't talk to me! I don't even think it's the same mouse! Pippa, did you put another mouse in that cage?"

I find myself trembling as badly as I would if a cat were coming. Pippa stands up. The sole of her sneaker is the only thing I can see now. From very far above me I hear her saying, "Run, Rodney."

And I do.

# Gestella

Time's the problem. Time and arithmetic. You've known from the beginning that the numbers would cause trouble, but you were much younger then – much, much younger – and far less wise. And there's culture shock, too. Where you come from, it's okay for women to have wrinkles. Where you come from, youth's not the only commodity.

You met Jonathan back home. Call it a forest somewhere, near an Alp. Call it a village on the edge of the woods. Call it old. You weren't old, then: you were fourteen on two feet and a mere two years old on four, although already fully grown. Your kind are fully grown at two years, on four feet. And experienced: oh, yes. You knew how to howl at the moon. You knew what to do when somebody howled back. If your four-footed form hadn't been sterile, you'd have had litters by then – but it was, and on two feet, you'd been just smart enough, or lucky enough, to avoid continuing your line.

But it wasn't as if you hadn't had plenty of opportunities, enthusiastically taken. Jonathan liked that. A lot. Jonathan was older than you were: thirty-five, then. Jonathan loved fucking a girl who looked fourteen and acted older, who acted feral, who *was* feral for three to five days a month, centered on the full moon. Jonathan didn't mind the mess that went with it, either: all that fur, say, sprouting at one end of the process and shedding on the other, or the aches and pains from various joints pivoting, changing shape, redistributing weight, or your poor gums bleeding all the time from the monthly growth and

21

recession of your fangs. "At least that's the only blood," he told you, sometime during that first year.

You remember this very clearly: you were roughly halfway through the four-to-two transition, and Jonathan was sitting next to you in bed, massaging your sore shoulder blades as you sipped mint tea with hands still nearly as clumsy as paws, hands like mittens. Jonathan had just filled two hot water bottles, one for your aching tailbone and one for your aching knees. Now you know he wanted to get you in shape for a major sportfuck – he loved sex even more than usual, after you'd just changed back – but at the time, you thought he was a real prince, the kind of prince girls like you weren't supposed to be allowed to get, and a stab of pain shot through you at his words. "I didn't kill anything," you told him, your lower lip trembling. "I didn't even hunt."

"Gestella, darling, I know. That wasn't what I meant." He stroked your hair. He'd been feeding you raw meat during the four-foot phase, but not anything you'd killed yourself. He'd taught you to eat little pieces out of his hand, gently, without biting him. He'd taught you to wag your tail, and he was teaching you to chase a ball, because that's what good four-foots did where he came from. "I was talking about – "

"Normal women," you told him. "The ones who bleed so they can have babies. You shouldn't make fun of them. They're lucky." You like children and puppies; you're good with them, gentle. You know it's unwise for you to have any of your own, but you can't help but watch them, wistfully.

"*I* don't want kids," he says. "I had that operation. I told you."

"Are you sure it took?" you ask. You're still very young. You've never known anyone who's had an operation like that, and you're worried about whether Jonathan really understands your condition. Most people don't. Most people think all kinds of crazy things. Your condition isn't communicable, for instance, by biting or any other way, but it is hereditary, which is why it's good that you've been so smart and lucky, even if you're just fourteen.

Well, no, not fourteen anymore. It's about halfway through Jonathan's year of folklore research – he's already promised not to write you up for any of the journals, and keeps assuring you he won't tell anybody, although later you'll realize that's for his protection, not yours – so that would make you, oh, seventeen or eighteen. Jonathan's still thirty-five. At the end of the year, when he flies you back to the United States with him so the two of you can get married, he'll be thirty-six. You'll be twenty-one on two feet, three years old on four.

Seven to one. That's the ratio. You've made sure Jonathan understands this. "Oh, sure," he says. "Just like for dogs. One year is seven human years. Everybody knows that. But how can it be a problem, darling, when we love each other so much?" And even though you aren't fourteen anymore, you're still young enough to believe him.

At first it's fun. The secret's a bond between you, a game. You speak in code. Jonathan splits your name in half, calling you Jessie on four feet and Stella on two. You're Stella to all his friends, and most of them don't even know that he has a dog one week a month. The two of you scrupulously avoid scheduling social commitments for the week of the full moon, but no one seems to notice the pattern, and if anyone does notice, no one cares. Occasionally someone you know sees Jessie, when you and Jonathan are out in the park playing with balls, and Jonathan always says that he's taking care of his sister's dog while she's away on business. His sister travels a lot, he explains. Oh, no, Stella doesn't mind, but she's always been a bit nervous around dogs – even though Jessie's such a *good* dog – so she stays home during the walks.

Sometimes strangers come up, shyly. "What a beautiful dog!" they say. "What a *big* dog!" "What kind of dog is that?"

"A Husky-wolfhound cross," Jonathan says airily. Most people accept this. Most people know as much about dogs as dogs know about the space shuttle.

Some people know better, though. Some people look at you, and frown a little, and say, "Looks like a wolf to me. Is she part wolf?"

"Could be," Jonathan always says with a shrug, his tone as breezy as ever. And he spins a little story about how his sister adopted you from the pound because you were the runt of the litter and no one else wanted you, and now look at you! No one would ever take you for a runt now! And the strangers smile and look encouraged and pat you on the head, because they like stories about dogs being rescued from the pound.

You sit and down and stay during these conversations; you do whatever Jonathan says. You wag your tail and cock your head and act charming. You let people scratch you behind the ears. You're a *good* dog. The other dogs in the park, who know more about their own species than most people do, aren't fooled by any of this; you make them nervous, and they tend to avoid you, or to act supremely submissive if avoidance isn't possible. They grovel on their bellies, on their backs; they crawl away backwards, whining.

Jonathan loves this. Jonathan loves it that you're the alpha with the other dogs — and, of course, he loves it that he's your alpha. Because that's another thing people don't understand about your condition: they think you're vicious, a ravening beast, a fanged monster from hell. In fact, you're no more bloodthirsty than any dog not trained to mayhem. You haven't been trained to mayhem; you've been trained to chase balls. You're a pack animal, an animal who craves hierarchy, and you, Jessie, are a one-man dog. Your man's Jonathan. You adore him. You'd do anything for him, even let strangers who wouldn't know a wolf from a wolfhound scratch you behind the ears.

The only fight you and Jonathan have, that first year in the States, is about the collar. Jonathan insists that Jessie wear a collar. "Otherwise," he says, "I could be fined." There are policemen in the park. Jessie needs a collar and an ID tag and rabies shots.

"Jessie," you say on two feet, "needs so such thing." You, Stella, are bristling as you say this, even though you don't have fur at the moment. "Jonathan," you tell him, "ID tags are for dogs who wander. Jessie will never leave your side, unless you throw a ball for her. And

I'm not going to get rabies. All I eat is Alpo, not dead raccoons: How am I going to get rabies?"

"It's the law," he says gently. "It's not worth the risk, Stella."

And then he comes and rubs your head and shoulders *that* way, the way you've never been able to resist, and soon the two of you are in bed having a lovely sportfuck, and somehow by the end of the evening, Jonathan's won. Well, of course he has: he's the alpha.

So the next time you're on four feet, Jonathan puts a strong chain choke collar and an ID tag around your neck, and then you go to the vet and get your shots. You don't like the vet's office much, because it smells of too much fear and pain, but the people there pat you and give you milk bones and tell you how beautiful you are, and the vet's hands are gentle and kind.

The vet likes dogs. She also knows wolves from wolfhounds. She looks at you, hard, and then looks at Jonathan. "A gray wolf?" she asks.

"I don't know," says Jonathan. "She could be a hybrid."

"She doesn't look like a hybrid to me." So Jonathan launches into his breezy story about how you were the runt of the litter at the pound: you wag your tail and lick the vet's hand and act utterly adoring.

The vet's not having any of it. She strokes your head; her hands are kind, but she smells disgusted. "Mr. Argent, gray wolves are endangered."

"At least one of her parents was a dog," Jonathan says. He's starting to sweat. "Now, *she* doesn't look endangered, does she?"

"There are laws about keeping exotics as pets," the vet says. She's still stroking your head; you're still wagging your tail, but now you start to whine, because the vet smells angry and Jonathan smells afraid. "Especially endangered exotics."

"She's a dog," Jonathan says.

"If she's a dog," the vet says, "may I ask why you haven't had her spayed?"

Jonathan splutters. "Ex*cuse* me?"

"You got her from the pound. Do you know how animals wind up at the pound, Mr. Argent? They land there because people breed them and then don't want to take care of all those puppies or kittens. They land there – "

"We're here for a rabies shot," Jonathan says. "Can we get our rabies shot, please?"

"Mr. Argent, there are regulations about breeding endangered species – "

"I understand that," Jonathan says. "There are also regulations about rabies shots. If you don't give my *dog* her rabies shot – "

The vet shakes her head, but she gives you the rabies shot, and then Jonathan gets you out of there, fast. "Bitch," he says on the way home. He's shaking. "Animal-rights fascist bitch! Who the hell does she think she is?"

She thinks she's a vet. She thinks she's somebody who's supposed to take care of animals. You can't say any of this, because you're on four legs. You lie in the back seat of the car, on the special sheepskin cover Jonathan bought to protect the upholstery from your fur, and whine. You're scared. You liked the vet, but you're afraid of what she might do. She doesn't understand your condition; how could she?

The following week, after you're fully changed back, there's a knock at the door while Jonathan's at work. You put down your copy of *Elle* and pad, bare-footed, over to the door. You open it to find a woman in uniform; a white truck with "Animal Control" written on it is parked in the driveway.

"Good morning," the officer says. "We've received a report that there may be an exotic animal on this property. May I come in, please?"

"Of course," you tell her. You let her in. You offer her coffee, which she doesn't want, and you tell her that there aren't any exotic animals here. You invite her to look around and see for herself.

Of course there's no sign of a dog, but she's not satisfied. "According to our records, Jonathan Argent of this address had a dog vaccinated last Saturday. We've been told that the dog looked very much like a wolf. Can you tell me where that dog is now?"

"We don't have her anymore," you say. "She got loose and jumped the fence on Monday. It's a shame: she was a lovely animal."

The animal-control lady scowls. "Did she have ID?"

"Of course," you say. "A collar with tags. If you find her, you'll call us, won't you?"

She's looking at you, hard, as hard as the vet did. "Of course. We recommend that you check the pound at least every few days, too. And you might want to put up flyers, put an ad in the paper."

"Thank you," you tell her. "We'll do that." She leaves; you go back to reading *Elle*, secure in the knowledge that your collar's tucked into your underwear drawer upstairs and that Jessie will never show up at the pound.

Jonathan's incensed when he hears about this. He reels off a string of curses about the vet. "Do you think you could rip her throat out?" he asks.

"No," you say, annoyed. "I don't want to, Jonathan. I liked her. She's doing her job. Wolves don't just attack people: you know better than that. And it wouldn't be smart even if I wanted to, it would just mean people would have to track me down and kill me. Now look, relax. We'll go to a different vet next time, that's all."

"We'll do better than that," Jonathan says. "We'll move."

So you move to the next county over, to a larger house with a larger yard. There's even some wild land nearby, forest and meadows, and that's where you and Jonathan go for walks now. When it's time for your rabies shot the following year, you go to a male vet, an older man who's been recommended by some friends of friends of Jonathan's, people who do a lot of hunting. This vet raises his eyebrows when he sees you. "She's quite large," he says pleasantly. "Fish and Wildlife might be interested in such a large dog. Her size will add another, oh, hundred dollars to the bill, Johnny."

"I see." Jonathan's voice is icy. You growl, and the vet laughs.

"Loyal, isn't she? You're planning to breed her, of course."

"Of course," Jonathan snaps.

"Lucrative business, that. Her pups will pay for her rabies shot, believe me. Do you have a sire lined up?"

"Not yet." Jonathan sounds like he's strangling.

The vet strokes your shoulders. You don't like his hands. You don't like the way he touches you. You growl again, and again the vet laughs. "Well, give me a call when she goes into heat. I know some people who might be interested."

"Slimy bastard," Jonathan says when you're back home again. "You didn't like him, Jessie, did you? I'm sorry."

You lick his hand. The important thing is that you have your rabies shot, that your license is up to date, that this vet won't be reporting you to Animal Control. You're legal. You're a *good* dog.

You're a good wife, too. As Stella, you cook for Jonathan, clean for him, shop. You practice your English while devouring *Cosmopolitan* and *Martha Stewart Living*, in addition to *Elle*. You can't work or go to school, because the week of the full moon would keep getting in the way, but you keep yourself busy. You learn to drive and you learn to entertain; you learn to shave your legs and pluck your eyebrows, to mask your natural odor with harsh chemicals, to walk in high heels. You learn the artful uses of cosmetics and clothing, so that you'll be even more beautiful than you are *au naturel*. You're stunning: everyone says so, tall and slim with long silver hair and pale, piercing blue eyes. Your skin's smooth, your complexion flawless, your muscles lean and taut: you're a good cook, a great fuck, the perfect trophy wife. But of course, during that first year, while Jonathan's thirty-six going on thirty-seven, you're only twenty-one going on twenty-eight. You can keep the accelerated aging from showing: you eat right, get plenty of exercise, become even more skillful with the cosmetics. You and Jonathan are blissfully happy, and his colleagues, the old fogies in the Anthropology Department, are jealous. They stare at you when they think no one's looking. "They'd all love to fuck you," Jonathan gloats after every party, and after every party, he does just that.

Most of Jonathan's colleagues are men. Most of their wives don't like you, although a few make resolute efforts to be friendly, to ask you to lunch. Twenty-one going on twenty-eight, you wonder if they somehow sense that you aren't one of them, that there's another side to you, one with four feet. Later you'll realize that even if they knew about Jessie, they couldn't hate and fear you any more than they already do. They fear you because you're young, because you're beautiful and speak English with an exotic accent, because their husbands can't stop staring at you. They know their husbands want to fuck you. The wives may not be young and beautiful any more, but they're no fools. They lost the luxury of innocence when they lost their smooth skin and flawless complexions.

The only person who asks you to lunch and seems to mean it is Diane Harvey. She's forty-five, with thin gray hair and a wide face that's always smiling. She runs her own computer repair business, and she doesn't hate you. This may be related to the fact that her husband Glen never stares at you, never gets too close to you during conversation; he seems to have no desire to fuck you at all. He looks at Diane the way all the other men look at you: as if she's the most desirable creature on earth, as if just being in the same room with her renders him scarcely able to breathe. He adores his wife, even though they've been married for fifteen years, even though he's five years younger than she is and handsome enough to seduce a younger, more beautiful woman. Jonathan says that Glen must stay with Diane for her salary, which is considerably more than his. You think Jonathan's wrong; you think Glen stays with Diane for herself.

Over lunch, as you gnaw an overcooked steak in a bland fern bar, all glass and wood, Diane asks you kindly when you last saw your family, if you're homesick, whether you and Jonathan have any plans to visit Europe again soon. These questions bring a lump to your throat, because Diane's the only one who's ever asked them. You don't, in fact, miss your family – the parents who taught you to hunt, who taught you the dangers of continuing the line, or the siblings with whom you tussled and fought over scraps of meat – because you've transferred all your loyalty to Jonathan. But two is an awfully small pack, and you're starting to wish Jonathan hadn't had that operation. You're starting to wish you could continue the line, even though you know it would be a foolish thing to do. You wonder if that's why your parents mated, even though they knew the dangers.

"I miss the smells back home," you tell Diane, and immediately you blush, because it seems like such a strange thing to say, and you desperately want this kind woman to like you. As much as you love Jonathan, you yearn for someone else to talk to.

But Diane doesn't think it's strange. "Yes," she says, nodding, and tells you about how homesick she still gets for her grandmother's kitchen, which had a signature smell for each season: basil and tomatoes in the summer, apples in the fall, nutmeg and cinnamon in winter, thyme and lavender in the spring. She tells you that she's growing thyme and lavender in her own garden; she tells you about her tomatoes.

She asks you if you garden. You say no. In truth, you're not a big fan of vegetables, although you enjoy the smell of flowers, because you enjoy the smell of almost anything. Even on two legs, you have a far better sense of smell than most people do; you live in a world rich with aroma, and even the scents most people consider noxious are interesting to you. As you sit in the sterile fern bar, which smells only of burned meat and rancid grease and the harsh chemicals the people around you have put on their skin and hair, you realize that you really do miss the smells of home, where even the gardens smell older and wilder than the woods and meadows here.

You tell Diane, shyly, that you'd like to learn to garden. Could she teach you?

So she does. One Saturday afternoon, much to Jonathan's bemusement, Diane comes over with topsoil and trowels and flower seeds, and the two of you measure out a plot in the backyard, and plant and water and get dirt under your nails, and it's quite wonderful, really, about the best fun you've had on two legs, aside from sportfucks with Jonathan. Over dinner, after Diane's left, you try to tell Jonathan how much fun it was, but he doesn't seem particularly interested. He's glad you had a good time, but really, he doesn't want to hear about seeds. He wants to go upstairs and have sex.

So you do.

Afterwards, you go through all of your old issues of *Martha Stewart Living*, looking for gardening tips.

You're ecstatic. You have a hobby now, something you can talk to the other wives about. Surely some of them garden. Maybe, now, they won't hate you. So at the next party, you chatter brightly about gardening, but somehow all the wives are still across the room, huddled around a table, occasionally glaring in your direction, while the men cluster around you, their eyes bright, nodding eagerly at your descriptions of weeds and aphids.

You know something's wrong here. Men don't like gardening, do they? Jonathan certainly doesn't. Finally one of the wives, a tall blonde with a tennis tan and good bones, stalks over and pulls her husband away by the sleeve. "Time to go home now," she tells him, and curls her lip at you.

You know that look. You know a snarl when you see it, even if the wife's too civilized to produce an actual growl.

You ask Diane about this the following week, while you're in her garden, admiring her tomato plants. "Why do they hate me?" you ask Diane.

"Oh, Stella," she says, and sighs. "You really don't know, do you?" You shake your head, and she goes on. "They hate you because you're young and beautiful, even though that's not your fault. The ones who have to work hate you because you don't, and the ones who don't have to work, whose husbands support them, hate you because they're afraid their husbands will leave them for younger, more beautiful women. Do you understand?"

You don't, not really, even though you're now twenty-eight going on thirty-five. "Their husbands can't leave them for me," you tell Diane. "I'm married to Jonathan. I don't *want* any of their husbands." But even as you say it, you know that's not the point.

A few weeks later, you learn that the tall blonde's husband has indeed left her, for an aerobics instructor twenty years his junior. "He showed me a picture," Jonathan says, laughing. "She's a big-hair bimbo. She's not *half* as beautiful as you are."

"What does that have to do with it?" you ask him. You're angry, and you aren't sure why. You barely know the blonde, and it's not as if she's been nice to you. "His poor wife! That was a terrible thing for him to do!"

"Of course it was," Jonathan says soothingly.

"Would you leave me if I wasn't beautiful anymore?" you ask him.

"Nonsense, Stella. You'll always be beautiful."

But that's when Jonathan's going on thirty-eight and you're going on thirty-five. The following year, the balance begins to shift. He's going on thirty-nine; you're going on forty-two. You take exquisite care of yourself, and really, you're as beautiful as ever, but there are a few wrinkles now, and it takes hours of crunches to keep your stomach as flat as it used to be.

Doing crunches, weeding in the garden, you have plenty of time to think. In a year, two at the most, you'll be old enough to be Jonathan's mother, and you're starting to think he might not like that. And you've already gotten wind of catty faculty-wife gossip about how quickly you're showing your age. The faculty wives see every wrinkle, even through artfully applied cosmetics.

During that thirty-five to forty-two year, Diane and her husband move away, so now you have no one with whom to discuss your wrinkles or the catty faculty wives. You don't want to talk to Jonathan about any of it. He still tells you how beautiful you are, and you still have satisfying sportfucks. You don't want to give him any ideas about declining desirability.

You do a lot of gardening that year: flowers – especially roses – and herbs, and some tomatoes in honor of Diane, and because Jonathan likes them. Your best times are the two-foot times in the garden and the four-foot times in the forest, and you think it's no coincidence that both of these involve digging around in the dirt. You write long letters to Diane, on e-mail or, sometimes, when you're saying something you don't want Jonathan to find on the computer, on old-fashioned paper. Diane doesn't have much time to write back, but does send the occasional e-mail note, the even rarer postcard. You read a lot, too, everything you can find: newspapers and novels and political analysis, literary criticism, true crime, ethnographic studies. You startle some of Jonathan's colleagues by casually dropping odd bits of information about their field, about other fields, about fields they've never heard of: forensic geography, agricultural ethics, poststructuralist mining. You think it's no coincidence that the obscure disciplines you're most interested in involve digging around in the dirt.

Some of Jonathan's colleagues begin to comment not only on your beauty, but on your intelligence. Some of them back away a little bit. Some of the wives, although not many, become a little friendlier, and you start going out to lunch again, although not with anyone you like as much as Diane.

The following year, the trouble starts. Jonathan's going on forty; you're going on forty-nine. You both work out a lot; you both eat right. But Jonathan's hardly wrinkled at all yet, and your wrinkles are getting harder to hide. Your stomach refuses to stay completely flat no matter how many crunches you do; you've developed the merest hint of cottage-cheese thighs. You forego your old look, the slinky, skintight look, for long flowing skirts and dresses, accented with plenty of silver. You're going for exotic, elegant, and you're getting there just fine; heads still turn to follow you in the supermarket. But the sportfucks are less frequent, and you don't know how much of this is normal aging and how much is lack of interest on Jonathan's part. He doesn't seem quite as enthusiastic as he once did. He no longer brings you herbal tea and hot water bottles during your transitions; the walks in the woods are a little shorter than they used to be, the ball-throwing sessions in the meadows more perfunctory.

And then one of your new friends, over lunch, asks you tactfully if anything's wrong, if you're ill, because, well, you don't look quite yourself. Even as you assure her that you're fine, you know she means that you look a lot older than you did last year.

At home, you try to discuss this with Jonathan. "We knew it would be a problem eventually," you tell him. "I'm afraid that other people are going to notice, that someone's going to figure it out – "

"Stella, sweetheart, no one's going to figure it out." He's annoyed, impatient. "Even if they think you're aging unusually quickly, they won't make the leap to Jessie. It's not in their worldview. It wouldn't occur to them even if you were aging a hundred years for every one of theirs. They'd just think you had some unfortunate metabolic condition, that's all."

Which, in a manner of speaking, you do. You wince. It's been five weeks since the last sportfuck. "Does it bother you that I look older?" you ask Jonathan.

"Of *course* not, Stella!" But since he rolls his eyes when he says this, you're not reassured. You can tell from his voice that he doesn't want to be having this conversation, that he wants to be somewhere else, maybe watching TV. You recognize that tone. You've heard Jonathan's colleagues use it on their wives, usually while staring at you.

You get through the year. You increase your workout schedule, mine *Cosmo* for bedroom tricks to pique Jonathan's flagging interest, consider and reject liposuction for your thighs. You wish you could have a facelift, but the recovery period's a bit too long, and you're not sure how it would work with your transitions. You read and read and read, and command an increasingly subtle grasp of the implications of, the interconnections between, different areas of knowledge: eco-tourism, Third-World famine relief, art history, automobile design. Your lunchtime conversations become richer, your friendships with the faculty wives more genuine.

You know that your growing wisdom is the benefit of aging, the compensation for your wrinkles and for your fading – although fading slowly, as yet – beauty.

You also know that Jonathan didn't marry you for wisdom.

And now it's the following year, the year you're old enough to be Jonathan's mother, although an unwed teenage one: you're going on fifty-six while he's going on forty-one. Your silver hair's losing its luster, becoming merely gray. Sportfucks coincide, more or less, with major national holidays. Your thighs begin to jiggle when you walk, so you go ahead and have the liposuction, but Jonathan doesn't seem to notice anything but the outrageous cost of the procedure.

You redecorate the house. You take up painting, with enough success to sell some pieces in a local gallery. You start writing a book about gardening as a cure for ecotourism and agricultural abuses, and you negotiate a contract with a prestigious university press. Jonathan doesn't pay much attention to any of this. You're starting to think that Jonathan would only pay attention to a full-fledged Lon Chaney imitation, complete with bloody fangs, but if that was ever in your nature, it certainly isn't now. Jonathan and Martha Stewart have civilized you.

On four legs, you're still magnificent, eliciting exclamations of wonder from other pet owners when you meet them in the woods. But Jonathan hardly ever plays ball in the meadow with you anymore; sometimes he doesn't even take you to the forest. Your walks, once measured in hours and miles, now clock in at minutes and suburban blocks. Sometimes Jonathan doesn't even walk you. Sometimes he just shoos you out into the backyard to do your business. He never cleans up after you, either. You have to do that yourself, scooping old poop after you've returned to two legs.

A few times you yell at Jonathan about this, but he just walks away, even more annoyed than usual. You know you have to do something to remind him that he loves you, or loved you once; you know you have to do something to reinsert yourself into his field of vision. But you can't imagine what. You've already tried everything you can think of.

There are nights when you cry yourself to sleep. Once, Jonathan would have held you; now he rolls over, turning his back to you, and scoots to the farthest edge of the mattress.

During that terrible time, the two of you go to a faculty party. There's a new professor there, a female professor, the first one the Anthropology Department has hired in ten years. She's in her twenties, with long black hair and perfect skin, and the men cluster around her the way they used to cluster around you.

Jonathan's one of them.

Standing with the other wives, pretending to talk about new films, you watch Jonathan's face. He's rapt, attentive, totally focused on the lovely young woman, who's talking about her research into ritual scarification in New Guinea. You see Jonathan's eyes stray surreptitiously, when he thinks no one will notice, to her breasts, her thighs, her ass.

You know Jonathan wants to fuck her. And you know it's not her fault, any more than it was ever yours. She can't help being young and pretty. But you hate her anyway. Over the next few days, you discover that what you hate most, hate even more than Jonathan wanting to fuck this young woman, is what your hate is doing to you: to your dreams, to your insides. The hate's your problem, you know; it's not Jonathan's fault, any more than his lust for the young professor is hers. But you can't seem to get rid of it, and you can sense it making your wrinkles deeper, shriveling you as if you're a piece of newspaper thrown into a fire.

You write Diane a long, anguished letter about as much of this as you can safely tell her. Of course, since she hasn't been around for a few years, she doesn't know how much older you look, so you simply say that you think Jonathan's fallen out of love with you since you're over forty now. You write the letter on paper, and send it through the mail.

Diane writes back, and not a postcard this time: she sends five single-spaced pages. She says that Jonathan's probably going through a midlife crisis. She agrees that his treatment of you is, in her words, "barbaric." "Stella, you're a beautiful, brilliant, accomplished woman. I've never known anyone who's grown so much, or in such interesting ways, in such a short time. If Jonathan doesn't appreciate that, then he's an ass, and maybe it's time to ask yourself if you'd be happier elsewhere. I hate to recommend divorce, but I also hate to see you suffering so much. The problem, of course, is economic: Can you support yourself if you leave? Is Jonathan likely to be reliable with alimony? At least – small comfort, I know – there are no children who need to be considered in all this. I'm assuming that you've already tried couples therapy. If you haven't, you should."

This letter plunges you into despair. No, Jonathan isn't likely to be reliable with alimony. Jonathan isn't likely to agree to couples therapy, either. Some of your lunchtime friends have gone that route, and the only way they ever got their husbands into the therapist's office was by threatening divorce on the spot. If you tried this, it would be a hollow threat. Your unfortunate metabolic condition won't allow you to hold any kind of normal job, and your writing and painting income won't support you, and Jonathan knows all that as well as you do. And your continued safety's in his hands. If he exposed you –

You shudder. In the old country, the stories ran to peasants with torches. Here, you know, laboratories and scalpels would be more likely. Neither option's attractive.

You go to the art museum, because the bright, high, echoing rooms have always made it easier for you to think. You wander among abstract sculpture and impressionist paintings, among still lifes and landscapes, among portraits. One of the portraits is of an old woman. She has white hair and many wrinkles; her shoulders stoop as she pours a cup of tea. The flowers on the china are the same pale, luminous blue as her eyes, which are, you realize, the same blue as your own.

The painting takes your breath away. This old woman is beautiful. You know the painter, a nineteenth-century English duke, thought so too.

You know Jonathan wouldn't.

You decide, once again, to try to talk to Jonathan. You make him his favorite meal, serve him his favorite wine, wear your most becoming outfit, gray silk with heavy silver jewelry. Your silver hair and blue eyes gleam in the candlelight, and the candlelight, you know, hides your wrinkles.

This kind of production, at least, Jonathan still notices. When he comes into the dining room for dinner, he looks at you and raises his eyebrows. "What's the occasion?"

"The occasion's that I'm worried," you tell him. You tell him how much it hurts you when he turns away from your tears. You tell him how much you miss the sportfucks. You tell him that since you clean up his messes more than three weeks out of every month, he can damn well clean up yours when you're on four legs. And you tell him that if he doesn't love you anymore, doesn't want you anymore, you'll leave. You'll go back home, to the village on the edge of the forest near an Alp, and try to make a life for yourself.

"Oh, Stella," he says. "Of course I still love you!" You can't tell if he sounds impatient or contrite, and it terrifies you that you might not know the difference. "How could you even *think* of leaving me? After everything I've given you, everything I've done for you – "

"That's been changing," you tell him, your throat raw. "The changes are the *problem*. Jonathan – "

"I can't believe you'd try to hurt me like this! I can't believe – "

"Jonathan, I'm *not* trying to hurt you! I'm reacting to the fact that you're hurting me! Are you going to stop hurting me, or not?"

He glares at you, pouting, and it strikes you that after all, he's very young, much younger than you are. "Do you have any idea how ungrateful you're being? Not many men would put up with a woman like you!"

"*Jonathan!*"

"I mean, do you have any idea how hard it's been for *me*? All the secrecy, all the lying, having to walk the damn dog – "

"You used to enjoy walking the damn dog." You struggle to control your breathing, struggle not to cry. "All right, look, you've made yourself clear. I'll leave. I'll go home."

"You'll do no such thing!"

You close your eyes. "Then what do you want me to do? Stay here, knowing you hate me?"

"I don't hate you! You hate me! If you didn't hate me, you wouldn't be threatening to leave!" He gets up and throws his napkin down on the table; it lands in the gravy boat. Before leaving the room, he turns and says, "I'm sleeping in the guestroom tonight."

"Fine," you tell him dully. He leaves, and you discover that you're trembling, shaking the way a terrier would, or a poodle. Not a wolf.

Well. He's made himself very plain. You get up, clear away the uneaten dinner you spent all afternoon cooking, and go upstairs to your bedroom. Yours, now: not Jonathan's anymore. You change into jeans and a sweatshirt. You think about taking a hot bath, because all your bones ache, but if you allow yourself to relax into warm water, you'll fall apart; you'll dissolve into tears, and there are things you have to do. Your bones aren't aching just because your marriage has ended; they're aching because the transition is coming up, and you need to make plans before it starts.

So you go into your study, turn on the computer, call up an Internet travel agency. You book a flight back home for ten days from today, when you'll definitely be back on two feet again. You charge the ticket to your credit card. The bill will arrive here in another month, but by then you'll be long gone. Let Jonathan pay it.

Money. You have to think about how you'll make money, how much money you'll take with you — but you can't think about it now. Booking the flight has hit you like a blow. Tomorrow, when Jonathan's at work, you'll call Diane and ask her advice on all of this. You'll tell her you're going home. She'll probably ask you to come stay with her, but you can't, because of the transitions. Diane, of all the people you know, might understand, but you can't imagine summoning the energy to explain.

It takes all the energy you have to get yourself out of the study, back into your bedroom. You cry yourself to sleep, and this time Jonathan's not even across the mattress from you. You find yourself wondering if you should have handled the dinner conversation differently, if you should have kept yourself from yelling at him about the turds in the yard, if you should have tried to seduce him first, if —

The ifs could go on forever. You know that. You think about going home. You wonder if you'll still know anyone there. You realize how much you'll miss your garden, and you start crying again.

Tomorrow, first thing, you'll call Diane.

But when tomorrow comes, you can barely get out of bed. The transition has arrived early, and it's a horrible one, the worst ever. You're in so much pain you can hardly move. You're in so much pain that you moan aloud, but if Jonathan hears, he doesn't come in. During the brief pain-free intervals when you can think lucidly, you're grateful that you booked your flight as soon as you did. And then you realize that the bedroom door is closed, and that Jessie won't be able to open it herself. You need to get out of bed. You need to open the door.

You can't. The transition's too far advanced. It's never been this fast; that must be why it hurts so much. But the pain, paradoxically, makes the transition seem longer than a normal one, rather than shorter. You moan, and whimper, and lose all track of time, and finally howl, and then, blessedly, the transition's over. You're on four feet.

You can get out of bed now, and you do, but you can't leave the room. You howl, but if Jonathan's here, if he hears you, he doesn't come.

There's no food in the room. You left the master bathroom toilet seat up, by chance, so there's water, full of interesting smells. That's good. And there are shoes to chew on, but they offer neither nourishment nor any real comfort. You're hungry. You're lonely. You're afraid. You can smell Jonathan in the room — in the shoes, in the sheets, in the clothing in the closet — but Jonathan himself won't come, no matter how much you howl.

And then, finally, the door opens. It's Jonathan. "Jessie," he says. "Poor Jessie. You must be so hungry; I'm sorry." He's carrying your leash; he takes your collar out of your underwear drawer and puts it on you and attaches the leash, and you think you're going for a walk now. You're ecstatic. Jonathan's going to walk you again. Jonathan still loves you.

"Let's go outside, Jess," he says, and you dutifully trot down the stairs to the front door. But instead he says, "Jessie, this way. Come on, girl," and leads you on your leash to the family room at the back of the house, to the sliding glass doors that open onto the back yard. You're confused, but you do what Jonathan says. You're desperate to please him. Even if he's no longer quite Stella's husband, he's still Jessie's alpha.

He leads you into the backyard. There's a metal pole in the middle of the backyard. That didn't used to be there. Your canine mind wonders if it's a new toy. You trot up and sniff it, cautiously, and as you do, Jonathan clips one end of your leash onto a ring in the top of the pole.

You yip in alarm. You can't move far; it's not that long a leash. You strain against the pole, the leash, the collar, but none of them give; the harder you pull, the harder the choke collar makes it for you to breathe. Jonathan's still next to you, stroking you, calm, reassuring. "It's okay, Jess. I'll bring you food and water, all right? You'll be fine out here. It's just for tonight. Tomorrow we'll go for a nice long walk, I promise."

Your ears perk up at "walk," but you still whimper. Jonathan brings your food and water bowls outside and puts them within reach.

You're so glad to have the food that you can't think about being lonely or afraid. You gobble your Alpo, and Jonathan strokes your fur and tells you what a good dog you are, what a beautiful dog, and you think maybe everything's going to be all right, because he hasn't stroked you this much in months, hasn't spent so much time talking to you, admiring you.

Then he goes inside again. You strain towards the house, as much as the choke collar will let you. You catch occasional glimpses of Jonathan, who seems to be cleaning. Here he is dusting the picture frames; here he is running the vacuum cleaner. Now he's cooking – beef stroganoff, you can smell it – and now he's lighting candles in the dining room.

You start to whimper. You whimper even more loudly when a car pulls into the driveway on the other side of the house, but you stop when you hear a female voice, because you want to hear what it says.

"...so terrible that your wife left you. You must be devastated."

"Yes, I am. But I'm sure she's back in Europe now, with her family. Here, let me show you the house." And when he shows her the family room, you see her: in her twenties, with long black hair and perfect skin. And you see how Jonathan looks at her, and you start to howl in earnest.

"*Jesus*," Jonathan's guest says, peering out at you through the dusk. "What the hell *is* that? A wolf?"

"My sister's dog," Jonathan says. "Husky-wolfhound mix. I'm taking care of her while my sister's away on business. She can't hurt you: don't be afraid." And he touches the woman's shoulder to silence her fear, and she turns towards him, and they walk into the dining room. And then, after a while, the bedroom light flicks on, and you hear laughter and other noises, and you start to howl again.

You howl all night, but Jonathan doesn't come outside. The neighbors yell at Jonathan a few times – *Shut that dog up, goddammit!* – but Jonathan will never come outside again. You're going to die here, tethered to this stake.

But you don't. Towards dawn you finally stop howling; you curl up and sleep, exhausted, and when you wake up the sun's higher and Jonathan's coming through the open glass doors. He's carrying another dish of Alpo, and he smells of soap and shampoo. You can't smell the woman on him.

You growl anyway, because you're hurt and confused. "Jessie," he says. "Jessie, it's all right. Poor, beautiful Jessie. I've been mean to you, haven't I? I'm so sorry."

He does sound sorry, truly sorry. You eat the Alpo, and he strokes you, the same way he did last night, and then he unsnaps your leash from the pole and says, "Okay, Jess, through the gate into the driveway, okay? We're going for a ride."

You don't want to go for a ride. You want to go for a walk. Jonathan promised you a walk. You growl.

"Jessie! Into the car, *now*! We're going to another meadow, Jess. It's farther away than our old one, but someone told me he saw rabbits there, and he said it's really big. You'd like to explore a new place, wouldn't you?"

You don't want to go to a new meadow. You want to go to the old meadow, the one where you know the smell of every tree and rock. You growl again.

"Jessie, you're being a *very bad dog!* Now get in the car. Don't make me call Animal Control."

You whine. You're scared of Animal Control, the people who wanted to take you away so long ago, when you lived in that other county. You know that Animal Control kills a lot of animals, in that county and in this one, and if you die as a wolf, you'll stay a wolf. They'd never know about Stella. As Jessie, you'd have no way to protect yourself except your teeth, and that would only get you killed faster.

So you get into the car, although you're trembling.

In the car, Jonathan seems more cheerful. "Good Jessie. Good girl. We'll go to the new meadow and chase balls now, eh? It's a big meadow. You'll be able to run a long way." And he tosses a new tennis ball into the backseat, and you chew on it, happily, and the car drives along, traffic whizzing past. When you lift your head from chewing on the ball, you can see trees, so you put your head back down, satisfied, and resume chewing. And then the car stops, and Jonathan opens the door for you, and you hop out, holding your ball in your mouth.

This isn't a meadow. You're in the parking lot of a low concrete building that reeks of excrement and disinfectant and fear, *fear*, and from the building you hear barking and howling, screams of misery, and in the parking lot are parked two white Animal Control trucks.

You panic. You drop your tennis ball and try to run, but Jonathan has the leash, and he starts dragging you inside the building, and you can't breathe because of the choke collar. You cough, gasping, trying to howl. "Don't fight, Jessie. Don't fight me. Everything's all right."

Everything's not all right. You can smell Jonathan's desperation, can taste your own, and you should be stronger than he is but you can't breathe, and he's saying, "Jessie, don't bite me, it will be worse if you bite me, Jessie," and the screams of horror still swirl from the building and you're at the door now, someone's opened the door for Jonathan, someone says, "Let me help you with that dog," and you're scrabbling on the concrete, trying to dig your claws into the sidewalk just outside the door, but there's no purchase, and they've dragged you inside, onto the linoleum, and everywhere are the smells and sounds of terror. Above your own whimpering you hear Jonathan saying, "She jumped the fence and threatened my girlfriend, and then she tried to bite me, so I have no choice, it's such a shame, she's always been such a good dog, but in good conscience I can't – "

You start to howl, because he's lying, *lying*, you never did any of that!

Now you're surrounded by people, a man and two women, all wearing colorful cotton smocks that smell, although faintly, of dog shit and cat pee. They're putting a muzzle on you, and even though you can hardly think through your fear – and your pain, because Jonathan's walked back out the door, gotten into the car, and driven away, Jonathan's *left* you here – even with all of that, you know you don't dare bite or snap. You know your only hope is in being a good dog, in acting as submissive as possible. So you whimper, crawl along on your stomach, try to roll over on your back to show your belly, but you can't, because of the leash.

"Hey," one of the women says. The man's left. She bends down to stroke you. "Oh, God, she's so scared. Look at her."

"Poor thing," the other woman says. "She's *beautiful*."

"I know."

"Looks like a wolf mix."

"I know." The first woman sighs and scratches your ears, and you whimper and wag your tail and try to lick her hand through the muzzle. Take me home, you'd tell her if you could talk. Take me home with you. You'll be my alpha, and I'll love you forever. I'm a *good* dog.

The woman who's scratching you says wistfully, "We could adopt her out in a minute, I bet."

"Not with that history. Not if she's a biter. Not even if we had room. You know that."

"I know." The voice is very quiet. "Wish I could take her myself, though."

"Take home a biter? Lily, you have kids!"

Lily sighs. "Yeah, I know. Makes me sick, that's all."

"You don't need to tell me that. Come on, let's get this over with. Did Mark go to get the room ready?"

"Yeah."

"Okay. What'd the owner say her name was?"

"Stella."

"Okay. Here, give me the leash. Stella, come. Come on, Stella."

The voice is sad, gentle, loving, and you want to follow it, but you fight every step, anyway, until Lily and her friend have to drag you past the cages of other dogs, who start barking and howling again, whose cries are pure terror, pure loss. You can hear cats grieving, somewhere else in the building, and you can smell the room at the end of the hall, the room to which you're getting inexorably closer. You smell the man named Mark behind the door, and you smell medicine, and you smell the fear of the animals who've been taken to that room before you. But overpowering everything else is the worst smell, the smell that makes you bare your teeth in the muzzle and pull against the choke collar and scrabble again, helplessly, for a purchase you can't get on the concrete floor: the pervasive, metallic stench of death.

# The Old World

"The ironic thing," Jenny says, "is that your dad always believed he was living in the middle of a huge conspiracy, and this time he's actually right."

That's already occurred to me. "He was probably right the other times, too," I tell her. "At least some of them." I'm trying to concentrate on the traffic ahead of us. Jenny offered to drive, and I should have let her. I thought driving would take my mind off the mess with Dad, but instead I'm just driving really badly. I try to switch lanes and wind up almost hitting a pickup truck in my blind spot. The kid behind the wheel, thirtyish and bearded, taps his horn, and when I'm safely back in my own lane, next to the truck, the woman beside him in the passenger seat rolls down her window.

"Hey," the passenger yells out, "you okay?"

"Fine," I call weakly. "Sorry about that."

"No problem! No harm, no foul! As long as you're okay!"

"I — just — blind spot," I yell back miserably. Next to me, Jenny sighs.

"Nate, stop the car. Let's switch. I should be driving."

"Okay. I'm sorry. I'll pull over."

"No, sweetie, just stop now. We're not going that fast, and there's a red light up there. It will be fine. You have too much on your mind, that's all."

So I stop the car, and we do the Chinese fire-drill. The cars behind us have stopped too, of course, but nobody's honking or yelling, because that's how we all are now. I can still remember the time when the kid in the pickup truck would have screamed at me or flipped me the bird or, God forbid, pulled out a gun and shot me, the time when the drivers behind us would have been cursing, honking, spitting, and reporting me to the cops.

Cops. I remember when there were cops. I remember when we needed cops.

I remember when being stopped in this much traffic would have meant that I was choking on exhaust, the days before all the car companies cheerfully switched over to hydrogen-cell technology, even though it required a huge investment in a new infrastructure, just because it was the fuel-efficient and environmentally correct thing to do.

My kids, Sam and Julie, don't remember those days at all.

My father's never left them. He's still living there, living then. Living in the old world, which has just been infiltrated by terrorists.

From the Truth Terrorist Manifesto

To the prisoners of Oldworld Manor:

We are from Outside. You don't know what we're talking about. The people who put you here don't want you believe that there's an Outside. They don't think you're strong enough to handle that information.

We disagree. We think you are strong enough. We want to free you. We want to give you genuine choices.

Most of you were big readers before the Change. (What Change, you ask? We're getting to that. Be patient.) You read everything because you were so passionately devoted to truth: even unpopular truth, the truths people tried to suppress, and even truths that contradicted your own worldviews. You read voraciously; you read everything. And so some of you may remember reading an obscure scientific article about two populations of animals, one on an island and one on the mainland. We ourselves have forgotten where this article appeared or what kind of animals they were: some sort of small mammal, we think. (Those of us who read it are very old now, as old as you are, and our memories aren't what they used to be.) Whatever its species, this was an animal that couldn't get back and forth easily between the two places. The two colonies were completely separate biologically, even though they were the same species. They had no communication with each other.

And then one day, both colonies suddenly started displaying a new tool-using behavior: using rocks to break clams open, maybe, something like that. The biologists studying the two colonies hadn't seen one animal in either place learn how to do this and teach it to the others. One day, all the animals in both places woke up and displayed the new behavior. They'd made a simultaneous evolutionary leap.

That's what happened to us twenty years ago. To people. This is the truth your jailors have been keeping from you, because they don't think you're strong enough to handle it.

For as long as there had been people at all, some of us had been haranguing the others to be kind, to be compassionate, to share resources instead of fighting over them: to cooperate, instead of competing. Don't lie, don't steal, don't kill. Don't cheat. But people did all those things anyway, and there were wars and plagues and tyrannies and general rottenness, and the people who wanted to play nicely with others kept being told that they were hopeless idealists who had their heads in the sand, because nature was really red in tooth and claw and nice guys finished last. And so forth and so on. You remember that. You know what we're talking about.

But it's different for your grandchildren, for all the people who weren't alive before the Change, or who were too young to remember what it was like back then. We oldsters can't make them believe that people could really be that stupid and wasteful and destructive, because looking back at it now, none of that behavior makes any sense. It had always been in our best interests to cooperate and share, but before the Change, most of us weren't able to understand that. We just didn't get it.

And then, one day twenty years ago — March 24, 2029 — we all woke up and got it, just like the two animal colonies who'd suddenly learned how to use rocks to break open clams. We all woke up wanting to be nice to each other. We all woke up grief-stricken over the lack of universal health care, over poverty and world hunger, global warming and irreversible climate change, warfare and injustice. We all woke up wanting to work together to fix those things. We all woke up with compassion and common sense. We'd all made a simultaneous evolutionary leap.

Except for a few of us, who hadn't or couldn't, who couldn't accept the new world. Like all of you, who've been locked into an elaborate insane asylum by people who really believe they have your best interests at heart.

We think they're wrong. We think you're strong enough to handle the truth, and we think it's our job to tell you the truth. That's why we've gone to a great deal of time, trouble, and expense to make sure that you're reading this. We're the Truth Terrorists.

We're thirty miles from Oldworld Manor. My stomach's one huge knot. "You know," Jenny says, "your father would probably be a Truth Terrorist himself, if he'd been able to adjust."

That's occurred to me, too. Before the Change, Dad was a journalist, specializing in politics and foreign affairs. He spent my childhood railing against fraud, corruption, and government conspiracies to cover up everything from the real effects of food additives to the real cost of whatever war we were fighting at the moment. He spent hours on the Internet tracking down cover-ups, and he wrote scathing stories about them that usually either didn't get printed or were simply dismissed as the ravings of a liberal lunatic. He marched and demonstrated and protested and wrote letters and signed petitions and got arrested a couple of times, and he was very likely being watched by the FBI, and once he wound up on an airline no-fly list, although it turned out that was a mistake and they'd really been targeting somebody else with the same name who'd gone to the Middle East a few times.

"Just because you're paranoid doesn't mean people aren't really out to get you," he always said darkly. He said that a lot. Coming from anyone else, it would have been a joke, but my father meant it. He used to apologize to me for having brought me into such a horrible world. He meant that, too. He'd call me into his dusty, paper-strewn study and make me sit down in front of his monitor so he could show me whatever latest government scandal he'd uncovered that no one else was paying attention to, and he'd rant and rave about the stupidity of the general public and the cowardice of the liberal media, and then – sobbing, his head in his hands – he'd beg my forgiveness for having conceived me in a moment of blind lust. "It's the only time we didn't use birth control, Nate, I swear to God, we were always so careful because we could tell even then that everything was going to hell in a handbasket, and how could we subject a child to that? But, well, we were a little drunk, and it was spring, and – "

"Dad," I always told him, "Dad, it's okay. I'm glad you conceived me. Really. Thank you for conceiving me. I'm glad I'm alive. I like being alive. You don't need to apologize. And there are some good things in the world too, Dad, really." And he'd always ask me what they were, and I'd have to come up with a list. "Ice cream and sunrises and, um, brave journalists and – and books! Books are really cool, Dad, come on, you like them too, even though you spend so much time on the computer, I know you do."

And he'd sigh and shake his head, and start crying again. "But so few people read anymore! Books are going the way of the record album!"

"The what?"

"The record album! Records! An obsolete form of media you've never seen or heard! You're so young, Nate. So young. I was idealistic once, too. You'll learn better."

My mother finally couldn't take it anymore; when I was thirteen, in 2015, she told my father that she was moving out and taking me with her. I had to listen to her ranting, too. "I can't believe the things he tells you! Nate, you have no idea how desperately I wanted you!

I told your father I was on the pill, even though I wasn't, and he kept using condoms *anyway*, not to mention all the lectures he gave me about evil pharmaceutical companies and the health hazards of oral contraception. I had to get him drunk to make him forget the condom that one time. It took everything I had before that to keep him from getting a vasectomy: I talked him out of that idea only by telling him that if we survived a nuclear war or biological catastrophe, we might have to help repopulate the planet. And then when I got pregnant, he wanted me to get an abortion! And I told him that he'd spent his entire conscious existence campaigning for a woman's right to choose, and I was choosing to have this child, dammit, and if he didn't want the baby he could just leave!"

"But he didn't," I always told her. "He didn't leave. So he must have really wanted me, somewhere deep down."

"Oh, honey, he adores you. He adores kids. That's why he was so determined not to have any, because he couldn't stand the idea of what they'd have to go through. But I told him that I was choosing to have the baby, and that he could choose to be its father or not, and of course then he was hooked. He hated negligent parents, and he never would have been able to live with himself if he thought he was a deadbeat dad."

Once I asked Mom why she'd married him in the first place. She sighed and shook her head and said, "Oh, Nate, it was the old story. I thought I could change him. I thought our love would make him happy; I thought that if I pointed out the bright side of things, he'd start to see them too; I thought he just had a chemical imbalance that medication could fix, except that he refused to go on the meds because they were really carcinogens produced by evil pharmaceutical companies. At one point I went to my doctor and got a prescription for Prozac for myself, and put it in your father's coffee every morning. I'm not proud of that, but that's how desperate I got."

"Wow. What happened?"

"Nothing. Not a blessed thing. I couldn't see any difference, except that he had a lot more trouble reaching climax, and that made him curse whatever the government was adding to the water, so I stopped giving him the Prozac, and then that side effect wore off and he said the government must have started adding Viagra to the water to counter the effects of the other chemicals. And of course he found some crackpot site on the net that reported that very thing, and good luck talking him out of it once anybody else had come up with the same idea. That's when he started triple-filtering the bottled water we bought." She shook her head and said, "Nate, please promise me something. Promise me that you'll never marry anyone you want to change. Don't marry any woman you don't love just the way she is."

"I promise," I said, and I kept my promise. I've always loved Jenny just the way she is, and she loves me too, and we love Sam and Julie. Every day I tell my kids how much I love them, how much their mother and I wanted them, how ecstatic we were when they were born. Sam's twenty-three now – he was born three years before the Change – and Julie's eighteen. They're great kids. They roll their eyes whenever I tell them how much I love them, the same way I rolled my eyes when I was their age and Dad gave me the same old, tired speeches. I guess some things never change, no matter how much the world does.

Things didn't change that much after the divorce; Dad still stayed close to us, because he didn't want to be a negligent father. Mom and I moved into a two-bedroom apartment, and Dad moved into a little studio with a loft bed for him and a foldout couch for me when I came to visit. I think he was happier after the divorce, because he could spend more time online with his conspiracy-theorist friends, and his entire house could be dusty and paper-strewn. Looking back on it now, I actually think that was the best time of his life, those fourteen years before the Change, because for all his terror and despair and bitterness, he was doing what he was best at: hunting for cover-ups, and finding them. He dutifully gave me money and sent checks to Mom – although as a banker, she made a lot more than he did – because he didn't want to be a deadbeat dad. He saw himself as a kind of knight or saint or prophet: one of a small band of clear-sighted freethinkers who knew the truth about a world that insisted on ignoring them. It was his way of being a hero.

Of course he had a terrible time when Mom got cancer, one of the fast-moving kinds that wouldn't slow down for anything the doctors threw at it. We all had a terrible time. Dad had never really stopped loving Mom, and I wept in Jenny's arms every night, and every morning we took Sam, who was just a baby then, to the hospice to visit Mom. I'm so glad she got to see Sam before she died, so glad she knew she had a grandchild. I wish she'd gotten to meet Julie, who looks just like her.

Dad wanted to visit too, but Mom wouldn't let him: she said he was too depressing. So every day after we saw Mom, Jenny would take Sam home and I'd go to my father's tiny apartment, and he'd weep and rail about Mom's illness.

"It's the damn Prozac she took all those years ago. I bet she never told you she was on Prozac. She never wanted to admit how depressing the world was, never wanted to look at what was really happening, but it got to her anyway, Nate, I know it did: she was too smart not to see the truth. So she got depressed and had to go on Prozac, and look at where she is now! You won't get me anywhere near that stuff, and I'm healthy as a horse."

"Dad," I said. It hurt to talk. "I don't think it's the Prozac. Millions of people have taken Prozac. They don't get cancer any more often than anyone else does."

"They will. Just wait. Just wait and see."

"Dad. You know, sometimes when you wait and see, good things actually happen. Like when I met Jenny, or when Sam was born."

He patted my hand. "You're in denial, Nate. I understand. It's where you need to be to cope with what's happening to your mother. I love you, Nate, you and Jenny and Sam. Make sure you only give Sam certified organic baby food."

"We love you too, Dad. And we're taking good care of Sam, don't worry."

I wish Mom had let Dad visit, even though I understand why she didn't. I know she thought about him, more and more towards the end. Her last words were about him. "Nate," she said, her voice a thready whisper, "take care of your father. I keep hoping that someday he'll be happy before he dies."

I couldn't see through my tears. "I will, Mom. Have you been happy, Mom? I love you, Mom." But she didn't answer; she couldn't. She took a last breath and died.

At the funeral, the minister said a bunch of stuff about how she was in a better world now, how we were all going to a better world. My father couldn't take it: he got up and left in the middle of the service. But it turns out that Mom missed the better world and that Dad got to see it, because it arrived two years later, on March 24, 2029.

## From the Truth Terrorist Manifesto

It took a while after the Change for everyone to figure out what was going on, and then we weren't able to fix everything. A lot of the damage was irreversible: the global warming that's wiped out huge portions of coastline on every continent, the HIV that decimated Africa even when all the pharmaceutical companies distributed drug cocktails for free, the species extinctions, beautiful animals no one will ever see again. So it's not like the Change made us all happy, because it sent a lot of people, the ones who'd never wanted to face those issues before, into tremendous pain and grief. They could no longer hide from what they'd done, from what we'd all done, and how it made them feel. A lot of people spent a lot of time in agony, because we'd done so much harm we couldn't undo. The suicide rate went way up for a while, before it disappeared almost completely.

The Change made all of us see everything more clearly: the way all of you always had. You are our spiritual forbears. You were the original Truth Terrorists, the ones who burned through all deceptions. That's why we're trying to free you now from the lie in which you've been imprisoned.

We couldn't fix everything. Things aren't perfect now. All any of us could do was promise to be better, to share and cooperate and be compassionate, to try our very best not to break things the way they'd been broken before. We kept that promise. We don't need police now, and poverty and hunger have been almost wiped out, along with suicide, and there aren't any more wars. But we still grieve for all those animals, and for all the people who died who didn't have to.

It took us a while to believe that the Change was real, even though the difference was so dramatic everywhere. When the papers are suddenly full of stories about incredible acts of philanthropy and ceasefires and cooperation between people and political parties who were previously at each other's throats, and when that's happening all over the world, and when it's all in the service of helping people who need help: well, let's just say that we all knew right away that something staggering was going on. There are still people who obsess about exactly how it happened, probably because they're afraid that if things changed so quickly, they could change back that quickly, too. Nobody really knows what the mechanism was; the spontaneous evolutionary leap theory is the one most of us have settled on, but religious people ascribe the Change to grace or miracle, to God rather than science, and there are people who think it was interference by kindly aliens, or even some side effect of a benevolent virus released into the atmosphere by saintly scientists. There are still plenty of conspiracy theorists around, but now they come up with stories about elaborate networks of justice and mercy and goodwill. And that just makes everyone else laugh. We *know* the people around us are plotting to perform acts of lovingkindness. That's been going on for twenty years now. It's not news. It's not anything anyone needs to keep a secret.

Except that some people *have* been keeping it a secret. From you, the original Truth Terrorists.

If we don't understand why most of us changed, we also don't understand why a few of us didn't. There were still a few criminals after the Change, although they've all been locked up in vastly improved prisons, prisons with excellent food and golf courses and maid service. (An improved prison is still a prison. We are doing this to free you because you're also in a prison, and you did nothing wrong to deserve to be there.) And there were still some people who weren't quite criminals but still didn't want to share or cooperate, who stayed selfish and greedy. They're harder to deal with than the actual criminals: mostly they just wind up being profoundly lonely, which is maybe how those people always wound up anyway.

And there were still some people who persisted in looking for the downside of everything, the dark side, the hidden agenda. Like all of you. The people who've put you here think that means you can't handle the truth. We, the Truth Terrorists, think we owe you the truth, as long as we present it in a form you recognize, in a shape that's familiar enough to be safe.

Ten miles away. I think I'm getting an ulcer, sitting here in the car. "Remember the early days?" Jenny asks wistfully. "When we thought he'd finally be happy?"

My stomach spasms. "When I thought Mom would finally get her wish. Of course I remember."

"Oh, God, Nate. I'm sorry. I shouldn't have brought it up."

"Don't be sorry," I tell her. "Do you think I don't think about that all the time? Do you think I haven't thought about it every day since Dad lost it? It's not like you're bringing up something I could forget."

Jenny and I had always thought Dad would be happy after the Change. This was the world he'd always wanted, wasn't it? We didn't realize right away how bad it was for him: everybody was disoriented and trying to readjust, and we were all dealing with huge social changes. Of course we saw that he wasn't increasingly happy and excited like nearly everybody else, and at first we just chalked it up to old habits dying hard. But he spent more time online than ever, and he called me more often, too, and he sounded more panicky every time he called. "Nate! Nate! Everybody seems to *believe* that Congress is really talking about dismantling the military so it can increase the education budget!"

"Well, sure, Dad. That's because they really *are* talking about it. I saw it on the news."

"Nate! Surely you can't believe that they'd do that! Why would they do that, Nate?"

"Because educating kids makes a lot more sense than killing people, and nobody wants to fight anymore."

I heard my father sputtering on the other end of the line. "Come on, Nate, nobody really thinks that way! Especially not in *Congress*!"

The day that bill actually went through – and obviously it took a while, because a lot of details had to be worked out – Dad called me in tears. His conspiracy-theorist friends believed the demilitarization was happening, too. He couldn't find anyone to agree with him that it all must be a giant hoax. "Nate, oh God, the world must be ending! What's wrong with everybody? Nate, I'm dizzy, I can't breathe, Nate – "

I hadn't heard him in such bad shape since Mom died. I was afraid he was having a heart attack. I called 911, and then Jenny and I put Sam in the car seat and rushed to the hospital, and sat with Dad in the ER for six hours while the doctors ran a bunch of tests. They finally decided that his heart was fine, that he was just having a panic attack.

Being in the hospital just made his panic worse, though, because so many things didn't make sense to him. Nobody asked him for an insurance card or proof that he could pay, because the healthcare system had already been reformed – that was one of the earliest things that got fixed after the Change, since so many people had been worrying about it for so long anyway – and the doctor and nurses spent a really long time with him, just sitting at his bedside and chatting, because they didn't have to treat gunshots or knife wounds anymore, plus there were fewer car accidents because we were all driving more carefully. Of course the emergency room still could have been busy with heart attacks and strokes and diabetes and cancer, but I guess it was a slow night, and most people were having less trouble with chronic conditions too, because of lower stress levels.

Anyway, the doctor was really friendly and sociable, and it sent poor Dad into another tizzy. "Nate!" he hissed at me when the doctor had gone to check on some tests, "is he a real doctor? He can't be a real doctor! Real doctors don't sit and chat like this! That only happens on TV!"

"I think he's a real doctor, Dad."

"Why aren't there more patients here? Nobody's screaming! There's always screaming in emergency rooms! Is this a real emergency room, Nate?"

"It's real, Dad. It's all real, really."

He'd started to cry in great gulping sobs, and I started to panic a bit too; I left Jenny to sit with Dad and went outside to find the doctor. He was sitting reading some printouts at the nursing station, where a bunch of nurses were playing poker because they had so little work to do. "Your father's having a panic attack," he told me kindly. "We'll send him home with some Ativan; it's an anti-anxiety drug. Does he have a history of psychiatric problems?"

"Not diagnosed ones, no." Jenny and I had talked before about whether he was paranoid schizophrenic, but he didn't hear voices, and he'd always had proof for his theories, even if other people ignored it or interpreted it differently. He always made sense, even if his take on things was a little extreme. But when I said that, the doctor's eyebrows went up.

"Undiagnosed ones, then? What do you think's going on?"

"Um, well…he's having trouble adjusting to the Change. It doesn't seem to have affected him, and he doesn't believe in it. He thinks it's a hoax of some sort." And I told the doctor about my father, and he listened and nodded and looked very compassionate. The nurses had looked up from their poker game, and were listening and nodding and looking compassionate too.

When I was done, the doctor sighed and said, "We've seen a few cases of this. People who hate the Change because it violates their belief system or invalidates what they spent their whole lives doing, before. Some cops are having a lot of trouble."

"Because they don't have jobs anymore," I said. "Sure. But my father's not a cop."

"You said he was an investigative journalist? There's not much left to investigate. And it goes even deeper than employment issues, or might: I'm not a psychiatrist and can't make an actual diagnosis, but we've seen a condition called 'conflict addiction.' There are people who spent their whole lives before the Change opposing things, protesting things, defining other people as enemies. And now they don't have anything to oppose or protest, and the people they thought were their enemies are acting like friends, and they can't deal with it."

"But this is the world he's always wanted," I said. "If you'd asked my father, before the Change, how he thought things should work, he'd have described exactly what's happening now."

The doctor nodded. "Right. It's the world he said he always wanted, but now that he has it, he doesn't know how to live in it. Because all of his modes of functioning involve protest and opposition. He has to learn an entirely new way of thinking and living. That's going to be hard work, and I have to warn you, not everyone can do it. Listen, I'll send him home with the Ativan, and I'll give you the name of a psychiatrist who specializes in this. If anyone can help him, Dr. Hurley can."

"He won't take the Ativan. He thinks pharmaceutical companies are trying to poison everybody."

"Well, I'm not surprised, after what you told me. If he won't take the Ativan, warm milk and a hot bath may help him relax."

So Jenny and I took Dad home, and he refused to take the Ativan, and we gave him warm milk and a hot bath, and I sat with him until he fell asleep. I told him over and over that he was all right, that his heart was fine, that Jenny and Sam and I loved him. And he held my hand and told me that he was feeling much better, and that he knew we loved him, and that he loved us, too.

Now I wish we'd brought him back to our house. I wish we'd kept more of an eye on him. I don't know why we didn't think to do that. If we'd brought him back to our house, maybe we could have kept him from watching the news the next morning, or at least shielded him from it. Not that it ultimately would have helped, I guess; something else would have gotten to him, eventually. But the next morning, the top news was that the major pharmaceutical companies had made a group announcement that they'd been guilty of unethical practices for years, that they'd been buying off doctors and tampering with clinical trials and withholding information from consumers, and that they were going to mend their ways and also offer financial compensation and free supplies of better drugs to patients who contacted them.

"Oh my God," Jenny said, as we sat at the kitchen table watching the TV. "You'd better call your dad, Nate."

"He'll be overjoyed," I said. "He's been saying all that for years; everybody's known it for years, anyway. He'll feel vindicated because they've finally admitted it. Won't he?"

"After what happened yesterday? I doubt it. Nate, call him."

I called. There was no answer. "Maybe he's in the shower," I said. "Maybe he went out to pick up some groceries."

"Maybe he's slit his wrists," Jenny said. "We have to go over there. Unless you want to call 911 first."

"Jenny, you're overreacting."

"I hope so." She picked up Sam, who was halfway through his breakfast banana. "Nate, let's go."

We went. There was no answer when we knocked on my father's door. "Maybe he took the Ativan and he's sleeping," I said.

"Sure. Use your key, Nate. We need to get in there."

I used my key. We found my father curled in a fetal position on the floor in front of the television. He was still in his pajamas and bathrobe. He didn't respond when we talked to him, touched him, waved our hands in front of his face. He was breathing, but he barely blinked. His eyes were fixed in a glassy stare, and a thin trickle of drool dripped from his mouth onto the rug. Jenny called 911 while I sat with Dad, begging him to talk to me. Sam sat next to me and sang his favorite song, "Itsy Bitsy Spider." Dad loved to hear Sam sing that song, and he always sang along, but today nothing happened.

So we wound up back at the hospital, where Dad had still more tests, all of which said that he was fine, physically. The emergency room was still eerily quiet, and at the nurses' station, the day shift was deep into a game of Scrabble. A group of paramedics played frisbee in the hallway. "I'm worried about you guys," I told the nurses; I'd wandered over to watch the game while Dad was having an MRI. "Are you going to lose your jobs? You need more sick people than this to keep your jobs, don't you?"

They all looked up at me and smiled, and I wondered if they'd been hitting the Ativan. "It's okay," one of them said. "There will always be sick people, even if there aren't a lot right now. You know, the flu. Allergies. People falling off ladders."

"And we can always go overseas to help people there," said another.

"Actually," said a third, "I've always wanted to be a painter. I might try that."

"Placebos," said the fourth. "That's all my letters, across two triple-word scores."

An energetic squabble erupted over whether the plural of "placebo" ended in "es" or only in "s," and I went back to Dad's room, relieved that the human race hadn't changed past all recognition. We could still be competitive, when it was just a game.

Because none of the medical tests had shown anything, the hospital called Dr. Hurley, who examined Dad and listened to our account of what had been happening. When we were done, he sighed and nodded and looked compassionate. "Yes, it sounds like conflict addiction to me. But right now, it's even more than that. Your father's gone catatonic. He's completely shut down because he can't cope with his environment. We're going to have to hospitalize him and give him food and water through a tube until he comes out of this."

"He'll come out of it, then?" I could have used some Ativan myself. Sam was sitting in a corner, happily coloring with some crayons a nurse had given him; I was jealous of his calm. "You're sure he'll come out?"

"I can't be sure of anything," Dr. Hurley said gently. "This is an

extreme case, one of the worst I've seen, although it's not unprece-
dented."

"What happened to the precedents?" Jenny asked. Of the two of
us, she's much better in a crisis. She takes in situations right away,
and she gets right to the core of things. "Did the precedents come out
of it? How were they treated? And if they came out of the catatonia,
what happened then?"

Dr. Hurley scratched his nose. He didn't look happy. "They, um,
they came out of it when they were played old news broadcasts. They
came out of it when something like their old environment, where they
felt safe and comfortable, was restored." He coughed. "Actually, there
are enough of these cases that the NIH has just made a very interesting proposal about how to deal with them. I can give you some arti
cles to read, if you'd like."

And that's how we learned about Oldworld Manor.

## From the Truth Terrorist Manifesto

This place where you've been living, Oldworld Manor, isn't the
real world. It's a prison, a demented funhouse, a very sophisticated
insane asylum. And this isn't the only such place; there are others, ten
or twelve around the country, and others in other parts of the world.

Your jailors want you to believe that Oldworld Manor is just business as usual, an unremarkable neighborhood on the same old planet.
For them, it's part psychiatric hospital and part theme park, a little
like colonial Williamsburg used to be, except dirtier and scarier looking. It isn't really scary, and the dirt is sanitized and completely harm-
less, but a lot of people have gone to a lot of effort to make sure that
you and the other full-time residents don't know that.

This is why your families always come to visit you, not the other
way around. This is why your efforts to travel, for the few of you still
young and healthy enough to do that, always seem to run into obsta-
cles: rampaging bears in the national forests you want to visit, hotel-
hostage crises or salmonella outbreaks in formerly glamorous capital

cities, foreign borders closed to Americans for health or military or ideological reasons.

None of that's true. It's just pretend, misinformation your jailors feed you to make sure you don't stray out of the Oldworld Manor universe. The only destinations you're allowed to reach are other Oldworld Manors.

Oldworld Manors are huge tourist attractions, and not just for you. Kids love to go on school trips there, because it's creepy and safe at the same time, like a horror movie. They know the place where you live is just pretend.

And there's a long waiting list of people who want to work at Oldworld Manor: people who want to dress up as cops pretending to catch people who've been paid to act like criminals; people to write and produce the fake newspapers and news broadcasts about rampaging bears and salmonella outbreaks and international security alerts; people to maintain the phony conspiracy-theory weblogs; people to staff the hospital, where the ER's always really crowded and there's lots of screaming, lots of fake bullet wounds and stabbings next to the real medical problems, because you Oldworld residents get the flu and break your legs, like everybody else.

Lots of people want to get into Oldworld Manor, because they want to pretend. But now we've gotten in. We aren't pretending. We think you deserve the right to enjoy the happiness of post-Change life. We think you're strong and capable enough to make that choice.

Jenny and I are here, finally. Do I even have a stomach anymore, or has it been replaced by a nuclear core in full meltdown?

We pull up to the gates and show our ID, and the guard waves us through. "I hope your dad will be okay," he calls to me through the window, and I thank him. But once we're on our way to the hospital, I say, "You'd think they'd check the ID cards more carefully now, since that's how — "

"Nate, please relax. I'm sure the guard was alerted that we were coming. They have our pictures on file; I'm sure he looked at those so he'd recognize us. And anyway, the damage is already done, here. You'd better believe they're tightening security at the other places."

I look through the window. On the sidewalk, a homeless man's panhandling for change: he's an actor, of course. There's a lot of garbage lying around, and we drive past boarded-up buildings and street signs peppered with bullet holes, all props. "I hope they catch the bastards," I say, and hatred twists in my gut. I haven't felt hatred for twenty years. I haven't felt hatred since before the Change: it shocks me.

"Nate." Jenny's voice has gotten quieter. "Look, the Truth Terrorists were – they were just telling the truth. God knows the idea's always been controversial. We argued about it too, remember? All those conversations about whether we were just enabling your father's addiction by putting him here, whether this was some sociological equivalent of Methadone."

"Of course I remember," I snap at her, and she shoots me an anguished glance. "And we finally decided that what we were doing by putting Dad here was saving his life. Do you remember that?"

"Nate – "

"And whoever messed with that had no right, no right at all! It was – it was – "

"It was deeply misguided," Jenny says. Now we're driving through a neighborhood of brownstones with STREET WATCH signs and cars double-parked along the street. Someone runs up to a Volvo and smashes the window, and the car alarm goes off as the actor yanks out the radio. "I agree with you completely. But we haven't seen your father yet. He could be all right. They said he's not catatonic, and that has to be a good thing, doesn't it?"

"They said he's raving! They had to put him in a *rubber room*, Jenny! They'd have used Thorazine or something if they weren't afraid of short-circuiting his adjustment process! Adjustment process: Who are they kidding? He's eighty years old in a rubber room. Does that sound to you like he's all right? Does that sound like adjustment?"

Jenny takes a hand off the wheel to reach over and squeeze my thigh. "Nate, they're doing the very best for him they know how."

"Yes, of course they are. Of course they are, because that's what everybody does now. And if they catch the scum who did this, I'm sure they'll put him or her or it into a wonderful prison with lots of therapy and counseling and job-skills training. Right now, I'd prefer lethal injection."

"You don't mean that."

"Don't tell me what I mean."

"Nate, I don't want to fight with you."

"Then don't."

Usually, Jenny would shut up at this point, but today she doesn't. She's upset too, even if she's not admitting it. "What's really going on is that you feel guilty about all these years of lying to your father, even if it was for a good reason, and you're taking your fear and anger out on a convenient target."

"Jenny, please shut up."

This time, she does. The drive to the hospital seems to take forever. Oldworld Manor has to be pretty huge, something like fifty miles across, to minimize the chances that residents will be able to wander outside, into the real world. Most of them, most of the conflict-addicted who couldn't cope with the Change, are really old – my father's one of the youngest of the bunch – and not really mobile, so it hasn't been a problem. But none of that matters now, because the problem isn't that one of them got out: the problem's that masked crusaders got in.

The hospital parking lot's much more crowded than usual, and when we walk into the lobby, I see a small mob of people, and hear yelling. "I want to know how this happened!" a woman bellows. "I want to know how you let this happen! My mother's just had a nervous breakdown because you people weren't careful enough!"

"I don't think she's an actor," I tell Jenny.

The man at the front of the crowd is wearing a white coat and a stethoscope, and wiping sweat off his face. "I'm so very, very sorry. We've done everything we could to prevent an incident like this, but the perpetrators were just too sophisticated for us. Whoever they were, they hacked into our computer system to create a fake family member, and then forged a fake family ID, and then used another fake ID to get access to our telecommunications center. And then they flooded the Oldworld media with messages saying that this is an artificial environment, that the residents had been lied to, and they got copies of the Truth Terrorist Manifesto on every computer screen and under every door – "

"We know all that!" I yell. "It's old news! We want to know when you're going to catch these people! We want to know when they're going to be punished! What do you know about them? What leads do you have?"

"Nate," Jenny said, her hand on my arm. I know I'm being irrational.

The guy in the white coat – I'm wondering if he's even a doctor, although I don't want to change the subject by asking – couldn't tell me any of that even if he knew it, because it would compromise the investigation. But I want him to stop telling us old news and give us something else.

It occurs to me that some cops just got their jobs back.

He mops his forehead again. "We don't know much. We're doing everything we can to track them down, I promise you. And we're doing everything we can to restore your loved ones to equilibrium in the meantime."

"Is it possible that some of your employees were plants?" I force myself not to howl in rage, not to curse. "How closely have you screened the people who work here?"

The supposed doctor mumbles something about excellent morale and loyal employees, about never imagining that Oldworld staff would want to sabotage the place, and Jenny tugs at my sleeve. "Nate. Come on. You already know all this, and it's not doing your blood pressure any good. We need to go see your father. Come on, now. I know you're scared, but you're going to feel much better after you've seen him."

"Later for you," I mutter under my breath at the white coat. Jenny's

right. I need to see my father, even though I don't want to. The terrorists don't have to face my father or the other residents. They don't
have to look at what they've done. But I do need to face him. I need to
know if he can forgive me.

I've never felt as much dread as I feel walking down the long white
hall towards the door of my father's padded cell. My stomach has
settled down, finally; instead, my blood vessels are all filled with ice
water. A group of beefy orderlies trail behind me and Jenny and Dr.
Noruba, Dad's physician. She's a slim young woman who's also wearing a white coat and stethoscope, but whom I believe to be a real doctor, because she's been treating Dad very capably for about five years
now. The orderlies are here so they can quell Dad if he gets violent.
I've insisted on seeing him, on being able to talk to him in person. I've
insisted that they open the door to the rubber room.

"He's very agitated," Dr. Noruba tells me for the millionth time. "I
want you to be prepared. We didn't want to drug him, especially given
his history of aversion to chemicals, but he's really very agitated."

"Yes, I know. I understand that."

When we get to the room, I look through the little window, but
don't see my father. Anxiety cramps my gut; I have visions of Dad having somehow hung himself from his hospital pajamas in some corner
of the room I can't see. "Open the door," I tell the orderlies. "Now."

They open it, looking grim. Jenny's hand is on my shoulder. "Dad!"
I call into the room. "Daddy, are you there?"

"Nate!" It's a hoarse croak. I rush inside, and, just as I suspected,
see him sitting in one of the corners I couldn't see from the window.
He's naked. Dr. Noruba should have warned me about that. I sup-
pose they wanted to prevent any chance that he might hang himself
with his hospital pajamas. I glance back at the door and see Jenny's
face framed in the small rectangle of clear plastic. She's biting her lip.
"Nate, did you and Jenny really put me here?"

I feel sick. I go over and sit next to him on the soft rubber floor.
When he looks at me, his blue eyes are as piercing as ever, even though
they're surrounded by wrinkles now. "Yes, Dad. We really did. I'm so

sorry. We thought it was the best thing. You were – you were so sick after the Change, Dad, and we were so scared, and we thought this would help you."

He reaches out to put a skinny hand on my arm, and squeezes. He's surprisingly strong. "Well now. So that's why I never got to go to your house for holidays, for all these years. That's why you and Jenny and the kids always came here. All those stories about house renovations and floods and fire and how you were passing by here on your way to somewhere else: I thought all that sounded fishy after a while."

"I guess it did," I tell him. "I'm sorry. Dad, we only did it because we love you – "

"And the children were in on this? Yes, they must have been. I remember Sam telling me stories about traffic accidents he'd seen, and Julie telling me stories about kids being bullied at school, and it always seemed odd to me that they saved up all of their bad news for their grandpa. They enjoyed it too much, for one thing. I used to wonder how you'd raised such morbid kids, when you were always such an infernal optimist."

"It skipped a generation," I say. It's a really feeble attempt at a joke, but to my surprise, my father laughs. It occurs to me with a jolt that he doesn't seem agitated at all. I blink. What was Dr. Noruba talking about? "Dad, Sam and Julie love you. You know that. We all just wanted to do what was best for you – "

"Ah," Dad says, and he leans closer to me and lowers his voice, and his eyes get even brighter, and his hand's still on my arm, but now it's shaking. He talks very fast. His old-man breath, that strange aroma of dentures and mothballs, is hot on my face. "But that's the thing, Nate. You wanted to do what was best for me, and the people who broke this place open wanted to do what was best for me, but nobody asked *me* what was best for me – "

"Dad," I tell him, "you were catatonic for a month. Do you remember that? We couldn't ask you. You couldn't talk. You had to be given food and water through tubes. And we'd been telling you the truth before that, but you couldn't handle it. We couldn't risk that happening again, Dad. I'm so sorry, and I hope you can forgive me, but I couldn't risk that. I love you too much. I couldn't stand seeing you like that."

"Nobody asked me what was best for me," Dad goes on, even more quickly, as if I haven't spoken at all. "And that's just the way it was before, Nate, you see? People doing things supposedly for other people's good, but really for their own agendas. All of this Change nonsense is a hoax, Nate. It's a load of crap. People haven't changed at all."

I look at his feverish face and glittering eyes, and I realize that Dr. Noruba was wrong. Well, of course. She's too young to remember the world before the Change. She doesn't know what any of her patients were like then.

My father isn't agitated. He's happy. This is exactly how he used to act, how he used to look, when he'd just uncovered a new conspiracy, when he'd found incontrovertible proof that The Public Had Been Lied To, unassailable evidence that power inevitably corrupted those who held it.

"Maybe you're right," I tell him, and I wonder if it's the truth or another lie. Am I just playing along to keep him happy, or do I really believe that we haven't changed? I remember the hatred I felt for the terrorists, and it occurs to me that even though crime really has vanished almost entirely, there has to be a reason so many people want to be fake criminals in places like this, even if it's just a game.

"Of course I'm right," he says, and he stands up now and starts pacing back and forth very quickly, the same way he used to pace in front of his computer when he was hot on the trail of another cover-up. "Nate. Is this room bugged? Are they listening to us?"

"I honestly don't know, Dad. Maybe."

He nods, comes closer to me, grabs me in a bearhug, and whispers into my ear. "We need to find them. The Truth Terrorists. We need to join them. There are other places like this?" I nod, and my father squeezes my neck. "We need to do the same thing at those places."

We? "Dad, learning the truth has hurt a lot of people. And you just told me that the terrorists were wrong not to ask you what was best for you."

"Shhh, Nate. Keep your voice down! We will ask. We'll find a way to ask, somehow. Or do it gradually to watch the effects on the patients. This was the Truth Terrorists' first project. There's always room for improvement. We'll join them so we can show them a better way."

We? He really does sound crazy now. "Dad – "

"So do you have room for me in this house of yours? The one that keeps burning down and getting flooded and renovated? It must be a mansion by now, with all those renovations." His eyes twinkle.

"Dad," I say, not even trying to keep my voice down. "Dad, you can't come home with us. You couldn't handle the Change last time. What makes you think you can handle it now?"

He gives me a pitying look. "Nate. Of course I can handle it. Things haven't changed at all. It's the same old world of lying and cover-ups, even from my family. I know that now."

And suddenly I remember one of the statements from the Manifesto. *We, the Truth Terrorists, think we owe you the truth, as long as we present it in a form you recognize, in a shape that's familiar enough to be safe.* And I remember what Jenny said: *your dad always believed he was living in the middle of a huge conspiracy, and this time he's actually right.*

I've just realized that these Terrorists are geniuses. They've done what Jenny and I and all the doctors could never do: they found a way to tell my father the truth in a form he could accept.

He smiles at me. "I'm so relieved, Nate. I feel better than I've felt in years. And you'll help me, won't you? You keep saying you've been doing all this to help me. Now you have a chance to do it for real. Sam and Julie can help, too. And maybe even Jenny, if we can talk her into it. They're all good researchers, aren't they?"

I swallow. My father wants me to help him by becoming a co-conspirator. He's using my family to make his own secret network, a homegrown terrorist cell. *Your father would probably be a Truth Terrorist himself, if he'd been able to adjust.* My smart Jenny.

And I'm on board. He's won me over. I'm about to become a terrorist. On some level, I think this is really sick. But on another, I feel my fingers and toes tingling, feel the thrill of the hunt, the joy of adrenaline. I realize that I feel better than I've felt in years.

"We'll ask them, Dad. After all, they have to have the chance to decide what's best for them."

Dad grins at me, and it occurs to me that my mother must be spinning in her grave. "That's my boy. Now, how do we break out of here?"

# Jo's Hair

You remember the story. Jo March, tomboy and hoyden, whose only beauty is her long chestnut hair, sells it for twenty-five dollars because her father lies ill in a hospital in Washington. He has not asked for twenty-five dollars, has not asked for anything, but Jo, good nineteenth-century daughter, knows that sacrifices are called for in such situations. Her father has sacrificed his comfortable home life to serve as a Civil War chaplain. Her mother has sacrificed her anger, and the other daughters their ambitions, little Beth will ultimately sacrifice her life. Jo, who does not yet wish to sacrifice her desires, sacrifices her hair instead: walks into a small shop where a small, oily man cuts off her mane and gives her a small roll of bills, which she sends proudly to her father.

Her father does not want it. He never spends the money. When he comes home he tells the assembled family that in all Washington he couldn't find anything beautiful enough to buy with Jo's money, and Jo, sitting in the firelight, blushes, her eyes grown dim. Her parents and sisters, watching her, think her proud of her father's praise; and because she wants to please them, she tries to think so too. Deep down, though, some part of her knows that her sacrifice has been rejected as worthless: too crass, too material, too redolent of the flesh and the body, of the very things good daughters should never exchange for money. Jo's father does not want her hair or anything her hair has purchased.

She understands all this, bright girl that she is, although she never speaks of it. She grows more hair, and thinks only occasionally of the mane she sold. Dutiful daughter, she learns instead to make approved sacrifices. She stops writing, marries an older man with whom she founds a school, devotes herself to home and family. She never goes to Europe, never has an illicit romance, tastes the forbidden only through the adventures of the rambunctious boys she has raised, who are free to venture into the world. Jo has learned the limits of decorum.

But what of Jo's hair?

Here is Jo's hair in the window of the shop where she left it. It has been combed, braided, powdered, oiled, woven fantastically with flowers, a thing for fairyfolk or vain young girls. Along comes just such a young girl, with her even more worldly mother, both of them eager to buy the beauty Jo has so nobly, and with so little effect, sold for a few paltry pieces of paper.

"Look, Mama!" cries our new heroine, pointing at the beautiful plait in the window. "Just the thing for the ball!"

"It will do," her mother says with a nod, surveying Jo's hair with eyes used to assessing silks, satins, fine bonbons, the incomes and social standing of potential husbands. For fifty dollars she boys the hair Jo sold for twenty-five, and that night the young girl attaches Jo's hair to her own thick chestnut locks, just a shade darker than Jo's, and waltzes ecstatically in a brilliant green silk gown beneath even more brilliant crystal chandeliers. By the end of that year, Jo's lovely hair has shone in the light from many chandeliers, from the moon in summer rose gardens, from the blinding sun of midday boating expeditions. It has been admired by the cream of society, by fawning servants, and by a most satisfyingly long list of suitors, including the extremely rich, handsome, and dissipated young man upon whom the new owner of Jo's hair, and her mama, have rested their hopes for lo! these many waltzes.

The same Christmas day that Jo's father tells her he could find nothing to buy with her hair, the dissipated young man steals his first kiss from the worldly young lady, and strokes the smooth plait of Jo's hair, little dreaming that it once belonged to a poor clergyman's daughter. On the day Jo's sister Meg, to Jo's great relief, becomes engaged to a poor but honest tutor, Jo's hair is the central ornament in a costume which, before that evening is out, has been complemented by a dazzling diamond ring beside which even Jo's hair fades into insignificance.

And now, after a decorous three-year wait, Meg and the tutor decorously marry, as Jo mourns the first break in the circle of sisters. On that same day, the worldly young lady dies in childbirth – we would, of course, never dream of questioning whether the stillborn child was actually her husband's – and Jo's hair becomes the stolen property of a servant who carries it off with her into another household. As Jo dismisses the wealthy, dashing neighbor who so desperately wants to marry her, the housemaid who wears Jo's hair attempts – with far less success – to repulse the dishonorable advances of her gentleman employer. Jo flees her neighbor's heartbreak by going to New York to write sensation stories; the disgraced housemaid flees to a lying-in home and, after abandoning her baby on the steps of a church, finds herself reduced to acting bit parts in bad melodramas.

Now Jo's hair smells of greasepaint and cheap gin and the old, tired dust that collects in theaters. Scolded by Professor Bhaer – her destiny, her doom, the only desire she is allowed – for writing immoral trash, Jo resolves to be virtuous and puts away her pen. Little does she suspect that her hair, forever beyond virtue now, lies in a moldy trunk of stage properties a mere mile from the boarding house where, obeying her fate, she met the professor.

She has more important things to worry about. Returning home to her family, she finds the saintly Beth dying a saintly death of tuberculosis. Grieving, Jo dutifully nurses her little sister, who counsels, as Victorian household saints always do, self-abnegation. "Be everything to Father and Mother when I'm gone," Beth says sweetly, "and if it's hard to work alone, remember that I don't forget you, and that you'll be happier in doing that than writing splendid books or seeing all the world."

Jo agrees, of course. How could she not? This is her first deathbed scene, and it moves her profoundly. Young as she is, she little guesses how many others there will be, how few things she will ever be able to do for herself if she devotes her life to keeping promises to the dead. Pierced by sorrow, valiantly struggling not to rebel against the drudgery of the life she has promised to lead, she stays at home and learns to dust.

Meanwhile, Jo's hair has, in a moment of sartorial desperation, been snatched out of its moldy backstage trunk by the woman who will eventually become the most famous diva of the age. As Beth dies, Jo's hair crosses the Atlantic on a luxury steamer. Jo wears mourning as her hair, adorned with blue gems, disembarks in London. Jo languishes at home, washing dishes and convinced that she is fated to be an old maid, as the actress wearing her hair sets out, in the company of a lord addicted to opium and the perfume of women's bodies, for the mysterious East. Professor Bhaer miraculously reappears, and proposes to Jo under an umbrella on a gray, pouring afternoon, while Jo's hair hides demurely beneath a veil in Istanbul.

She marries Friedrich, of course – what choice does she have? – and embarks upon the Plumfield years, raising her sons and other people's sons, any sons she can find, raising them and teaching them and watching them leave her to marry, to go into business, to go West. Meanwhile, more people die: her mother, Meg's husband, various prim spinster neighbors. Jo, good Victorian wife, becomes an old hand at deathbed scenes.

Most of them are quite dull. Only one, of the many she must endure through the years, holds any interest for this tale. As Jo's father lies dying, he gives her back the twenty-five dollars she sent him, so very long ago, when she sold her hair. All these years, he has kept the roll of yellowed bills in a little leather bag. "Spend it on your boys," he tells her, and weeping, she promises him that she will, just as she promised

Beth so long ago to live for her parents instead of herself.

But Jo doesn't spend the money on her boys. Instead, for a reason she cannot fully explain even to herself, she chooses not to spend the money at all. She wears the little bag around her neck, where it weighs on her like a millstone. If she were asked, she would say that, like her father, she cannot find anything beautiful enough to buy with the money. She isn't asked, however. No one notices or cares. Her countless boys have other interests, and Friedrich seems curiously distracted.

As it turns out, he has become infatuated with a local dairymaid, a recent immigrant from Germany who looks like a Valkyrie and makes superb sauerkraut, a skill Jo has never mastered. In due course, Friedrich and his new love run off to Berlin, where they open a restaurant. Jo struggles onward, heroically trying to run Plumfield alone. She acknowledges, although only to herself, a guilty relief when at last the school burns down, sacrificed to the wickedness of a blaspheming boy who insisted on smoking cigars in bed.

Jo herself has, at last, sacrificed everything her father and Beth could have wished: her hopes, her health, her ambition, her idealism, any purely personal desires. She has been ground down to a suffering kernel of patience, that Victorian household staple – as crucial as bread, salt, and oil for the lamps – the woman who gives all and asks for nothing. In the process, she has outlived the era that molded her, has outlived the century itself. Jo has remained at home through the invention of Studebakers and submarines, of light bulbs and airplanes, of motion pictures and federal income tax. Her lifetime has seen the sinking of the *Titanic*, the extinction of the passenger pigeon, and the hideous convulsions of the First World War.

When she was young and strong, all of this would have thrilled her; now it only inspires terror. Jo is obsolete, and she knows it. Selfless Victorian wives are going the way of the passenger pigeon. Friedrich has left her, her boys are scattered to the corners of the earth, and the women of her family who might have cared for her are dead, worn down by work and childbearing. Old and ailing now, Jo throws herself upon the mercy of a world she no longer understands, and repairs to the county poorhouse.

Jo's hair, meanwhile, has found its way into harems and whorehouses, palaces and parades: it has traveled by elephant through dim, steaming jungles, by camel across the Sahara, by whaleboat across the Atlantic. It has been presented to the queen in Buckingham Palace and crossed the Rockies on a mule; it has been admired in Paris salons and Colorado saloons. It has been mute witness to adulteries, betrayals, murders, political plots, the death of men in duels and women in childbirth. It has seen the world's greatest cities and smallest villages. Children have pulled on it, lovers have caressed it, heathen healers have cast spells with it, taking it for some holy shaman's charm.

As we rejoin Jo's hair, a dog in Windswept, Kansas, carries it away from its owner, a wandering scissor salesman who won it from a California undertaker in a poker game. The dog buries it under a tree. A few days later, a very young Kansas pirate, seeking gold, notices the signs of recent digging and unearths Jo's hair. Disappointed not to have found more glittering treasure, but as confident as any savage that this relic must have arcane magical powers, he gives it to his mother for her birthday.

"What a strange thing," she says, holding Jo's hair gingerly between thumb and forefinger.

"Don't you like it, Mama?"

"It's pretty." she says, eyeing the thick, dirty plait and feeling ashamed of her own sparse locks. "I'd say it's been knocking about a bit, though. The lady who grew it must've been a stunner. I wonder why she cut it off?"

"Maybe she was an imprisoned princess," says the small pirate hopefully.

His mother grunts. "Don't get many of those around here, dearie. Those books you read will be rotting your brain. A nun, maybe. Who knows?" She puts Jo's hair into a drawer, not wishing to hurt her son's feelings. If only she had some nice hair of her own to cut off. She's heard that people pay good money for hair.

In the county home, Mother Bhaer lies marooned in a thin white bed, her wrinkled hands plucking at the coverlet in front of her, her wrinkled white head – all its hair lost, long ago, to illness, age, grief – covered by a wrinkled white cap. A thin line of drool descends from one side of her mouth. She has just soiled the sheets.

In her more lucid intervals, she realizes that she has indeed achieved her ambition of becoming like Beth, for here she is, dying, tended by others. She knows now that everyone becomes like Beth, whatever they do in their lives or don't do. Had she written all the splendid books she ever wanted to write, had she traveled to her heart's content, still she would have arrived here at last. She has cheated herself for nothing; her self-denial has left her only the small pouch around her neck, holding the twenty-five dollars she has never spent.

For the moment, she has forgotten about the money, forgotten the meaning of the slight, familiar weight on her chest. For long stretches now, she forgets where she is and where she has been, forgets that she is dying, forgets, blessedly, all the things she has lost and the many more she has never had. She lies on her narrow bed, her eyes glazed; sometimes she calls out names – Friedrich, Beth, Marmee – and then, head cocked, fails silent, as if listening for an answer from a beloved voice. The voices that answer are never ones she knows.

And now here comes another voice Jo doesn't know, someone new to change the bedclothes, to feed Jo gruel and carry the bowl away afterwards, to open the window when the room needs airing and close it again when Jo gets too cold. "Good morning, Mother Bhaer," the new voice says, too loudly, and fragments of Jo's past come rushing upon her like pieces of an unwelcome dream.

"Please don't call me that. Call me Jo."

The new voice hasn't heard her. "There now, mum, we'll have you all comfy in a jiffy," it says, and lifts Jo to yank the linens off the bed. Jo sees now a beaming, ruddy face, very young, as guileless as a yearling colt's. When the young woman turns to reach for the clean sheets, Jo sees swinging below her white cap a thick chestnut braid.

"What beautiful hair you have," Jo says wonderingly. It reminds her of something, but she can't quite remember what.

The young woman laughs, deftly changing the bed beneath Jo's prone body. "This thing? This old rat's tail? Oh, it's a hairpiece, mum. My aunt in Kansas sent it to me for a lark; her son found it buried under a tree. Just fancy that. I don't even know why I wear it – the pins stick into my head and it itches something furious. Probably has bugs. It smells queer enough."

She proceeds to pull out the pins until the offending appendage comes free. She tosses it carelessly onto the clean bed next to Jo, and Jo considers asking her to put the thing somewhere else – if it does have bugs, Jo certainly doesn't want it there – but instead she reaches out and begins to stroke the braid as she would an animal. Then she lifts it to her cheek, caressing it.

"Don't it smell queer?" the nurse says. "My aunt said she couldn't figure out what it smelled like. Nothing you'd call bad, exactly – just strange. Hair *do* pick up smells like nobody's business, don't it? What do you think it smells like, mum?"

It smells like sunlight and cinnamon, like ambergris and attar of rose, like battlefields and bedrooms. It smells like musk and milk, fresh ink and old ivory; like pine needles, incense, horsedung, curry, and beer, like old books and new timber. It smells like mustard and meadow grass and moonshine, like savannahs and sourdough and the restless sea.

Jo feels her eyes filling with tears. "I'll give you twenty-five dollars for this," she says.

The nurse stares at her. "For *that?* That old thing? Oh now, mum, I'd be robbing you, I couldn't – "

"Yes, you could." Jo snaps, already fumbling with the bag around her neck. "Here. Take it. Buy something you want. Buy something beautiful."

She thrusts the money into the young woman's hand and sends her away. After all these years, Jo at last knows that there was a reason why her father never spent the twenty-five dollars on himself, and why Jo never spent it on anyone else. A hank of dirty hair has renewed her faith in Providence.

The nurse, guiltily clutching the leather bag, lingers outside the door, her conscience battling with the part of her that has long coveted a grand feathered hat in one of the fancy stores downtown. Surely the old woman must be cracked, to give twenty-five dollars for a filthy, nasty plait of hair like that. And what if she suddenly comes to her senses, accuses the nurse of cheating or robbing her?

The nurse hefts the little bag in her hand: suspiciously light, this little bag. Maybe there's nothing inside. Maybe the old lady made that up about the twenty-five dollars. I'll just take a look, the nurse thinks, curious now. She opens the bag and shakes out what's inside: a few folded, faded, fragile pieces of paper, cracking and crumbling as she touches them. They may have been money once, but they won't buy anything now.

Poor old thing, the nurse thinks, overcome by pity, poor crazy old woman, her money's not even any good anymore. I won't tell her. I'll let her keep the hair, and I'll let her think she paid for it. These old people need their pride.

Every good tale needs three of something. Here, then, is our third deathbed scene: Jo, stretched out on her thin white bed with a look of peace after all these weary months. It is the dark hour before dawn, the same hour at which Beth died so many years ago. Someone has combed Jo's hair out onto the pillow, and the local minister – complacently aware of his virtue in having dragged himself here from a warm bed – is amazed to discover that the wrinkled white cap has hidden, all this time, a rich crop of chestnut hair, thick and shining, hair any girl would be proud to show off in a ballroom.

From somewhere comes a faint smell of horses, of French perfume, of the sea; the minister wrinkles his nose and waves a hand in front of his face. The new nurse must have left this stink in the room, little strumpet under her starched white uniform, so many of the young ones are like that, pretending to be pious when really —

His mind begins to wander into speculations about the lascivious curves beneath the new nurse's white frock. Fortunately for the state of his soul, the old woman on the bed stirs and suddenly opens her eyes, looking fixedly at something across the room.

"What is it?" demands the minister softly, recalled to his duty. Sometimes these old people, especially the women, have visions of Heaven when they die. That kind of thing has gone out of fashion now, and the minister misses it. He can still remember the days when entire families would crowd around the deathbed, waiting eagerly for a glimpse of the Beyond. He has heard the dying describe the loving face of God, the Shining Ones gathered to welcome them home, blessed Sweet Jesus waiting on the broad banks of that final river. He always respected those visions; with one son dead in a mangled motorcar and another never returned from the battlefields of Europe, he wants more desperately than ever to believe them. "Dear Mother Bhaer, can you tell me what you see?"

She doesn't answer, but begins to weep: tears of joy, the minister knows, a triumph of faith in the hereafter. He feels joy hovering in the room like so many ministering angels. "Tell me," he pleads solemnly, his voice taking on the exhortatory fullness it acquires only in the pulpit and at deathbeds. He leans forward and gazes prayerfully upwards, certain that he is about to receive some new assurance of Paradise. "Before you go, dear, dear Mother Bhaer, tell me what you see!"

"All the world," says Jo March, and smiles at him, and dies.

# Going After Bobo

I was the only one home when the GPS satellites finally came back online. It was already dark outside by then, and it had been snowing all afternoon. I'd been sitting at the kitchen table with my algebra book, trying to concentrate on quadratic equations, and then the handheld beeped and lit up and the transmitter signal started blipping on the screen, and I looked at it and cursed and ran upstairs to double check the signal position against my topo map. And then I cursed some more, and started throwing on warm clothing.

I'd spent five days staring at my handheld, praying that the screen would light up again, please, please, so I'd be able to see where Bobo was. The only time he'd ever stayed away from home overnight, and it was when the satellites were out. Just my luck.

Or maybe David had planned it that way. Bobo had been missing since Monday, the day the satellites went down, and David had probably opened the door for him when I wasn't looking, like always, and then given him an extra kick, gloating because he knew I wouldn't be able to follow Bobo's signal.

I hadn't been too worried yet, on Monday. Bobo was gone when I got back from school, but I thought he'd come home for dinner, the way he always did. When he didn't, I went outside and called him and checked in neighbors' yards. I started to get scared when I couldn't find him, but Mom said not to worry, Bobo would come back later, and even if he didn't, he'd probably be okay even if he stayed out overnight.

But he wasn't back for breakfast on Tuesday, either, and by that night I was frantic, especially since the satellites were still down and I had no idea where Bobo was and I couldn't find him in any of the places where he usually hung out. Wednesday and Thursday and Friday were hell. I carried the handheld with me everyplace, waiting for it to light up again, hunched over it every second, even at school, while Johnny Schuster and Leon Flanking carried on in the background the way they always did. "Hey, Mike! Hey Michael — you know what we're doing after school today? We're driving down to Carson, Mike. Yeah, we're going down to Carson City, and you know what we're going to do down there? We're going to — "

Usually I was pretty good at just ignoring them. I knew I couldn't let them get to me, because that was what they wanted. They wanted me to fight them and get in trouble, and I couldn't do that to Mom, not with so much trouble in the family already. I didn't want her to know what Johnny and Leon were saying; I didn't want her to have to think about Johnny and Leon at all, or why they were picking on me. Our families used to be friends, but that was a long time ago, before my father died and theirs went to jail. Johnny and Leon think it was all my father's fault, as if their own dads couldn't have said no, even if my dad was the one who came up with the idea. So they're mean to me, because my father isn't around anymore for them to blame.

It was harder to ignore them the week the satellites were down. Mom's bosses were checking up on her a lot more, because their handhelds weren't working either. We got calls at home every night to make sure she was really there, and when she was at work, somebody had to go with her if she even left the building. Just like the old days, before the handhelds. And God only knew what David was up to. I guess he was still going to his warehouse job, driving a forklift and moving boxes around, because his boss would have called the probation office if he hadn't shown up. But he wasn't coming home when he was supposed to, and every time he did come home, he and Mom had screaming fights, even worse than usual.

So I had five days of not knowing where Bobo was, while Johnny and Leon baited me at school and Mom and David yelled at each other at home. And then finally the satellites came back online on Friday. The GPS people had been talking about how they might have to knock the whole system out of orbit and put up another one – which would have been a mess – but finally some earthside keyboard jockey managed to fix whatever the hackers had done.

Which was great, except that down here in Reno it had been snowing for hours, and according to the GPS, I was going to have to climb 3,200 feet to reach Bobo. Mom came in just as I was stuffing some extra energy bars in my pack. I knew she wouldn't want me going out, and I wasn't up to fighting with her about it, so I'd been hoping the snow would delay her for a few hours, maybe even keep her down in Carson overnight. I should have known better. That's what Mom's new SUV was for: getting home, even in shitty weather.

She looked tired. She always looks tired after a shift.

"What are you doing?" she said, and looked over my shoulder at the handheld screen, and then at the topo map next to it. "Oh, Jesus, Mike. It's on top of Peavine!"

I could smell her shampoo. She always smells like shampoo after a shift. I didn't want to think about what she smells like before she showers to come home.

"*He's* on top of Peavine," I said. "Bobo's on top of Peavine."

Mom shook her head. "Honey – no. You can't go up there."

"Mom, he could be *hurt*! He could have a broken leg or something and not be able to move and just be lying there!" The signal hadn't moved at all. If it had been lower down the mountain, I would have thought that maybe some family had taken Bobo in, but there still weren't any houses that high. The top of Peavine was one of the few places the developers hadn't gotten to yet.

"Sweetheart." Mom's voice was very quiet. "Michael, turn around. Come on. Turn around and look at me."

I didn't turn around. I stuffed a few more energy bars in my pack, and Mom put her hands on my shoulders and said, "Michael, he's dead."

I still kept my back to her. "You don't *know* that!"

"He's been gone for five days now, and the signal's on top of Peavine. He has to be dead. A coyote got him and dragged him up there. He's never gone that high by himself, has he?"

She was right. In the year he'd had the transmitter, Bobo had never gone anywhere much, certainly not anywhere far. He'd liked exploring the neighbors' yards, and the strips of wild land between the developments, where there were voles and mice. And coyotes.

"So he decided to go exploring," I said, and zipped my pack shut. "I have to go find out, anyway."

"Michael, there's nothing to find out. He's dead. You know that."

"I do *not* know that! I don't know anything." *Except that David's a piece of shit.* I did turn around, then, because I wanted to see her face when I said, "He hasn't been home since Monday, Mom, so how do I know what's happened? I haven't even *seen* him."

I guess I was up to fighting, after all. It was an awful thing to say, because it would only remind her of what we were all trying to forget, but I was still happy when she looked away from me, sharply, with a hiss of indrawn breath. She didn't curse me out, though, even though I deserved it. She didn't even leave the room. Instead she looked back at me, after a minute, and put her hands on my shoulders again. "You can't go out there. Not in this weather. It wouldn't even be safe to take the suv, or I'd drive you – "

"He could be lying hurt in the snow," I said. "Or holed up somewhere, or – "

"Michael, he's dead." I didn't answer. Mom squeezed my shoulders and said gently, "And even if he *were* alive, you couldn't reach him in time. Not all that way; not in this weather. Not even in the suv."

"I just want to know," I said. I looked right at her when I said it. I wasn't saying it to be mean, this time. "I can't stand not knowing."

"You do know," she said. She sounded very sad. "You just won't let yourself know that you know."

"Okay," I told her, my throat tight. "I can't stand not seeing, then. Is that better?"

She took her hands off my shoulders and sighed. "I'll call Letty, but it's not going to do any good. Is your brother home?"

"No," I said. David should have been home an hour before that. I wondered if he even knew that the satellites were back up.

Mom frowned. "Do you know where he is?"

"Of course not," I said. "Do you think I care? Call the sheriff's office, if you want to know where he is."

Mom gave me one of her patented warning looks. "Michael — "

"He let Bobo out," I said. "You know he did. He did it on purpose, just like all the other times. Do you think I care where the fuck he is?"

"I'm going to go call Letty," Mom said.

David hated Bobo the minute we got him. He was my tenth birthday present from Mom and Dad. The four of us went to the petstore to pick him out, but when David saw the kittens, he just wrinkled his nose and backed up a few feet. David was always doing things like that, trying to be cool by pretending he couldn't stand the rest of us.

David and I used to be friends, when we were younger. We played catch and rode our bikes and dug around in the dirt pretending we were gold miners, and once David even pulled me out of the way of a rattlesnake, because I didn't recognize the funny noise in the bushes and had gone to see what it was. I was six then, and David was ten. I'll never forget how pale he was after he yanked me away from the rattling, how scared he looked when he yelled at me never, *ever* to do that again.

The four-year difference didn't matter back then, except that it meant David knew a lot more than I did. But once he got into high school, David didn't want anything to do with any of us, especially his little brother. And all of a sudden he didn't seem so smart to me anymore, even though he thought he was smarter than shit.

I named my new kitten Bobcat, because he had that tawny coat and little tufts on his ears. His name got shortened to Bobo pretty quickly, though, and that's what we always called him — everybody except David, who called him "Hairball." By the time Dad died, Bobo was a really big cat: fifteen pounds, anyway, which was some comfort when David started "accidentally" letting Bobo out of the house. I figured he could hold his own against most other cats, maybe even against owls. I tried not to think about cars and coyotes, and people with guns.

He started going over the fence right away, but he was good about coming home. He always showed up for meals, even if sometimes he brought along his own dessert: dead grasshoppers, and mice and voles, and once a baby bird. Dr. Mills says that when cats bring you dead prey, it's because they think you're their kittens, and they're trying to feed you.

Bobo was a good cat, but David kept letting him out, no matter how much I yelled at him about it. Mom tried to ground David a couple of times, but it didn't work. David just laughed. He kept letting Bobo out, and Bobo kept going over the fence. It took me four months of allowance, plus Christmas and birthday money, to save up enough for the transmitter chip and the handheld. David laughed about that, too.

"He's just a fucking *cat*, Mike. Jesus Christ, what are you spending all your money on that transmitter thing for?"

"So I can find him if he gets lost," I said, my stomach clenching. Even then, I could hardly stand to talk to David.

"If he gets lost, so what? They have a million more cats at the pound."

*And you'd let them all out if you could, wouldn't you?* "They don't have a million who are mine," I said, and Mom looked up from chopping onions in the kitchen. It was one of her days off.

"David, leave him alone. You're the one who should be paying for that transmitter, you know." And they got into a huge fight, and David stomped out of the house and roared off in his rattletrap Jeep, and when all the dust had settled, Mom came and found me in my room. She sat down on the side of the bed and smoothed my hair back from my forehead, as if I was seven again instead of thirteen, and Bobo jumped down from where he'd been lying on my feet. He'd been licking the place where Dr. Mills had put the transmitter chip in his shoulder. Dr. Mills said that licking would help the wound heal, but that if Bobo started biting it, he'd have to wear one of those weird plastic collars that looks like a lampshade. I hadn't seen him biting it yet, but I was keeping an eye on him. When Mom sat on the bed, he resettled himself under my desk lamp, where the light from the bulb warmed the wood, and went back to licking.

Bobo always liked warm places. Dr. Mills says all cats do.

Mom stroked my forehead, and watched Bobo for a little while, and then said, "Michael — sometimes you can know exactly where people are, and still not be able to protect them." As if I didn't know that. As if any of us had been able to protect Dad from his own stupidity, even though the pit bosses knew exactly where he was every time he dealt a hand.

I knew Mom was thinking about Dad, but there was no point talking about it. Dad was gone, and Bobo was right in front of me. "I'd keep him inside if I could, Mom! If David — "

"I know," she said. "I know you would." And then she gave me a quick kiss on the forehead and went downstairs again, and after a while, Bobo got off the desk and came back to lie on my feet. Watching him lick his shoulder, I wondered what it felt like to have a transmitter.

I'm the only one in the family who doesn't know.

Letty's Mom's best friend; they've known each other since second grade. Letty works for the BLM, and they have really good topo maps, so she could tell me exactly where Bobo was: just inside the mouth of an abandoned mine.

"He could have crawled there to get out of the snow," I said. The transmitter signal still hadn't moved. Mom and Letty exchanged looks, and then Mom got up. "I'm going upstairs now," she said. "You two talk."

"He *could* have," I said.

"Oh, Michael," Mom said. She started to say something else,

but then she stopped. "Talk to Letty," she said, and turned and left the room.

I listened to Mom's footsteps going upstairs, and after a minute Letty said, "Mike, it's not safe to go out there now. You know that, right? It wouldn't be safe even in a truck. Not in this weather. And in the snow, you can know exactly where something is and still not be able to get at it."

"I know," I said. "Like that hiker last year. The one whose body they didn't find until spring." Except that the hiker hadn't had a transmitter, so they hadn't known where he was. It didn't matter. For ten days after he went missing, the cops and the BLM had search teams and helicopters all over the mountain, and never mind the weather.

"Yes," Letty said, very quietly. "Exactly." She waited for me to say something, but I didn't. "That guy was dying, you know. He was in a lot of pain all the time. His wife said later she thought maybe that was why he went out in a storm like that, while he could still go out at all."

Letty stopped and waited again, and I kept my head down. "He went out in bad weather," she said finally, "near dark. It's snowing now, and you were getting ready to hike up the mountain when your mom got home at seven-thirty. Michael?"

"Bobo could still be alive," I said fiercely. "It's not like anybody else *cares*. It's not like the state's going to spend thousands of dollars on a search and rescue!"

"So you were thinking – what?" Letty said. "That you'd go up there and get everybody hysterical, and get a search going, and while they were at it, they'd bring Bobo back? Was that the plan?"

"No," I said. I felt a little sick. I hadn't thought about any of that. I hadn't even thought about how I was going to get Bobo back down the mountain once I found him. "I just – I just wanted to get Bobo, that's all. I thought I could go up there and it would be okay. I've hiked in snow before."

"At night?" Letty asked. Then she sighed. "Mike, you know, a lot of people care about Bobo. Your mom cares, and I care, and Rich Mills cares. He was a sweet cat, and we know you love him. But we care about you, too."

"I'm fine," I told her. I wasn't sitting in the mouth of a mine during a snowstorm. I wasn't registered with the sheriff's office.

"You wouldn't be fine if you went up on Peavine tonight," Letty said. "That's the point. And even if Bobo's still alive — and I don't think he can be, Michael — you can't help him if you're frozen to death in a gully somewhere. Okay?"

I stared at the handheld, at the stationary signal. I thought about Bobo huddled in the mouth of the mine, getting colder and colder. He hated being cold. "Is it true that when you freeze to death," I said, "you feel warm at the end?"

"That's what I hear," Letty said. "I don't plan to test it."

"I don't either. That wasn't what I meant."

"Good. Don't do anything stupid, Mike. Search and rescue might not be able to get you out of it."

I felt like I was suffocating. "I was putting food in my pack. An entire box of energy bars. Ask Mom."

Letty shrugged. "Energy bars won't keep you from freezing."

"I *know* that."

"Good. And one more thing: don't you pay any mind to those Schuster and Flanking kids. They're slime."

I jerked my head up. How did she know about that? She raised an eyebrow when she saw my face, and said, "People talk. Folks at my office have kids in your school. The bullies are slime, Michael, and everybody knows it. Don't let them give you grief. Your mother's a good person."

"I know she is." I wanted to ask Letty if she'd told Mom about Johnny and Leon, wanted to beg her not to tell Mom, but the way adults did things, that probably meant that telling Mom would be the first thing she'd do.

Letty nodded. "Good. Just ignore them, then."

It was easy for her to say. She didn't have to listen to them all the time. "That wasn't why I was going out," I told her. "I was going after Bobo."

"I know you were," Letty said. "I also know nothing's simple." She folded her topo map and stood up and said, "I'd better be getting on home, before the weather gets any worse. Tell your Mom I'll talk to her tomorrow. And try to have a good weekend." She ruffled my hair before she went, the way Mom had when Bobo got the chip. Letty hadn't done that since I was little. I didn't move. I just sat there, looking at the blip on the handheld.

After a while I went up to my room. David hadn't come back yet, not that I cared, and Mom's door was closed. I knew she was sleeping off the shift. I also knew she'd be out of bed and downstairs in two seconds if she heard David coming in or me going out. She'd hung the front and back doors with bells, brass things from Nepal or someplace she'd gotten at Pier One. You couldn't go out or come in without making a racket, and you couldn't take the bells off the door without making one, either. "You learn to sleep lightly when you have babies," Mom told me once, as if either David or I had been babies for years. And our windows were old, and pretty noisy in their own right. And it was snowing harder.

So I just sat on my bed and stared out the window at the snow, trying not to think. My window faces east, away from Peavine, towards downtown. I couldn't see the lights from the casinos because of the snow, but I knew they were there. After a while it stopped snowing, and a few stars came out between the clouds, and so did the neon: the blue and white stripes of the Peppermill, which stands apart from everything else, south of downtown, and the bright white of the Hilton a bit north of that – "the Mother ship," Mom always calls it – and then, clustered downtown, the red of Circus Circus and the green of Harrah's, which Mom calls Oz City, and the flashing purple of the Silverado, where Dad used to work.

Dad loved this view; he was so proud that we could look down on the city. He couldn't stop crowing about it to all his friends. I remember when he brought George Flanking and Howard Schuster, Leon and Johnny's dads, into my room so they could look out my window, too. So they could see "the panorama." That was what Dad called it. We'd never been able to see anything from our old windows, except more trailers across the way. "I'm going to get us out of this box," Dad said when we lived there. "We're going to live in a real house, I swear we are." And then we moved here, to a real house, and pretty soon that wasn't big enough for him, either.

I shut my blinds and flopped down on my bed. Someplace a dog had started to bark, and then another joined in, and another and another, until the whole damn neighborhood was going nuts. And then I heard what must have set them off: the yipping howl of a coyote, trotting between houses looking for prey.

When we bought our house five years ago, the street ended a block from here, and that was where the mountain started. Winter mornings, sometimes, we'd see coyotes in our driveway. Now the developers have built another hundred houses up the street, with more subdivisions going up all the time: fancy houses, big, the kind we could never afford, the kind that made Dad's eyes narrow, that made him spend hours hunched over his desk. The kind he talked about when he went out drinking with George and Howard, I guess. I don't know who's buying those big houses; casino and warehouse workers can't afford places like that. Mom could, maybe, if she weren't saving for nursing school. The only people I can think of who might live there are the ones who work for the development companies.

So we don't get coyotes in our driveway anymore, but they're still around. They travel in back of the houses, next to the six-foot fences people put around their yards. There's still sagebrush between the subdivisions, and rabbits, and you can still follow those little strips of wildness to the really wild places, up on the mountain.

Coyotes are unbelievably smart, and they'll eat anything if they have to, and it doesn't bother them when people cut the land into pieces. They like it, because the boundaries between city and wilderness are where rodents live, and rodents are about coyotes' favorite food, aside from cats. So when we cut things up for them, there are more edges where they can hunt. It doesn't hurt that we've killed most of the wolves, who eat coyotes when they can, or that coyotes look so much like dogs. They can sneak in just about anyplace. Dr. Mills says there are coyotes living in New York City now, in Central Park. There are millions of them, all over the country.

Ranchers and farmers hate them because they're so hard to kill, and because even if you kill them, there are always more. But I can't hate them, not even for eating cats. They're smart and they're beautiful, and they're just trying to get by, and as far as I can tell, they're doing a better job of it than we are. They know how to work the system. That's what Dad thought he was doing, but he wasn't smart enough.

I lay there, listening to that coyote and to all the dogs, still trying not to think, but thinking anyway: about what a weird town this is, where you get casinos and coyotes both, where the developers are covering everything with new subdivisions, but there's still a mountain where you can die. After a while it got quiet again, and I peeked out the window and saw more snow. A while after that I heard the bells jangling downstairs, and heard Mom's feet hitting her bedroom floor and thudding down the stairs. When she and David started yelling at each other, I pulled my pillow over my head and finally managed to go to sleep.

It wasn't snowing when I woke up on Saturday, but it looked like it might start again any minute. The transmitter signal still hadn't moved, and when I thought about Bobo out there in the cold, I felt my own heart freezing in my chest. I heard voices from downstairs, and smelled coffee and bacon. Mom and David were both home, then. I threw on clothing and grabbed the handheld and ran down to the kitchen.

"Good morning," Mom said, and handed me a plate of bacon and eggs. She was wearing sweats and looked pretty relaxed. David was wearing his bathrobe and scowling, but David always scowls. I wondered what he was doing up so early. "Any change on the screen, Mike?"

"No," I said. I knew she didn't think there ever would be, and I wondered why she'd asked. David's face had gone from scowling to murderous, but that was all right, because I planned to be out the door as soon as possible.

"Okay," Mom said. "We're all going up there after breakfast."

"We are?" I said.

"Your brother's coming whether he wants to or not, and I asked Letty to come too. Rich Mills has to work this morning. Unless you'd rather not have all those people, honey."

"It's okay," I said. So that's what David was doing up. Mom was making him come as punishment, so he could see what he'd done, and Letty was coming because she had the maps, and maybe to help Mom keep me and David apart if we tried to kill each other. And Mom wouldn't think it was important to have Dr. Mills there, because she didn't think Bobo was still alive. I put down my plate and gulped down some coffee and said, "I'm going to go put the carrying case in the SUV."

"You're going to eat first," Mom said. "Sit down."

I sat. Driving up Peavine in the snow wasn't exactly Mom's idea of a day off; the least I could do was not give her any lip. David bit into his toast and said around a mouthful of bread, "I'm not going."

That was fine with me, but I wasn't going to say so in front of Mom. It was their fight. "You're coming," she told him. "And if Bobo's still alive you're paying the vet bills, and if he's not, you're buying your brother another cat. And if we get another cat you'll damn well help us keep it in the house, or I'll call the sheriff's office myself and tell them to take you off probation and put you in jail, David, I swear to God I will!"

She would, too. Even David knew that much. He scowled up at her and said, "The cat didn't *want* to stay in the house."

"That's not the issue," Mom said, and I stuffed my face full of eggs to keep from screaming at David that he'd hated Bobo, that he'd wanted Bobo to die, and that I hoped he'd die, too: alone, in the cold.

I remembered one of the first times David had let Bobo out. Bobo didn't have the transmitter yet, and I was in the backyard calling his name. Suddenly I saw something race over the fence and he ran up to me, mewing and mewing, his tail all puffy. I picked him up and carried him inside and he stayed on my lap, with his face stuck into my armpit like he was hiding, for half an hour, until finally he calmed down and stopped shaking and jumped down to get some food. I'd hoped that whatever had spooked him so badly would keep him from wanting to go out again, even if David opened all the doors and windows, but I guess he forgot how scared he'd been. "He didn't want to freeze to death, either," I said.

David pushed his chair back from the table and said, "Look, whatever happened to your fucking cat, it's not my fault, and I'm not wasting my day off going up there." He looked at Mom and said, "Do whatever you want: it doesn't matter. I might as well be in prison already."

"Bullshit," Mom said. "If you go to prison, you'll lose a lot more than a Saturday. Do you have any idea how lucky you are not to be there already? Especially after the stunts you've been pulling this week?" Nevada's a zero-tolerance drug state, even for minors, so when David got caught driving stoned last year, with most of a lid of pot in the glove compartment of his Jeep, Mom had to use every connection she had to get him probation instead of jail. It would have been a "juvenile facility," since David was still a few weeks short of eighteen, but Mom says her connections said that wouldn't make much difference. Juvenile facilities are worse, if anything.

Mom didn't say who her connections are, and I don't want to know. Whoever they are, I figure they didn't help David entirely out of the goodness of their hearts. I figure they were scared of what Mom could tell people about them, even if what she does is legal.

"I told you," David said, "I've just been hanging out with some guys from work. You know: eating dinner, playing pool? I was in town."

"Right," Mom said. "And there's no way anybody could check

that with the satellites down, is there? That's what you were count-ing on."

David rolled his eyes. "What time did the damn GPS go back up last night? Six-thirty or something? We were still eating then. We were at that pizza place in the mall. Call the sheriff's office and ask them, if you don't believe me." He jerked a thumb at my handheld and said, "How stupid do you think I am? I knew it could come back online any second. What, I'm going to take off for Mexico or something?"

Mom didn't bother to answer. She and I were the smart ones in the family: David took after Dad. Anybody stupid enough to get caught with that much pot was stupid enough to do just about anything else, as far as I could tell, but the only time I'd even started to say anything like that, right after his arrest, David had just glared at me and said, "Yeah, well, if you'd had to look at what I had to look at, you'd smoke dope too, baby brother."

As if I hadn't wanted to look. As if I hadn't kept trying to go out-side. As if even now I didn't keep imagining what it had looked like, a million different ways, enough to keep me awake, sometimes.

But even then, I knew that David had only said it to make me feel guilty. He knew just how to get at everybody. Now he gestured at the handheld again and said bitterly, "I can't wipe my ass without those people knowing about it."

He was needling Mom, because that's what Dad had always said about dealing blackjack at the Silverado. The dealers were under sur-veillance all the time: from pit bosses, from hidden cameras. "You can't get away from it," Dad said. "It's like working in a goddamn box, with the walls closing in on you." But Dad chose his box, and so did David.

"That's not the issue," Mom told David again. "It's more than stay-ing in county limits, David. You're supposed to come home straight after work. You know that."

"So you're my jailor now? Just like the casino was Dad's and the Lyon County cops are — "

"Stop it," Mom said, her voice icy. "I'm not your jailor. I'm the one who kept you out of jail. You agreed to the terms of the probation!"

"Like you agreed to all those terms when you decided to go down to Carson and play *nurse*?"

Mom was out of her chair then, and David was out of his, and they stood nose to nose, glaring at each other, and I knew that there was no way we were all going up on Peavine today, because they wouldn't be able to sit in the same car even if David had wanted to go, even if I'd wanted him there. Nothing David says to Mom ever makes any real sense, but he knows exactly how to get to her. Sometimes he has to keep at it for a while, but Mom always snaps eventually, even if the same thing has happened a million times before. Just like Bobo being scared by something outside, and still going out again when David gave him the chance. David knows exactly how to get people to hurt themselves.

They were still eye to eye, like cats circling each other before a fight, when the doorbell rang. "I'll get it," I said. Maybe it was Letty, and I could warn her about what was happening before she came inside.

It was a cop. "Good morning, son. I'm looking for David. That your brother?"

"Yeah," I said, but my legs felt like wood, and I didn't seem to be able to get out of the way.

"Don't worry," he said. "It's just a routine drug test."

That was supposed to happen on Fridays. So David had skipped his drug test, too. My stomach shriveled some more. "Will he have to go to jail?" I said. The house would be a lot quieter if David was in jail, but school would be worse. If David went to jail, he'd probably be in the same place as George Flanking and Howard Schuster, and I didn't want to think too much about that.

The cop's face softened. "No. Not if he's clean. He'll get a warning, that's all."

And then Mom, behind me, said, "Michael, let him *in*," and my legs came alive and I got out of the doorway, fast, and the cop came in, tipping his hat to Mom.

"Morning, ma'am." I wondered if Mom was remembering the last time the cops were at our house. I wondered if this cop was one of her connections. I wonder that about all kinds of people: my teachers and all the cops and storekeepers and Dr. Mills, even. I hate wondering it, but that's another thing I can't talk to Mom about. It would just hurt her. It would just make me like David, or like Aunt Tina, who hasn't even talked to us since Mom started working down in Carson.

The fight Aunt Tina picked with Mom was as bad as any of David's: worse, maybe, because she doesn't even live with us. She wasn't even here when Dad died. It was none of her business. "Oh, Sherry! How can you do *that*, of all things? With your boys the ages they are, after what their father did? How will they be able to hold their heads up, knowing – "

"Knowing that their mother's keeping a roof over their head? My secretarial job doesn't pay enough, Tina, not by itself – and if you know what else I can do to earn a hundred thousand a year, go right ahead and tell me!"

It was perfectly legal, and it would let Mom earn enough money to go to nursing school at UNR and get a job none of us would have to be embarrassed about. That's what she kept telling us. A year, she'd said, or two at the most. But it had already been two years, and she hadn't saved enough to quit yet, because the hundred thousand didn't include food or clothing or insurance, or all the tests Mom has to have to make sure she's still healthy. She has drug tests, too. She gets more tests than David does, even though she's not a criminal and never did anything wrong, and she has to pay for all of hers. And when she's in Carson she can't go into a casino or a bar by herself, and she can't be seen in a restaurant with a man, and she has to be registered with the Lyon County Sheriff's Office – because technically, she's not in Carson at all. Her job's not legal in big towns: not in Reno, not in Vegas, not even in lousy little Carson City, the most pathetic excuse for a state capitol you ever saw. Mom has to work right outside Carson, in Lyon County, which is still plenty close enough to be convenient for her connections.

It used to be that the women at Mom's job couldn't even leave the buildings where they work without somebody going with them, but now they have transmitters, instead. And it used to be that they had to work every day for three weeks, living at the job, and then get one week off, but some of them got together and lobbied to change that, because so many of them were single mothers, and they wanted to be able to go home to their kids at night. But they still can't live in the same county where they work, which is why Mom has to commute between Reno and Carson. Highway 395's the only way to get down there, and those thirty-five miles can get really bad in the winter. That's why Mom had to buy the SUV. The SUV wasn't included in the hundred thousand, either.

Mom doesn't know that I know a lot of this. I've heard her and Letty talking about it, especially about all the tests. Letty's afraid Mom's going to get something horrible and die, but Mom keeps pooh-poohing her. "For heaven's sake, Letty; it's not like they don't have to wear condoms!"

I got out of the cop's way and tried not to think about him wearing a condom. It's hard not to get really mad at Dad whenever I think things like that. It's hard not to get even madder at David. He has it easier than Mom does, and it's not fair. She's not the criminal.

I followed the cop into the kitchen. Mom was chitchatting about the weather and pouring him a cup of coffee; David was disappearing down the hall to the bathroom, carrying a little plastic cup. I looked at the drug kit, sitting on the table next to our half-eaten breakfasts. "Only takes two minutes," the cop told me, "and then I'll be out of here and leave you folks to your weekend. Ma'am, you mind if I take my jacket off?"

"Of course not," she said, and he did, and when I saw the gun in its holster I took a step back, even though of course the cop would be wearing a gun, all cops wear guns. Nearly everybody around here owns guns anyway, except us. And Mom bit her lip and the cop stepped back too, away from me, raising his hands. He looked sad.

"Hey, hey, son, it's all right. I'll put the jacket back on."

"You don't have to," I said, my face burning. "I'm going up to my room, anyway." I wanted to get out of there before David came back out of the bathroom with his precious bodily fluids. I didn't want to stand around and find out what the drug tests said. So I went upstairs, wondering if there was anybody in the entire fucking town who didn't know everything about anything that had ever happened to us.

I flopped down on my bed again, waiting for the jangle of bells that would mean the cop had left. It came pretty quickly, and then there was another right after it, and I didn't hear any yelling, so I figured everything was okay. The phone had rung, somewhere in there. One of David's loser friends, probably. Maybe he'd gone out. Maybe I wouldn't have to deal with him today. I wanted to be out on the mountain, climbing up to Bobo, but I knew the SUV would get there more quickly than I could, even with the delay.

But when I went back downstairs, David was in the living room watching TV and Mom and Letty were sitting at the kitchen table, looking worried. I looked at Mom and she said, "Relax. Your brother's clean."

"Okay," I said. She and Letty had probably been talking about me. "Are we leaving soon?"

Mom looked down at the table. "Michael, honey, I'm sorry. We can't leave right away. I'm waiting for a call from the doctor."

I squinted at her. "From the *doctor?*"

"I'm fine," Mom said. "It's nothing, really. She's looking at some test results, that's all, and I may need to take some antibiotics. But I don't want to miss the call. We'll go right after that, okay?"

"I'm going now," I said. *I thought they had to wear condoms.* "He's been up there since last night, Mom!"

Letty started to stand up. "Mike, I'll drive you – "

"You don't have to," I said. Right then, as much as I wanted to reach Bobo quickly, I wanted to be alone even more. "You can catch up with me after the doctor calls. Stay and talk to Mom." Stay and keep Mom and David out of each other's hair, I meant, and maybe Letty knew that, because she nodded and sat back down.

"Okay. We'll follow you as soon as we can. Be careful."

"Don't worry," I said. "It's not like you don't know where I'm going."

It felt good to be out, away from Mom and David, where I could finally breathe again. I cut over to the wild strip on the edge of our subdivision and started working my way up, past the new construction sites where the dumptrucks and jackhammers were roaring away, even on Saturday, up to where all the signs say BUREAU OF LAND MANAGEMENT and NATIONAL FOREST SERVICE. The signs don't mean much, because the Forest Service and the BLM can sell the land to developers anytime they want. Right now, though, the signs meant that I was on the edge of wildness stretching for miles, all the way to Tahoe.

When the construction noises faded, I started hearing the gunfire. Shooters come up on Peavine for target practice; you can always find rifle shells on the trails, and there are all kinds of abandoned cars and washing machines and refrigerators that people have hauled up here and shot into Swiss cheese. Sometimes the metal has so many holes you wonder how it holds its shape at all. "Redneck lace," Dad used to call it – Dad who'd grown up in a trailer, and was so proud that he'd gotten us out of one; Dad, who couldn't stand being called a redneck, even though he came up on Peavine every weekend with George Schuster and Howard Flanking, so they could drink beer and shoot skeet.

After he died, I couldn't come up on the mountain for a long time. But gunfire's one of those things you can't get away from here, any more than you can avoid new subdivisions, and Peavine's the only place I can come to be alone, really alone. I can hike up here for hours and never see anybody else. The gunfire's far away, and nearby are sagebrush and rabbits and hawks. In the summer you see lizards and snakes, and in the winter, in the snow, you see the fresh tracks of deer and antelope. I've seen prints that looked like mountain lion; I've seen prints that looked like dog, but were probably coyote.

I hiked hard, pushing myself, taking the steepest trails. It takes me three hours to get to the top of Peavine in good weather, and today I wanted the most direct route I could find. When you're slogging up a fifteen percent grade in the snow, it's harder to think about how miserable your cat would be, stuck up here in weather like this, and it's harder to think about what you want to do to your brother for letting him out. It's harder to think about who you know might be wearing condoms, or how condoms can break even when they're used right. It's harder to think about how angry you are that your mother's connections don't have to be tested before she is, to make sure she doesn't catch anything.

Mom never lied to me. She wouldn't say "some antibiotics" if she really meant "years of AIDS drugs." She wouldn't say it was nothing if she was scared she might be infected with something that could kill her. I was angry anyway, because nothing was fair.

So that fifteen percent grade was just what I needed. If Mom and Letty followed me, they'd be coming the easy way, up the road. They'd probably be angry if they couldn't find me, but they'd also get to the mine before I did, and they'd be able to drive Bobo back down. I hadn't been able to bring the carrying case with me, but I wouldn't be able to get it back down the mountain with Bobo in it anyway, not by myself. I hoped Mom had remembered to put the carrying case in the SUV. I hoped Bobo would still be in any kind of shape to need the carrying case at all.

*I'm sorry*, I told him as I climbed. *I'm sorry I didn't come after you sooner. I'm sorry I couldn't protect you from David. I'm sorry about whatever scared you. Bobo, please be alive. Please be okay.*

After a while, it started to snow. I kept going. I was wearing my warmest thermals and I was covered in Gore-Tex, and I had enough food in the pack for three days. And if Mom and Letty drove up in the snow and couldn't find me because I'd come back down, they'd really start freaking. So I headed on up, except that as soon as I could, I cut over to the road. I didn't see any fresh tire marks, which meant they were still behind me. I tromped along, checking the GPS every once in a while to make sure the signal hadn't moved, and then

I heard a horn and turned around and saw headlights.

It was Dr. Mills. "Hey, Mike. I drove by your house when I got off work, and your mom said you'd headed up here." I scrambled into his truck; he had the heater blasting, and it felt good. "I hope you don't mind that your mom didn't come. My old truck can take the wear better than that fancy Suburban she has, and there's only so much room in here."

There was still plenty of room in the front seat. I glanced back at the flatbed: Dr. Mills had brought a carrying case, but of course on the way down, we'd want to be able to have Bobo in front with us, where it was warm. The part about Mom could have meant just about anything, depending on whether it was his excuse or hers. If it was hers, she could have been hoping that Dr. Mills would run a male-bonding father-figure trip on me, or she could have still been waiting for the doctor to call, or she and Letty could have been trying to force David to stay in the house somehow. Or all of the above. If it was his – I didn't want to think about what it meant for him to be saving wear on her SUV, or not wanting her in the truck at all. Dr. Mills is married. I didn't want to think about him driving down to Carson.

So I looked at the handheld again. "He's in an old mine up here," I said.

"Mmm-hmmm. That's what your mom told me. How long since he's moved?"

"Not since the satellites came back up," I said, and Dr. Mills nodded. He stayed quiet for a long time, and finally I said, "You think he's dead, don't you? That's what Mom thinks."

The snow was coming down harder now, the windshield wipers squeaking in a rhythm that kept trying to lull me to sleep. Dr. Mills could have told me he didn't want to go on; he could have turned around. He didn't do that. He knew I had to see as much as I could. "Michael," he said finally, "I've been a vet for fifteen years, and I've seen plenty of miracles. Animals are amazing. But I have to tell you, I think it would take a miracle for Bobo not to be dead."

"Okay," I said, trying to keep my voice steady.

"With coyotes," he said, "usually it's quick. They break the necks of their prey, the same as cats do with birds and mice. So unless Bobo got away for a few minutes and then got caught again, he wouldn't have suffered long."

"Okay," I said, and looked at my hands. I wondered how long it would take me to break David's neck, and how much I could make him suffer while I did it. And then I thought, there goes David again, making me want to do something stupid, something that would only mean I was hurting myself.

It took us ten more minutes to get to the mine, and by then the snow was coming down so hard that we could hardly see a foot ahead of the truck. We got out and started walking towards where the mine should have been, snow stinging our faces. It was really cold. I couldn't see anything but snow: no rocks, not even the scrubby pines that grow up here. And within about ten feet I realized that the mine entrance was completely buried, and that even if we'd been able to find it, we'd probably need to dig through five feet of snow to get to Bobo.

"Michael," Dr. Mills yelled into my ear, over the wind. "Michael, I'm sorry. We have to go back."

I tried to say, "I know," but my voice wouldn't work. I turned around and headed towards the truck, and when I was back inside it I started shivering, even when the heat was blasting again. I sat in the front seat, with the empty space between me and Dr. Mills where Bobo should have been, and shivered and hugged myself. Finally I said, "You get warm, just before you freeze to death. If the coyotes didn't kill him — or if he went up on his own — "

"He's not in pain," Dr. Mills said. "That's a cliché, isn't it? But it's true. Michael, wherever he is now, he doesn't hurt. I can promise you that." And then he started telling me about some poem called "The Heaven of Animals," where the animals remain true to their natures. The predators still hunt and exult over their kill, and their prey rise up again every morning, perfectly renewed, joyously taking their proper part in the chase.

I guess it's a nice idea, but all I could think about was Bobo, shivering, hiding his head under my arm because he was scared.

So we drove on down the mountain, and pretty soon the snow stopped coming down so hard, and when we got back down to the developments, there was hardly any snow at all. You could still hear the construction equipment, and gunfire far off. Maybe the target shooters had moved farther down to get away from the snow. Dr. Mills hadn't said anything for a while, but when we started hearing the guns, he looked over at me.

Don't, I thought. Don't say it. Don't say anything. Just take me home, Dr. Mills, please. Don't say it.

"I never told you," he said, very quietly, "how sorry I am about what happened to your dad."

I stared straight ahead, thinking about Bobo, thinking about the hiker who'd died on Peavine. I wondered how long it would take the snow to melt.

When Bobo was a kitten, Dad used to dangle pieces of string for him. He always dangled them just high enough so Bobo couldn't get at them, and he'd laugh and laugh, watching Bobo jump. "We're going to enter this cat in the *Olympics*," he said. "Look at him! He must've made three feet that time!"

Bobo had lots of toys he could play with anytime he wanted, balls and catnip mice and crumpled-up pieces of paper I'd toss on the floor for him. But the minute Dad dangled that string, he'd stop playing with the stuff he could catch and go after the thing he couldn't have.

"Just like you," Mom always told him, watching them. "Just like you, Bill, jumping at what you'll never be able to get."

"Aw, now, Sherry! Why can't we have a Lexus? Why can't we have one of those fancy home theaters, huh?"

I thought he was kidding. Maybe Mom did, too.

When Dr. Mills dropped me off at home, David was gone, which was a good thing, because I don't know what I would have done if I'd had to look at him. Mom and Letty were still there. They tried to talk to me.

I didn't want to talk. I went straight up to my room and took off all the Gore-Tex and went to bed. I didn't want to think about what we didn't need anymore: the toys and the litter box and Bobo's food and water bowls. I knew I'd have to throw it all away. Mom had told David he had to get me another cat, but how could I get another cat? David would just let it out again. When I got into bed, I remembered that the handheld was still in my jacket pocket, and somehow that hurt more than anything else. I pulled my pillow over my head and turned my face to the wall. The pillow blocked out a lot, but I still heard the phone, and I still heard the jangling bells when Letty left, and I still heard them again when David came in. I couldn't block out the sounds of him and Mom yelling at each other, no matter how hard I tried.

I got up and tried to do homework, but that just made me think about how I was going to have to go to school on Monday morning. I tried to read, but all the words seemed flat and tasteless, like week-old bread. So finally I just sat on my bed, staring out at the casinos. They looked so small from here, little boxes you could pick up and throw like dice. And then I heard a coyote, off in the other direction.

Being good is one of the smallest boxes there is: Mom knows that, and so do I, and so did Dad. Mom was the only one who never complained about it, but what did I know? Maybe she hated it as much as I did. I didn't see how she could like it. Maybe she felt like Dad said he'd always felt, like the walls were closing in on her. "If I could just get outside," he always told me. "Working in that damn casino, no daylight anywhere, all those people watching you all the time, you just want to go outside and take a walk, Mike, you know what I mean?"

After Dr. Mills drove me up to the mine, I knew what Dad meant. I sat there with the walls closing in on me, and I couldn't breathe. I needed more room. I wanted to be outside with the coyotes, running around the outside of the boxes, invisible. Even if you try to watch a coyote to see what it's doing, even if you try to track it, it will disappear on you. It will fade into the grass, into the sagebrush, into shadows. And you'll know that wherever it is, it's laughing.

Sunday was quiet. David stayed in front of the TV, and I finally got my homework done, and Mom cleaned the house, humming to herself while she worked. She had to be on antibiotics for ten days, and she couldn't work until the infection was gone. "Ten-day vacation," she told me cheerfully, but she didn't get paid vacations any more than she got anything else. All it meant was ten days' pay out of the nursing-school fund.

Once I asked her what would happen if the Lyon County sheriff's office saw her transmitter signal outside the building where she works. What if they tracked it and found her in a bar, or in a casino, or in a restaurant with a man? Would she go to jail?

She'd shaken her head and said very gently, "No, honey, I'd just lose my job. And I'd never do that, because it would be stupid." Because it would be like what Dad did, she meant. "Don't worry."

When I got up on Monday morning, my stomach hurt already. I hadn't been able to sleep very well, because I kept thinking about Bobo buried in the snow. I kept wondering about what I hadn't been able to see, worrying that maybe there'd been some way to save him and I hadn't figured it out.

I couldn't stand the idea of going to school. I couldn't stand facing Johnny and Leon; I couldn't stand the idea of going through all that and not being able to come home and have Bobo comfort me, curling up on my stomach the way he always did to get warm. I'd always been able to tell Bobo everything I couldn't talk about to anybody else, and now he was gone.

But I had to go to school, so I wouldn't upset Mom.

I had an algebra test first period. I knew the material; I could have done all the problems, but I couldn't make my hands move. I just sat there and stared at the paper, and when Mrs. Ogilvy called time, I handed it in blank.

She looked at it, and both her eyebrows went up. "Michael?"

"I didn't feel like it," I said.

"You didn't — Michael, are you sick? Do you want to go to the nurse?"

"No," I said, and walked away, out into the hall, to my next class, which was English. We were talking about Julius Caesar. I sat against the back wall and fell asleep, and when the bell rang I got up and went to biology, where we were dissecting frogs. Biology was always bad, because Johnny and Leon were in there. They grabbed the lab station next to mine, and whenever they thought they could get away with it they whispered, "Hey, Mike, know what we're gonna do after school? Hey, Mike — we're gonna drive down to Carson. We're gonna drive down to Carson *and fuck your mother*."

Donna Mauro, my lab partner, said, "They are *such* jerks."

"Yeah," I said, but I couldn't even look at Donna, because I was too ashamed. I knew everybody in school knew what my mother did, but that didn't mean I liked it when Johnny and Leon reminded them. I wondered if one of Donna's parents worked for the BLM and had talked to Letty, but it could have been just about anybody.

I stared down at the frog. We were supposed to be looking for the heart. I pretended it was Johnny instead, and sliced off a leg. Then I pretended it was Leon, and sliced off the other leg.

Donna just watched me. "Um, Mike? What are you doing?"

"I thought I'd have frog legs for lunch," I said. My voice sounded weird to me, tinny. "Want one?"

"Um — Mike, that's cool, but we have to find the heart now."

I handed her the scalpel. "Here. You find the heart."

And then I turned and walked away.

It was really easy, actually. I just walked out of the room, like I had to go to the bathroom but had forgotten to ask permission. Behind me I could hear Mr. Favaro, our teacher, saying something, and Donna answering, but the voices didn't really reach me. I felt like I was inside a bubble: I could see outside, but everything was muffled, and no one could get inside. They'd just bounce off.

It was wonderful.

I walked along the hall, and Mr. Favaro ran up behind me, gabbling something. I had to listen really carefully to make out what he was saying. It sounded like he was on the moon. "Mike? Michael? Is there something you need to tell me?"

I considered this. "No," I said. If I'd been Leon or Johnny or one of the bad kids, Mr. Favaro probably would have yelled at me and told me to get back inside the room, *now*, but he was spooked because it was me acting this way. So he gabbled some more, and I ignored him, and finally he ran away in the other direction, towards the principal's office.

I just walked out the door. My jacket was back in my locker, but it was pretty warm out, at least in the sun, and I wasn't cold. The bubble kept me warm. I started walking down a gully that angled past the football field. I could hear voices behind me; I didn't stop to try to figure out what they were saying. But then a van pulled up alongside the gully, and people got out, and the voices started again. "Michael. Michael Michael Michael Michael Michael."

"*What*?" I said. Ms. Dellafield was there, the principal, and Mr. Ambrose, the school nurse, and two guidance counselors whose names I could never remember. They all looked really scared. I blinked at them. "I just wanted to take a walk," I said, but they were in a semicircle around me, pushing at the edges of the bubble, herding me towards the van. "You don't have to do this," I told them. "Really. I'm fine. I was just taking a walk."

They didn't listen. They kept herding me towards the van, and then I was inside it, and the door was closing.

They drove me back to school, and then they herded me into Mr. Ambrose's office, and then Ms. Dellafield went to call Mom while Mr. Ambrose and the two guidance counselors stood there and watched me, like they were going to tackle me if I tried to move. "Why are you doing this?" I kept asking them. "I was just going for a walk." It didn't make any sense. I'd seen other kids walk out of classes: they'd never gotten this kind of attention. "I'll go back to biology, okay? I'll dissect my frog. You don't have to call my mother!"

And at the same time I thought, thank God Mom's home today. Thank God she's not down in Carson, so that Ms. Dellafield doesn't have to hear them say whatever they say when they answer the phone there, not that there's any chance that Ms. Dellafield doesn't know where Mom works, since everybody else knows it. But even all that didn't bother me as much as usual, because the bubble was still basically holding. Mr. Ambrose and the guidance counselors kept asking me how I was, and I kept telling them I was fine, thank you, and how are all of you today? And they kept looking more and more worried, as if I'd answered them in another language, one where "fine" meant "my eyeballs are about to explode." So I sat there feeling fine, if a little far away, and thinking, these people are really weird.

And finally, after about half an hour, I heard voices outside Mr. Ambrose's office, and then the door opened and Mom came in. She was leaning on David. David had his arm around her, and he was really pale. It was the same way he'd looked after he pulled me away from the rattlesnake.

I squinted at him and said, "What are you doing here? What happened?"

"She called me," David said. He sounded like he was choking. "At work. When they called her. So we could come over here together."

I looked at Mom. She was crying, and then I got really scared. "What's going on?" I said. "Mom, what's wrong? Are you okay? Did something happen to Letty?" Maybe Mom had called Ms. Dellafield and said something had happened and they had to find me. But that wouldn't explain the van and the guidance counselors, would it? If something had happened to Letty, wouldn't Mom have driven over here to tell me herself?

Everybody just stared at me. Mom stopped crying, and wiped her eyes, and said very quietly, "Michael, the question is, are you okay?"

"I'm *fine*! Why does everybody keep asking me that? I was just going for a walk! Why doesn't anybody believe me?"

And Mom started crying again and David shook his head and said, "Oh, you stupid — "

"David." Ms. Dellafield sounded very tired. "Don't."

I felt like I was going crazy. "Would somebody please tell me what's going on? I was just — "

"Michael," Mom said, "that's what your father said, too."

I blinked. The room had gotten impossibly quiet, as if nobody else was even breathing. Mom said, "He said he was just going for a walk, and then he went out into the yard. Don't you remember?"

I looked away from all of them, out the window. I didn't remember that. I didn't remember anything that had happened that day, before the shot. It didn't matter: everyone else at school knew the story, and they'd remembered it for me. "I really was just going for a walk," I said, and then, "I don't even have a gun."

Ms. Dellafield said I should take the rest of the day off, so Mom and David and I drove home together, in David's Jeep. When Ms. Dellafield called Mom at home, Mom had been too upset even to drive, so she'd called David and he'd left work and picked her up and driven her to school. He drove us all home, too. He drove really carefully. Once a squirrel ran into the road and David slowed down until it got out of his way. I'd never seen him drive like that before. And when we were walking into the house, Mom tripped, and David reached out to steady her.

The last time I'd seen Mom and David leaning on each other, they'd been coming in from the yard. I remembered that part. My ears had still been ringing, but Letty wouldn't let me go, no matter how hard I fought. She'd been eating lunch with us when it happened. "Let me see," I kept telling her, trying to break free. "Let me go out there! I want to see what happened!"

But Letty wouldn't let go, because the first thing that happened after the shot was that Mom and David ran out into the yard, and David started screaming, and then Mom yelled at Letty, "Keep Michael inside! Don't let him come out here!"

And they came back inside, and Mom called the police, and I kept saying, "I want to go see," and David kept shaking his head and saying, "No you don't, Michael, you don't want to see this, you really don't," and Letty wouldn't let go of me. And the cops came and asked everybody questions, and then Letty took me to her house, and by the time I got home, Mom and David had cleaned up the backyard, picked up all the little pieces of bone and brain, so that there was nothing left to see at all.

Dad was stupid. You can't beat the house: anybody who's ever been anywhere near a casino knows that. But he and George and Howard were trying. They'd worked out a system, the newspaper said; George or Howard, never both at once, would go in and play at Dad's table, and Dad would touch a cheek or scratch an ear, always a different signal, so they'd know when to double their bets. And then when they won, they'd split the take with him. They tried to be smart. They didn't do it very often, but it was often enough for the pit bosses and the cameras to catch on. And somehow, when Dad came home that day, he knew he'd been caught. He knew the walls were closing in.

George and Howard went to jail. I guess Dad knew he'd have to go there too. I guess he thought that was just too small a box.

Nobody said anything for a long time, after we got home from school. Mom started unloading the dishwasher, moving in little jerks like somebody in an old silent movie, and David sat down at the kitchen table, and I went to the fridge and got a drink of juice. And finally David said, "Why the hell did you do that?"

He didn't sound angry, or like he was trying to piss me off. He just sounded lost. And I hadn't been trying to do anything; I'd just been going for a walk, but I'd said that at least a million times by now and it was no good. Nobody believed me, or nobody cared. So instead I said, "Why did you keep letting Bobo out?"

And Mom, with her back to us, stopped moving; she stood there, holding a plate, looking down at the open dishwasher. And David said, "I don't know."

Mom turned and looked at him, then, and I looked at Mom. David never admitted there was anything he didn't know. He stared down at the table and said, "You kept saying you wanted to go outside. You kept – you were *fighting* to go outside. The cat wanted to go out, Michael. He did." He looked up, straight at me; his chin was trembling. "You didn't even have to look at it. It wasn't fair."

His voice sounded much younger, then, and I flashed back on that day when he saved me from the rattlesnake, when we were still friends, and all of a sudden my bubble burst and I was back in the world, where it hurt to breathe, where the air against my skin felt like sandpaper. "So you wanted me to get my wish by having to look at Bobo?" I said. "Is that it? Like I wanted any of it to happen, you fuckhead? Like – "

"Shhhh," Mom said, and came over and hugged me. "Shhhh. It's all right now. It's all right. I'm sorry. I'm sorry. David – "

"Forget it," David said. "None of it matters anymore, anyway."

"Yes it does," Mom said. "David, I made you do too much. I – "

"I want to go for a walk now," I said. I was going to scream if I couldn't get outside; I was going to scream or break something. "Can we just go for a walk? All of us? You can watch me, okay? I promise not to do anything stupid. Please?"

Mom and David have gotten along a lot better since then. Letty and I talked about it, once. She said they'd probably been fighting so much because David was mad at Mom for making him help her in the yard when Dad died, and Mom felt guilty about it, and didn't even know she did, and kept lashing out at him. And none of us were talking about anything, so it festered. Letty said that what I did at school that day was exactly what I needed to do to remind Mom and David how much they could still lose, to make them stop being mad at each other. And I told her I hadn't been trying to do anything, and anyway I hadn't even remembered what Dad had said before he went out into the yard. She said it didn't matter. It was instinct, she said. She said people still have instincts, even when they live in boxes, and that we can't ever lose them completely, not if we're still alive at all. Look at Bobo, she told me. You got him from a petstore. He'd never even lived outside, but he still wanted to get out. He still knew he was supposed to be hunting mice.

In June, when the snow melted from the top of Peavine, I hiked back up to the mine. I'd been back on the mountain before that, of course, but I hadn't gone up that high: maybe because I thought I wouldn't be able to see anything yet, maybe because I was afraid I would. But that Saturday I woke up, and it was sunny and warm, and Mom and David were both at work, and I thought, okay. This is the day. I'll go up there by myself, to see. To say goodbye.

All those months, the transmitter signal hadn't moved.

So I hiked up, past the developments, through rocks and sagebrush, scattering basking lizards. I saw a few rabbits and a couple of hawks, and I heard gunfire, but I didn't see any people.

When I got to the mine, I peered inside and couldn't see anything. I'd brought a flashlight, but it's dangerous to go inside abandoned mines. Even if it's safe to breathe the air, even if you don't get trapped, you don't know what else might be in there with you. Snakes. Coyotes.

So I shone the flashlight inside and looked for anything that might have been a cat once. There were dirt and rocks, but I couldn't even see anything that looked like bones. The handheld said this was the place, though, so I scrabbled around in the dirt a little bit, and played the flashlight over every surface the beam would reach, and finally, maybe two feet inside the mine, I saw something glinting in a crevice in the rock.

It was the chip: just the chip, a tiny little piece of silver circuitry, sitting there all by itself. Maybe there'd been bones too, for a while, and something had carried them off. Or maybe something had eaten Bobo and left a pile of scat here, with the chip in it, and everything had gone back into the ground except the chip. I don't know. All I knew was that Bobo was gone, and I still missed him, and there wasn't even anything that had been him to bring back with me.

I sat there and looked at the chip for a while, and then I put the handheld next to it. And then I went and sat on a rock outside the mine, in the sun.

It was pretty. There were wildflowers all over the place, and you could see for miles. And I sat there and thought, I could just leave. I could just walk away, walk in the other direction, clear to Tahoe, walk away from all the boxes. I don't have a transmitter. Nobody would know where I was. I could walk as long as I wanted.

But there are boxes everywhere, aren't there? Even at Tahoe, maybe especially at Tahoe, where all the rich people build their fancy houses. And if I walked away, Mom and David wouldn't know where I was. They wouldn't even have a transmitter signal. And I knew what that felt like. I remembered staring at the dark screen, when the satellites were offline. I remembered staring at it, and trying not to cry, and praying. *Please, Bobo, come back home. Please come back, Bobo. I love you.*

So I sat there for a while, looking out over the city. And then I ate an energy bar and drank some water, and headed back down the mountain, back home.

# Beautiful Stuff

Rusty Kerfuffle stood on a plastic tarp in an elegant downtown office. The tarp had been spread over fine woolen carpet; the walls were papered in soothing monochrome linen, and the desk in front of Rusty was gleaming hardwood. There was a paperweight on the desk. The paperweight was a crystal globe with a purple flower inside it. In the sunlight from the window, the crystal sparkled, and the flower glowed. Rusty desired that paperweight with a love like starvation, but the man sitting behind the desk wouldn't give it to him

The man sitting behind the desk wore an expensive suit and a tense expression; next to him, an aide vomited into a bucket. "Sir," the aide said, raising his head from the bucket long enough to gasp out a comment. "Sir, I think this is going to be a public relations disaster."

"Shut up," said the man behind the desk, and the aide resumed vomiting. "You. Do you understand what I'm asking for?"

"Sure," Rusty said, trying not to stare at the paperweight. He knew how smooth and heavy it would feel in his hands; he yearned to caress it. It contained light and life in a precious sphere: a little world.

Rusty's outfit had been a suit, once. Now it was a rotting tangle of fibers. His ear itched, but if he scratched it, it might fall off. He'd been dead for three months. If his ear fell off in this fancy office, the man behind the desk might not let him touch the paperweight.

The man behind the desk exhaled, a sharp sound like the snort of a horse. "Good. You do what I need you to do and you get to walk around again for a day. Understand?"

"Sure," said Rusty. He also understood that the walking part came first. The man behind the desk would have to re-revive Rusty, and all the others, before they could do what had been asked of them. Once they'd been revived, they got their day of walking whether they followed orders or not. "Can I hold the paperweight now?"

The man behind the desk smiled. It wasn't a friendly smile. "No, not yet. You weren't a very nice man when you were alive, Rusty."

"That's true," Rusty said, trying to ignore his itching ear. His fingers itched too, yearning for the paperweight. "I wasn't."

"I know all about you. I know you were cheating on your wife. I know about the insider trading. You were a morally bankrupt shit-head, Rusty. But you're a hero now, aren't you? Because you're dead. Your wife thinks you were a saint."

This was, Rusty reflected, highly unlikely. Linda was as adept at running scams as he'd ever been, maybe more so. If she was capitalizing on his death, he couldn't blame her. He'd have done the same thing, if she'd been the one who had died. He was glad to be past that. The living were far too complicated.

He stared impassively at the man behind the desk, whose tie was speckled with reflections from the paperweight. The aide was still vomiting. The man behind the desk gave another mean smile and said, "This is your chance to be a hero for real, Rusty. Do you understand that?"

"Sure," Rusty said, because that was what the man wanted to hear. The sun had gone behind a cloud: the paperweight shone less brightly now. It was just as tantalizing as it had been before, but in a more subdued way.

"Good. Because if you don't come through, if you say the wrong thing, I'll tell your wife what you were really doing, Rusty. I'll tell her what a pathetic slimebag you were. You won't be a hero anymore."

The aide had raised his head again. He looked astonished. He opened his mouth, as if he wanted to say something, but then he closed it. Rusty smiled at him. I may have been a pathetic slimebag, he thought, but I never tried to blackmail a corpse. Even your cringing assistant can see how morally bankrupt that is. The sun came out again, and the paperweight resumed its sparkling. "Got it," Rusty said happily.

The man behind the desk finally relaxed a little. He sat back in his chair. He became indulgent and expansive. "Good, Rusty. That's excellent. You're going to do the right thing for once, aren't you? You're going to help me convince all those cowards out there to stop sitting on their butts."

"Yes," Rusty said. "I'm going to do the right thing. Thank you for the opportunity, sir." This time, he wasn't being ironic.

"You're welcome, Rusty."

Rusty felt himself about to wiggle, like a puppy. "Now can I hold the paperweight? Please?"

"Okay, Rusty. Come and get it."

Rusty stepped forward, careful to stay on the tarp, and picked up the paperweight. It was as smooth and heavy and wonderful as he had known it would be. He cradled it to his chest, the glass pleasantly cool against his fingers, and began swaying back and forth.

Rusty had never understood the science behind corpse revival, but he supposed it didn't matter. Here he was, revived. He did know that the technique was hideously expensive. When it was first invented, mourning families had forked over life savings, taken out second mortgages, gone into staggering debt simply to have another day with their lost loved ones.

That trend didn't last long. The dead weren't attractive. The technique only worked on those who hadn't been embalmed or cremated, because there had to be a more-or-less intact, more-or-less chemically unaltered body to revive. That meant it got used most often on accident and suicide victims: the sudden dead, the unexpected dead, the dead who had gone without farewells. The unlovely dead, mangled and wounded.

The dead smelled, and they were visibly decayed, depending on the gap between when they had died and when they had been revived.

They shed fingers and noses. They left behind pieces of themselves as mementos. And they had very little interest in the machinations of the living. Other things drew them. They loved flowers and animals. They loved to play with food. Running faucets enchanted them. The first dead person to be revived, a Mr. Otis Magruder, who had killed himself running into a tree while skiing, spent his twenty-four hours of second life sitting in his driveway making mud pies while his wife and children told him how much they loved him. Each time one of his relations delivered another impassioned statement of devotion, Otis nodded, and said, "Uh-huh." And then he ran his fingers through more mud, and smiled. At hour eighteen, when his wife, despairing, asked if there was anything she could tell him, anything she could give him, he cocked his head and said, "Do you have a plastic pail?"

Six hours later, when Otis was mercifully dead again, his wife told reporters, "Well, Otis was always kind of spacy. That's why he ran into that tree, I guess." But it turned out that the other revived dead — tycoons, scientists, gangsters — were spacy too. The dead didn't care about the same things the living did.

These days, the dead were revived only rarely, usually to testify in criminal cases involving their death or civil cases involving the financial details of their estates. They made bad witnesses. They became distracted by brightly colored neckties, by the reflection of the courtroom lights in the polished wood of the witness box, by the gentle clicking of the clerk's recording instrument. It was very difficult to keep them on track, to remind them what they were supposed to be thinking about. On the other hand, they had amazingly accurate memories, once they could be cajoled into paying attention to the subject at hand. Bribes of balloons and small, brightly colored toys worked well; jurors became used to watching the dead weep in frustration while scolding lawyers held matchbox cars and neon-hued stuffed animals just out of reach. But once the dead gave the information the living sought, they always told the truth. No one had ever caught one of the dead lying, no matter how dishonest the corpse might have been while it was still alive.

It had been very difficult for the man behind the desk to break through Rusty's fascination with the paperweight. It had taken a lot to get Rusty's attention. Dirt about Rusty's affairs and insider deals hadn't done it. None of that mattered anymore. It was a set of extraneous details, as distant as the moon and as abstract as ethics, which also had no hold on Rusty.

Rusty's passions and loyalties were much more basic now.

He stood in the elegant office, rocking the paperweight as if it were a baby, crooning to it, sometimes holding it at arm's length to admire it before bringing it back safely to his chest again. He had another two hours of revival left this time; the man behind the desk would revive him and the others again in a month, for another twenty-four hours. Rusty fully intended to spend every minute of his current two hours in contemplation of the paperweight. When he was revived again in a month, he'd fall in love with something else.

"You *idiot*," said the man who had been sitting behind the desk. He wasn't behind a desk now; he was in a refrigerated warehouse, a month after that meeting with Rusty. He was yelling at his aide. Around him were the revived dead, waiting to climb into refrigerated trucks to be taken to the rally site. It was a lovely, warm spring day, and they'd smell less if they were kept cool for as long as possible. "I don't want *them*." He waved at two of the dead, more mangled than any of the others, charred and lacerated and nearly unrecognizable as human bodies. One was playing with a paperclip that had been lying on the floor; the other opened and closed its hand, trying to catch the dust motes that floated in the shafts of light from the window.

The aide was sweating, despite the chill of the warehouse. "Sir, you said — "

"I know what I said, you moron!"

"Everyone who was there, you said — "

"Idiot." The voice was very quiet now, very dangerous. "Idiot. Do you know why we're doing this? Have you been paying *attention*?"

"S-sir," the aide stuttered. "Yes sir."

"Oh, really? Because if you'd been paying *attention, they* wouldn't be here!"

"But — "

"Prove to me that you understand," said the dangerously quiet voice. "Tell me why we're doing this."

The aide gulped. "To remind people where their loyalties lie. Sir."

"Yes. And where *do* their loyalties lie? Or where *should* their loyalties lie?"

"With innocent victims. Sir."

"Yes. Exactly. And are those, those *things* over there" — an impassioned hand waved at the two mangled corpses — "are they innocent victims?"

"No. Sir."

"No. They aren't. They're the monsters who were responsible for all these *other* innocent victims! They're the *guilty* ones, aren't they?"

"Yes sir."

"They *deserve* to be dead, don't they?"

"Yes sir." The aide stood miserably twisting his hands.

"The entire point of this rally is to demonstrate that some people *deserve* to be dead, isn't it?"

"Yes sir!"

"Right. So why in the name of everything that's holy were those *monsters* revived?"

The aide coughed. "We were using the new technique. Sir. The blanket-revival technique. It works over a given geographical area. They were mixed in with the others. We couldn't be that precise."

"Fuck that," said the quiet voice, succinctly.

"It would have been far too expensive to revive all of them individually," the aide said. "The new technique saved us — "

"Yes, I know how much it saved us! And I know how much we're going to lose if this doesn't work! Get rid of them! I don't want them on the truck! I don't want them at the rally!"

"Sir! Yes, sir!"

The aide, once his boss had left, set about correcting the situation. He told the two unwanted corpses that they weren't needed. He tried to be polite about it. It was difficult to get their attention away from the paperclip and the dust motes; he had to distract them with a penlight and a Koosh ball, and that worked well enough, except that some of the other corpses got distracted too, and began crowding around the aide, cooing and reaching for the Koosh ball. There were maybe twenty of them, the ones who had been closest; the others, thank God, were still off in their own little worlds. But these twenty all wanted that Koosh ball. The aide felt like he was in a preschool in hell, or possibly in a dovecote of extremely deformed and demented pigeons.

"Listen to me!" he said, raising his voice over the cooing. "Listen! You two! You with the paperclip and you with the dust motes! We don't want you, okay? We just want everyone else! You two, do *not* get on the trucks! Have you got that? Yes? Is that a nod? Is that a yes?"

"Yesh," said the corpse with the paperclip, and the one who'd been entranced by the dust motes nodded.

"All right then," said the aide, and tossed the Koosh ball over their heads into a corner of the warehouse. There was a chorus of happy shrieks and a stampede of corpses. The aide took the opportunity to get out of there, into fresh air. His Dramamine was wearing off. He didn't know if the message had really gotten through or not, but fuck it: this whole thing was going to be a public-relations disaster, no matter who got on the trucks. He no longer cared if he kept his job. In fact, he hoped he got fired, because that way he could collect unemployment. As soon as the rally was over, he'd go home and start working on his resume.

Back in the warehouse, Rusty had a firm grip on the Koosh ball. He had purposefully stayed at the back of the crowd. He knew what he had to do, and he had been concentrating very hard on staying focused, although it was difficult not to be distracted by all the wonderful things around him: the aide's tie, a piece of torn newspaper on the floor, the gleaming hubcaps of the trucks. His mind wasn't working as well as it had been during his first revival, and it took all his energy to concentrate. He stayed at the back of the crowd and kept his eyes on the Koosh ball, and when the aide tossed it into the corner, Rusty was the first one there. He had it. He picked it up, thrilling at its texture, and did the hardest thing he had ever done: he sacrificed the pleasure of the Koosh ball. He forced himself to let go of it for the greater good. He tossed it into the back of the nearest truck and watched his twenty fellows rush in joy up the loading ramp. Were the two unwanted corpses there? Yes, they were. In the excitement, they had forgotten their promise to the aide.

Rusty ran to the truck. He climbed inside with the others, fighting his longing to join the exuberant scramble for the Koosh ball. But instead, Rusty Kerfuffle, who was not a hero and had not been a very nice man, pulled something from his pocket. He had a pocket because the man with the quiet voice had given him a new blue blazer to wear, so he'd be more presentable, and inside the pocket was the glass paperweight with a purple flower inside. Rusty had been allowed to keep the paperweight last time, because no one else wanted to touch it now. "It has fucking corpse germs all over it," the man with the quiet voice had told him, and Rusty had trembled with joy. He wouldn't have to fall in love with something else after all; he could stay in love with this.

Rusty used the paperweight now to distract the two unwanted corpses, and several of the others closest to him, from the Koosh ball. And then he started talking to them – although it was very, very hard for him to stay on track, because all he wanted to do was fondle the paperweight – and waited for the truck doors to be closed.

Outside the warehouse, it was spring: a balmy, fragrant season. The refrigerated trucks rolled past medians filled with cheerful flowers, past sidewalks where pedestrians strolled, their faces lifted to the sun, past parks where children on swings pumped themselves into the air in ecstasies of flight. At last the convoy of trucks pulled into a larger park, the park at the center of the city, and along tree-lined roads to a bandstand in the very center of that park. The man with the quiet voice stood at the bandstand podium, his aide beside him. One side of the audience consisted of people waving signs in support of the man with the quiet voice. The other side consisted of people waving signs denouncing him. Both sides were peppered with reporters, with cameras and microphones. The man with the quiet voice stared stonily down the center aisle, and read the speech prepared by his aide.

"Four months ago," he said, "this city suffered a devastating attack. Hundreds of innocent people were killed. Those people were your husbands and wives, your children, your brothers and sisters, your friends. They were cut down in the prime of their lives by enemies to whom they had done no harm, who wanted nothing more than to destroy them, to destroy all of us. They were cut down by pure evil."

The man with the quiet voice paused, waiting for the crowd to stir. It didn't. The crowd waited, watching him. The only thing that stirred was the balmy spring wind, moving the leaves. The man at the podium cleared his throat. "As a result of that outrageous act of destruction, the brave leaders of our great nation determined that we had to strike back. We could not let this horror go unanswered. And so we sent our courageous troops to address the evil, to destroy the evil, to stamp out the powers that had cut down our loved ones in their prime."

Again he paused. The audience stirred now, a little bit. Someone on one side waved a sign that said, WE WILL NEVER FORGET! Someone on the other side waved a sign that said, AN EYE FOR AN EYE MAKES THE WHOLE WORLD BLIND. The cameras whirred. The birds twittered. The refrigerated trucks rolled up to the edge of the bandshell, and the man at the podium smiled.

"I supported the courageous decision of our brave leaders," he said. His voice was less quiet now. "There was only one way to respond to this devastating grief, this hideous loss, this violation of all that we hold dear and sacred. This was the principled stance taken by millions of people in our great nation. But certain others among us, among you" — here he glared at the person who had waved the second sign — "have claimed that this makes me unworthy to continue to hold office, unworthy to continue to be your leader. If that is true, then many of the leaders of this country are also unworthy."

His voice had risen to something like a crescendo. The woman standing next to the man who had waved the second sign cupped her hands around her mouth and called out cheerfully, "No argument there, boss!" A few people laughed; a few people booed; the cameras whirred. The man at the podium glared, and spoke again, now not quietly at all.

"But it is *not* true! The leaders of this city, of this state, of this nation must be brave! Must be principled! Must be ready to fight wrong wherever they find it!"

"Must be ready to send innocent young people to kill other innocent young people," the same woman called back. The booing was louder now. The man at the podium smiled, grimly.

"Let us remember who is truly innocent. Let us remember who was truly innocent four months ago. If they could speak to us, what would they say? Well, you are about to find out. I have brought them here today, our beloved dead, to speak to us, to tell us what they would have us do."

He gave a signal. The truck doors were opened. The corpses shambled out, blinking in the glorious sunshine, gaping at trees and flowers and folding chairs and whirring cameras. The crowd gave a gratifying gasp, and several people began to sob. Others began to retch. Additional aides in the audience, well prepared for all eventualities, began handing out packets of tissues and barf bags, both imprinted with campaign slogans.

Rusty Kerfuffle, doggedly ignoring the trees and flowers and folding chairs and cameras, doggedly ignoring the knowledge that his beloved paperweight was in his pocket, moved towards the podium, dragging the unwanted corpses with him. In the van, he had accomplished the very difficult task of removing certain items of clothing from other corpses and outfitting these two, so maybe the man with the quiet voice wouldn't realize what he was doing and try to stop him. At least for the moment, it seemed to be working.

The man with the quiet voice was saying something about love and loss and outrage. His aides were trying to corral wandering corpses. More people in the audience were retching. Rusty, holding an unwanted corpse's hand in each of his – the three of them like small children crossing a street together – squinted his eyes almost shut, so he wouldn't see all the distracting things around him. Stay focused, Rusty. Get to the podium.

He got to the podium. Three steps up and he was on the podium, the unwanted corpses beside him. The man with the quiet voice turned and smiled at him. "And now, ladies and gentleman, I give you Rusty Kerfuffle, the heroic husband of Linda Kerfuffle, whom you've all seen on television. Linda, are you here?"

"Darling!" gasped a woman in the crowd. She ran towards the podium, but was overtaken by retching halfway there. Rusty wondered how much she was being paid.

An aide patted Linda on the back and handed her a barf bag. The aide on the platform murmured, "public relations disaster," too softly for the microphones. The quiet man coughed and cleared his throat and poked Rusty in the back.

Rusty understood that this was his cue to do something. "Hi, Linda," said Rusty. He couldn't tell if the microphones had picked that up, so he waved. Linda waved back, took a few steps closer to the podium, and was overcome with retching again.

The aide on the platform groaned, and the man with the quiet voice forged grimly ahead. "I have brought back Rusty and these other brave citizens and patriots, your lost loved ones, to tell you how important it is to fight evil, to tell you about the waste and horror of their deaths, to implore you to do the right thing, since some of you have become misled by propaganda."

Rusty had just caught a glimpse of a butterfly, and it took every ounce of his will not to turn to run after it, to walk up to the microphone instead. But he did his duty. He walked up to the microphone, pulling his two companions.

"Hi," he said. "I'm Rusty. Wait, you know that."

The crowd stared at him, some still retching. Linda was wiping her mouth. Some people were walking away. "Wait," Rusty called after them. "It's really important. It really is." A few stopped and turned, standing with their arms folded; others kept walking. Rusty had to say something to make them stop. "Wait," he said. "This guy's wrong. I wasn't brave. I wasn't patriotic. I cheated on my wife. Linda, I cheated on you, but I think you knew that. I think you were cheating on me too. It's okay; it doesn't matter now. I cheated on other stuff, too. I cheated on my taxes. I was guilty of insider trading. I was a morally bankrupt shithead." He pointed at the man with the quiet voice. "That's his phrase, not mine, but it fits." There: now he couldn't be blackmailed.

Most of the people who'd been walking away had stopped now: good. The man with the quiet voice was hissing. "Rusty, what are you doing?"

"I'm doing what he wants me to do," Rusty said into the microphone. "I'm, what was that word, *imploring* you to do the right thing."

He stopped, out of words, and concentrated very hard on what he was going to say next. He caught a flash of purple out of the corner of his left eye. Was that another butterfly? He turned. No: it was a splendid purple bandana. The aide on the platform was waving it at Rusty. Rusty's heart melted. He fell in love with the bandana. The bandana was the most exquisite thing he had ever seen. Who wouldn't covet the bandana? And indeed, one of his companions, the one on the left, was snatching at it.

Rusty took a step towards the bandana, and then forced himself to stop. No. The aide was trying to distract him. The aide was cheating. The bandana was a trick. Rusty still had his paperweight. He didn't need the bandana.

Heartsick, nearly sobbing, Rusty turned back to the podium,

dragging the other corpse with him. The other corpse whimpered, but Rusty prevailed. He knew that this was very important. It was as important as the paperweight in his pocket. He could no longer remember why, but he remembered that he had known once.

"Darling!" Linda said, running towards him. "Darling! I forgive you! I love you! Dear Rusty!"

She was wearing a shiny barrette. She never wore barrettes. It was another trick. Rusty began to tremble. "Linda," he said into the microphone. "Shut up. Shut up and go away, Linda. I have to say something."

Rusty's other companion, the one on his right, let out a small squeal and tried to lurch towards Linda, towards the barrette. "No," Rusty said, keeping desperate hold. "You stay here. Linda, take that shiny thing off! Hide it, Linda!"

"Darling!" she said, and the right-hand corpse broke away from Rusty and hopped off the podium, towards Linda. Linda screamed and ran, the corpse trotting after her. Rusty sighed; the aide groaned again; the quiet man cursed, softly.

"Okay," Rusty said, "so here's what I have to tell you." Some of the people in the crowd who'd turned to watch Linda and her pursuer turned back towards Rusty now, but others didn't. Well, he couldn't do anything about that. He had to say this thing. He could remember what he had to say, but he couldn't remember why. That was all right. He'd say it, and then maybe he'd remember.

"What I have to tell you is, dying hurts," Rusty said. The crowd murmured. "Dying hurts a lot. It hurts – everybody hurts." Rusty struggled to remember why this mattered. He dimly remembered dying, remembered other people dying around him. "It hurts everybody. It makes everybody the same. This guy, and that other one who ran away, they hurt too. This is Ari. That was Ahmed. They were the ones who planted the bomb. They didn't get out in time. They died too." Gasps, some louder murmurs, louder cursing from the man with the quiet voice. Rusty definitely had everyone's attention now.

He prodded Ari. "It hurt," Ari said.

"And?" said Rusty.

"We're sorry," said Ari.

"Ahmed's sorry too," said Rusty. "He told me. He'd have told you, if he weren't chasing Linda's shiny hair thing."

"If we'd known, we wouldn't have done it," Ari said.

"Because?" Rusty said, patiently.

"We did it for the wrong reasons," Ari said. "We expected things to happen that didn't happen. Paradise, and, like, virgins." Ari looked shyly down at his decaying feet. "I'm sorry."

"More," Rusty said. "Tell them more."

"Dying hurts," said Ari. "It won't make you happy. It won't make anybody happy."

"So please do the right thing," said Rusty. "Don't kill anybody else."

The man with the quiet voice let out a howl and leaped towards Rusty. He grabbed Rusty's free arm, the right one, and pulled; the arm came off, and the man with the quiet voice started hitting Rusty over the head with it. "You fucking incompetent! You traitor! You said you'd tell them — "

"I said I'd do the right thing," Rusty said. "I never said my version of the right thing was the same as yours."

"You lied!"

"No, I didn't. I misled you, but I told the truth. What are you going to do, kill me?" He looked out at the crowd and said, "We're the dead. You loved some of us. You hated others. We're the dead. We're here to tell you: please don't kill anybody else. Everybody will be dead soon enough, whether you kill them or not. It hurts."

The crowd stared; the cameras whirred. None of the living there that day had ever heard such long speeches from the dead. It was truly a historic occasion. A group of aides had managed to drag away the man with the quiet voice, who was still brandishing Rusty's arm; Rusty, with his one arm, stood at the podium with Ari.

"Look," Rusty said. He let go of Ari's hand and reached around to pull the paperweight out of his pocket. He held it up in front of the crowd. Ari cooed and reached for it, entranced, but Rusty held it above his head. "Look at this! Look at the shiny glass. Look at the flower. It's beautiful. You have all this stuff in your life, all this beautiful stuff. Sunshine and grass and butterflies. Barrettes. Bandanas. You don't have that when you're dead. That's why dying hurts."

And Rusty shivered, and remembered: he remembered dying, knowing he'd never see trees again, never drink coffee, never smell flowers or see buildings reflected in windows. He remembered that pain, the pain of knowing what he was losing only when it was too late. And he knew that the living wouldn't understand, couldn't understand. Or maybe some of them did, but the others would only make fun of them. He finished his speech lamely, miserably, knowing that everyone would say it was just a cliché. "Enjoy the beautiful stuff while you have it."

The woman who had heckled the man with the quiet voice was frowning. "You're advocating greed! That's what gets people killed. People murder each other for stuff!"

"No," Rusty said. He was exhausted. She didn't understand. She'd probably never understand unless she died and got revived. "Just enjoy it. Look at it. Don't fight. You don't get it, do you?"

"No," she said. "I don't."

Rusty shrugged. He was too tired; he couldn't keep his focus anymore. He no longer cared if the woman got it or not. The man with the quiet voice had been taken away, and Rusty had done what he had wanted to do, although it seemed much less important now than it had even a month ago, when he was first revived. He remembered, dimly, that no one had ever managed to teach the living anything much. Some of them might get it. He'd done what he could. He'd told them what mattered.

His attention wandered away from the woman, away from the crowd. He brought the paperweight back down to chest level, and then he sat down on the edge of the platform, and Ari sat with him, and they both stared at the paperweight, touching it, humming in happiness there in the sunshine.

The crowd watched them for a while, and then it wandered away, too. The other corpses had already wandered. The dead meandered through the beautiful budding park, all of them in love: one with a sparrow on the walk, one with a silk scarf a woman in the audience had given him, one with an empty, semi-crushed milk carton she had plucked out of a trashcan. The dead fell in love, and they walked or they sat, carrying what they loved or letting it hold them in place. They loved their beautiful stuff for the rest of the day, until the sun went down; and then they lay down too, their treasures beside them, and slept again, and this time did not wake.

# Elephant

The contractions have started. They hurt as much as everyone said they would, and they'll be worse before it's over. Between spasms, which are about ten minutes apart now, I find myself wondering if this is the child's revenge for all the pain she's already suffered.

During the contractions I can't think about anything except the pain. Pain has always done that to me, making me oblivious to anything else, so that now I can't even be properly grateful for Joni, with her oranges and sponges and constant reassurance, who's seen me through all this, who would think I was insane if she knew the whole story. Maybe I am. During the contractions or between them, I find it hard to tell.

Somebody in one of the childbirth classes asked me once if I could pinpoint the moment of conception. "Yes," I said, but no one would have believed me if I talked about it, not even Joni, who unwittingly started it during that phone conversation.

Oh, God, that horrible day — it was raining and cold, one of those days when I hated the city and my job and myself, myself even worse than usual because I hadn't done anything right at work and I couldn't seem to do anything to get anyone to smile at me, or say hello, or be pleasant — all day it was like that, like being in a vacuum, and then I got home and went and put out the garbage and the bag broke, spilling coffee grounds and tuna cans and wadded up paper towels all over the floor ... so I called Joni out in the suburbs, because I was terrified that if I didn't talk to someone I'd really go mad, right there; and she listened, two-year-old Joshua squealing in the background, as I poured out everything. It was a lousy connection on top of everything else and even as I talked I hated myself for calling her, for going through the old routine both of us know so well, for taking her away from her happy child and her considerate husband and her white clapboard house with the garden and the car and the two cats.

"I'm sorry," I said when I was done with all of it, and my voice was shaking because I'd started crying again. "Oh, shit, I'm sorry, why am I bothering you with this – I don't know how you put up with it anyway. I don't know how I can ask people to like me when I'm like this."

Joni sighed. "Cara, whatever happened to the little kid in you who *expects* to be liked?" She couldn't have expected an answer, because we both knew what had happened.

"Dead," I said, anyway, and Joni grunted; I could imagine her shaking her head on the other end of the phone in New Jersey.

"Cara, that never dies. Never. It just doesn't. Everybody's got that inside, somewhere."

*Bullshit*, I thought. I didn't say anything and she tried to tell me about Joshua's nursery school, except Joshua himself interrupted again, wanting juice, and then she had to go because dinner was ready.

I saw the commercial later that night. I was sitting on the couch in front of the *Late Late Show*, because I was afraid that if I went to sleep I'd have nightmares. I'd finished crying but I had a splitting headache, which always happens after I cry. I dozed off a little bit and all of a sudden there was the sound of a blow and a child's wail, and I yelled myself and came awake tense, ready to run away, every nerve wired. It was only a commercial, one of those "prevent child abuse" things, with a number to call if you knew a kid who was being hurt, but it didn't matter that it was just TV, because of the kid's scream.

That scream was echoing inside me somewhere, and I sat there shaking and remembered Joni talking about the kid inside me, the one who expects to be liked, and I suddenly realized no, no, that kid isn't dead, she's the one who's screaming, dear God, she's in me now – and I saw her. I saw her face, which had been mine when I was six or seven, very pale and tense, and I felt her huddling away inside me somewhere, trying to keep from being hurt, cowering against my ribcage. She was covered with bruises – bruises dealt out brutally, methodically, in places where they'd hurt like hell but wouldn't show, the way it was before Daddy died, and I knew who was beating her up, that skinny kid inside me.

I was.

I was, because you can't expect to be liked without getting hit for it, without getting stomped on and hurt, and she was the reason I'd suffered so much, gone through so much hell; she was the part of me that kept expecting life to be decent despite all the evidence, that kept putting me in a position to have people spit in my face and ignore me. She wasn't dead at all.

She was dying, though, and in pain, and I sat on the couch and cried again, harder this time, because I'd done it to her and I'd had it done to me and I knew what it felt like, and I just sat there, crying, hugging myself, thinking, I'm sorry, oh, God, I'm sorry. I didn't know; I never meant to hurt you. I'll get you out of there, I promise. You don't deserve that. Nobody should have to be in such a lousy place. I'm sorry! I'll set you free if I can. I promise. I promise.

Five weeks later, after a routine pelvic exam, the Ob/Gyn told me I was pregnant. He swore it up and down and sideways, said both the urinalysis and the pelvic proved it conclusively. I told him he was crazy, that it was impossible, and he told me I hadn't been careful enough, or maybe I'd been careful and gotten pregnant anyway because it can always happen, can't it?

And I thought, not to me, you bastard, not to Cara who hasn't had sex for four years because every unmarried man in New York is gay and I can't stand intercourse unless I'm dead drunk, anyway.

The doctor started talking about abortions, and I was listening until I remembered the TV commercial and the kid cowering inside my gut and the promise I'd made to it, and even though being pregnant was still impossible, it might make sense. I went home to get drunk, but I got sick first, and then I remembered that morning sickness doesn't have to happen in the morning, and I panicked. Just panicked, dead cold sweaty fear, but there'd been something in some psych course I'd had in school about how sometimes women who want to be pregnant get all the symptoms except the baby. I couldn't remember if they could get symptoms convincing enough to fool a doctor, and I had to know, so I dug into the old cartons in my closet trying to find the textbook.

It wasn't there — maybe I'd given it to Joni, maybe it had gotten thrown out — but I found a poetry book from some lit class and remembered there was a poem I liked in it, one of the few things I'd liked in school, and flipped through the pages until I found it. It was a poem about an elephant, by somebody named Carlos Drummond de Andrade. It starts out, "I made an elephant from the little I have," and talks about how he builds the elephant out of glue and wood from old furniture, and how the elephant goes out into the world looking for friends and nobody pays any attention to it and finally it comes back home, exhausted, and falls apart, just "collapses like paper," because it's been searching for something it can't find. It lies there in a messy heap on the rug, "like a myth torn apart," with feathers and cotton and everything else that had been stuffed into it spilling all over the place.

The last line is: "Tomorrow I begin again."

God, that last line! No wonder I'd liked that poem — it sounded like what coming home from work had been every day I could remember, every single shitty day. I remembered the kid and thought, hey, hey, are you still there? I couldn't feel her cowering anymore, just myself feeling sick and swollen and horrible, like when I'm about to get my period except it really was too late, at that point. And I realized that I wanted to be pregnant, that I wanted to get the kid out of me, send her into the world so she could find people who'd know how to love her — even if she wasn't real, even if she was just something I'd invented out of goddamned paper towels and coffee grounds.

I switched OB/Gyns, because after I'd said being pregnant was impossible the first one wouldn't have believed my new story, which was that I wanted to be a single mother and had paid a stranger to get me pregnant.

I invited Joni into the city one weekend, and didn't even have to tell her because she knew when she looked at me, God knows how because I wasn't showing at that point. But she knew, Joni who'd been my best friend since first grade and had always known everything.

She knew better than to believe the story I told, though. "You want to have a baby?" she asked gently, shaking her head. "Cara? You never said anything about it. You've never even liked kids — "

"I changed my mind," I told her. It hurt to swallow. I'd never consciously lied to Joni about anything, but if I told her the truth I'd lose her, too — Joni who was the only person I'd ever completely trusted.

"You *paid* someone? How do you find someone for that?"

"Ad in the *Voice*."

"Jesus, Cara, that's got to be illegal — do you have a lawyer?"

"No."

"Who's the father?"

"We didn't use real names. That was part of it. We met at a hotel."

"Oh, my God." Joni rubbed her eyes, shook her head again, said, "Why didn't you tell me about this? Why didn't you say anything?" And a moment later, with morbid curiosity, "How much did you pay him?"

I made up a figure. I couldn't tell Joni that I was planning to give the baby up for adoption, because that would blow the *Voice* story to hell. But I could tell she still didn't believe me; she sounded worried all the time, and when I was ten weeks along she finally said, "Cara, are you sure about this? There's still time to change your mind … it's not easy to make a good home for a kid, even when you're married and everything."

"I'm sure," I said. After I'd had the baby I'd tell her I'd changed my mind, that I'd thought about it and she was right, I couldn't give it a good enough home. How could I tell Joni I was having a child precisely because I couldn't give it a home at all, couldn't give anything or anyone a home, couldn't make a home for myself?

She appointed herself my surrogate partner. She enrolled me in exercise and natural childbirth classes, nagged me about nutrition, made me swear by anything I'd ever believed in not to drink, not to smoke, not to take even the most innocent drugs. She went with me for my check-ups, for the sonogram and the amniocentesis and the monitors which picked up a steady, thriving fetal heartbeat. I don't know how she afforded the time away from Dave and Joshua then, how she can afford it now; but I went along with all of it, because I owed the beaten child at least that much.

When the results from the amniocentesis came back, the doctor asked me if I wanted to know the sex of my baby. "It's a girl," I told him.

He laughed. "Bingo. You had a fifty-fifty chance of being right."

Even with the heartbeat and all the tests, every night before I went to sleep I became convinced that I was playing a huge hoax, that the symptoms were fake and there was no baby at all – even though I felt it kicking, even though my belly was growing like that of any pregnant woman.

And I found myself, to my horror, beginning to want the child. The charade of setting up a nursery pleased me as nothing has done in years. I began noticing children everywhere I went – infants in strollers, toddlers in playgrounds, women with babies in stores. When I talked to Joni on the phone I'd listen to hear what Joshua was doing in the background. I started reading baby books and worrying about chicken pox.

I love this unseen baby more than I've ever loved anything, and I don't know what to do with that, I who have always been so afraid to love. I'm afraid that at the last minute I'll waver and keep the child instead of giving it up – for all the wrong reasons, for the attention it will bring me – and that sooner or later I'll subject it to the very torment from which I'm trying to free it, just because I don't know any other way to act. I don't know if the promise I made, that night in front of the television, is one I can keep.

Yesterday I asked Joni if she remembered our phone conversation about the child inside us who expects to be liked. "You can't separate yourself from it?" I asked her. "You can't send it away?"

"Never," she said with a smile, and I closed my eyes because I knew she was trying to be reassuring, and I had no way of making her understand that she was being just the opposite.

The contractions are closer together now and I've been moved into the delivery room, Joni by my side telling me how to breathe, when to push, all the doctors and nurses looking down at me with cheer and encouragement. Their faces are shining. I can only imagine what mine looks like. I'm so afraid.

Soon it will all be over, and I don't know how it will end, what will happen to me and what I've created. When the baby comes out I wonder if she'll look like me; I wonder if she'll be covered with bruises and will never be able to trust anyone. I'm afraid to let her go, to dismiss the only part of me which has ever been good, and I'm afraid that if I don't give her away I'll destroy her and myself.

And there's the other possibility, although all the facts argue against it, although Joni and the nurses are urging me to push one last time, because the doctor just announced that he can see the baby's head: that when she comes out she'll collapse like paper, a myth torn apart, and tomorrow I'll have to begin again.

# Ever After

"Velvet," she says, pushing back her sleep-tousled hair. "I want green velvet this time, with lace around the neck and wrists. Cream lace — not white — and sea-green velvet. Can you do that?"

"Of course." She's getting vain, this one; vain and a little bossy. The wonder has worn off. All for the best. Soon now, very soon, I'll have to tell her the truth.

She bends, here in the dark kitchen, to peer at the back of her mother's prized copper kettle. It's just after dusk, and by the light of the lantern I'm holding a vague reflection flickers and dances on the metal. She scowls. "Can't you get me a real mirror? That ought to be simple enough."

I remember when the light I brought filled her with awe. Wasting good fuel, just to see yourself by! "No mirrors. I clothe you only in seeming, not in fact. You know that."

"Ah." She waves a hand, airily. She's proud of her hands: delicate and pale and long-fingered, a noblewoman's hands; all the years before I came she protected them against the harsh work of her mother's kitchen. "Yes, the prince. I have to marry a prince, so I can have his jewels for my own. Will it be this time, do you think?"

"There will be no princes at this dance, Caitlin. You are practicing for princes."

"Hah! And when I'm good enough at last, will you let me wear glass slippers?"

"Nonsense. You might break them during a gavotte, and cut your-

141

self." She knew the story before I found her; they always do. It enters their blood as soon as they can follow speech, and lodges in their hearts like the promise of spring. All poor mothers tell their daughters this story, as they sit together in dark kitchens, scrubbing pots and trying to save their hands for the day when the tale becomes real. I often wonder if that first young woman was one of ours, but the facts don't matter. Like all good stories, this one is true.

"Princess Caitlin," she says dreamily. "That will be very fine. Oh, how they will envy me! It's begun already, in just the little time since you've made me beautiful. Ugly old Lady Alison – did you see her giving me the evil eye, at the last ball? Just because my skin is smooth and hers wrinkled, and I a newcomer?"

"Yes," I tell her. I am wary of Lady Alison, who looks too hard and says too little. Lady Alison is dangerous.

"Jealousy," Caitlin says complacently. "I'd be jealous, if I looked like she does."

"You are very lovely," I say, and it is true. With her blue eyes and raven hair, and those hands, she could have caught the eye of many princes on her own. Except, of course, that without me they never would have seen her.

Laughing, she sits to let me plait her hair. "So serious! You never smile at me. Do magic folk never smile? Aren't you proud of me?"

"Very proud," I say, parting the thick cascade and beginning to braid it. She smells like smoke and the thin, sour stew which simmers on the hearth, but at the dance tonight she will be scented with all the flowers of summer.

"Will you smile and laugh when I have my jewels and land? I shall give you riches, then."

So soon, I think, and my breath catches. So soon she offers me gifts, and forgets the woman who bore her, who now lies snoring in the other room. All for the best; and yet I am visited by something very like pity. "No wife has riches but from her lord, Caitlin. Not in this kingdom."

"I shall have riches of my own, when I am married," she says grandly; and then, her face clouding as if she regrets having forgotten, "My mother will be rich too, then. She'll like you, when we're rich. Godmother, why doesn't she like you now?"

"Because I am stealing you away from her. She has never been invited to a ball. And because I am beautiful, and she isn't anymore."

What I have said is true enough, as always; and, as always, I find myself wondering if there is more than that. No matter. If Caitlin's mother suspects, she says nothing. I am the only chance she and her daughter have to approach nobility, and for the sake of that dream she has tolerated my presence, and Caitlin's odd new moods, and the schedule which keeps the girl away from work to keep her fresh for dances.

Caitlin bends her head, and the shining braids slip through my fingers like water. "She'll come to the castle whenever she wants to, when I'm married to a prince. We'll make her beautiful too, then. I'll buy her clothing and paint for her face."

"There are years of toil on her, Caitlin. Lady Alison is your mother's age, and all her riches can't make her lovely again."

"Oh, but Lady Alison's mean. That makes you ugly." Caitlin dismisses her enemy with the ignorance of youth. Lady Alison is no meaner than anyone, but she has borne illnesses and childlessness and the unfaithfulness of her rich lord. Her young nephew will fall in love with Caitlin tonight – a match Lord Gregory suggested, I suspect, precisely because Alison will oppose it.

Caitlin's hair is done, piled in coiled, lustrous plaits. "Do you have the invitation? Where did I put it?"

"On the table, next to the onions."

She nods, crosses the room, snatches up the thick piece of paper and fans herself with it. I remember her first invitation, only six dances ago, her eagerness and innocence and purity, the wide eyes and wonder. *I? I have been invited to the ball?* She refused to let go of the invitation then; afraid it might vanish as suddenly as it had come, she carried it with her for hours. They are always at their most beautiful that first time, when they believe most fully in the story and are most awe-stricken at having been chosen to play the heroine. No glamour we give them can ever match that first glow.

"Clothe me," Caitlin commands now, standing with her eyes closed in the middle of the kitchen, and I put the glamour on her and her grubby kitchen-gown is transformed by desire and shadow into sea-green velvet and cream lace. She smiles. She opens her eyes, which gleam with joy and the giddiness of transformation. She has taken easily to that rush; she craves it. Already she has forsaken dreams of love for dreams of power.

"I'm hungry," she says. "I want to eat before the dance. What was that soup you gave me last night? You must have put wine in it, because it made me drunk. I want some of that."

"No food before you dance," I tell her. "You don't want to look fat, do you?"

No chance of that, for this girl who has starved in a meager kitchen all her life; but at the thought of dancing she forgets her hunger and takes a few light steps in anticipation of the music. "Let me stay longer this time – please. Just an hour or two. I never get tired anymore."

"Midnight," I tell her flatly. It won't do to change that part of the story until she knows everything.

So we go to the dance, in a battered carriage made resplendent not by any glamour of mine but by Caitlin's belief in her own beauty. This, too, she has learned easily; already the spells are more hers than mine, although she doesn't yet realize it.

At the gates, Caitlin hands the invitation to the footman. She has grown to relish this moment, the thrill of bending him to her will with a piece of paper, of forcing him to admit someone he suspects – quite rightly – doesn't belong here. It is very important that she learn to play this game. Later she will learn to win her own invitations, to cajole the powerful into admitting her where, without their permission, she cannot go at all.

Only tonight it is less simple. The footman glances at the envelope, frowns, says, "I'm sorry, but I can't admit you."

"Can't admit us?" Caitlin summons the proper frosty indignation, and so I let her keep talking. She needs to learn this, too. "Can't admit us, with a handwritten note from Lord Gregory?"

"Just so, mistress. Lady Alison has instructed — "

"Lady Alison didn't issue the invitation."

The footman coughs, shuffles his feet. "Just so. I have the very strictest instructions — "

"What does Lord Gregory instruct?"

"Lord Gregory has not — "

"Lord Gregory wrote the invitation. Lord Gregory wants us here. If Lord Gregory learned we were denied it would go badly for you, footman."

He looks up at us; he looks miserable. "Just so," he says, sounding wretched.

"I shall speak to her for you," I tell him, and Caitlin smiles at me and we are through the gates, passing ornate gardens and high, neat hedges. I lean back in my seat, shaking. Lady Alison is very dangerous, but she has made a blunder. The servant could not possibly refuse her husband's invitation; all she has done is warn us. "Be very careful tonight," I say to Caitlin. "Avoid her."

"I'd like to scratch her eyes out! How dare she, that jealous old — "

"Avoid her, Caitlin! I'll deal with her. I don't want to see you anywhere near her."

She subsides. Already we can hear music from the great hall, and her eyes brighten as she taps time to the beat.

The people at the dance are the ones who are always at dances; by now, all of them know her. She excites the men and unnerves the women, and where she passes she leaves a trail of uncomfortable silence, followed by hushed whispers. I strain to hear what they are saying, but catch only the usual comments about her youth, her beauty, her low birth.

"Is she someone's illegitimate child, do you think?"

"A concubine, surely."

"She'll never enter a convent, not that one."

"Scheming husband-hunter, and may she find one soon. I don't want her taking mine."

The usual. I catch sight of Lady Alison sitting across the wide room. She studies us with narrowed eyes. One arthritic hand, covered with jeweled rings, taps purposefully on her knee. She sees me watching her and meets my gaze without flinching. She crosses herself.

I look away, wishing we hadn't come here. What does she intend to do? I wonder how much she has learned simply by observation, and how much Gregory let slip. I scan the room again and spot him, in a corner, nursing a chalice of wine. He is watching Caitlin as intently as his wife did, but with a different expression.

And someone else is watching Caitlin, among the many people who glance at her and then warily away: Randolph, Gregory's young nephew, who is tall and well-formed and pleasant of face. Caitlin looks to me for confirmation and I nod. She smiles at Randolph – that artful smile there has never been need to teach – and he extends a hand to invite her to dance.

I watch them for a moment, studying how she looks up at him, the angle of her head, the flutter of her lashes. She started with the smile, and I gave her the rest. She has learned her skills well.

"So," someone says behind me, "she's growing accustomed to these late nights."

I turn. Lady Alison stands there, unlovely and shrunken, having crossed the room with improbable speed. "Almost as used to them as you," she says.

I bow my head, carefully acquiescent. "Or you yourself. Those who would dance in these halls must learn to do without sleep."

"Some sleep during the day." Her mouth twitches. "I am Randolph's aunt, mistress. While he stays within these walls his care lies in my keeping, even as the care of the girl lies in yours. I will safeguard him however I must."

I laugh, the throaty chuckle which thrills Gregory, but my amusement is as much an act as Caitlin's flirtatiousness. "Against dancing with pretty young women?"

"Against being alone with those who would entrap him with his own ignorance. He knows much too little of the world; he places more faith in fairy tales than in history, and neither I nor the Church have been able to persuade him to believe in evil. I pray you, by our Lord in heaven and his holy saints, leave this house."

"So you requested at the gates." Her piety nauseates me, as she no doubt intended, and I keep my voice steady only with some effort. "The Lord of this castle is Lord Gregory, Lady Alison, by whose invitation we are here and in whose hospitality we will remain."

She grimaces. "I have some small power of my own, although it does not extend to choosing my guests. Pray chaperone your charge."

"No need. They are only dancing." I glance at Caitlin and Randolph, who gaze at each other as raptly as if no one else were in the room. Randolph's face is silly and soft; Caitlin's, when I catch a glimpse of it, is soft and ardent. I frown, suddenly uneasy; that look is a bit too sudden and far too unguarded, and may be more than artifice.

Lady Alison snorts. "Both will want more than dancing presently, I warrant, although they will want different things. Chaperone her – or I will do it for you, less kindly."

With that she turns and vanishes into the crowd. I turn back to the young couple, thinking that a chaperone would indeed be wise tonight; but the players have struck up a minuet, and Caitlin and Randolph glide gracefully through steps as intricate and measured as any court intrigue. The dance itself will keep them safe, for a little while.

Instead I make my way to Gregory, slowly, drifting around knots of people as if I am only surveying the crowd. Alison has positioned herself to watch Caitlin and Randolph, who dip and twirl through the steps of the dance; I hope she won't notice me talking to her husband.

"She is very beautiful," says Gregory softly when I reach his side. "Even lovelier than you, my dear. What a charming couple they make. I would give much to be Randolph, for a few measures of this dance."

He thinks he can make me jealous. Were this any other ball I might pretend he had succeeded, but I have no time for games tonight. "Gregory, Alison tried to have us barred at the gate. And she just threatened me."

He smiles. "That was foolish of her. Also futile."

"Granted," I say, although I suspect Lady Alison has resources of which neither of us are aware. Most wives of the nobility do: faithful servants, devoted priests, networks of spies in kitchens and corridors.

Gregory reaches out to touch my cheek; I draw away from him, uneasy. Everyone here suspects I am his mistress, but there is little sense in giving them public proof. He laughs gently. "You need not be afraid of her. She loves the boy and wishes only to keep him cloistered in a chapel, with his head buried in scripture. I tell her that is no sport for a young man and certainly no education for a titled lord, who must learn how to resist the blandishments of far more experienced women. So he and our little Caitlin will be merry, and take their lessons from each other, with no one the worse for it. See how they dance together!"

They dance as I have taught Caitlin she should dance with princes: lingering over the steps, fingertips touching, lips parted and eyes bright. Alison watches them, looking worried, and I cannot help but feel the same way. Caitlin is too obvious, too oblivious; she has grown innocent again, in a mere hour. I remember what Alison said about history, and fairy tales; if Caitlin and Randolph both believe themselves in that same old story, things will go harshly for all of us.

"Let them be happy together," Gregory says softly. "They have need of happiness, both of them — Randolph with his father surely dying, and the complexities of power about to bewilder him, and Caitlin soon to learn her true nature. You cannot keep it from her much longer, Juliana. She has changed too much. Let them be happy, for this one night; and let their elders, for once, abandon care and profit from their example."

He reaches for my hand again, drawing me closer to him, refusing to let go. His eyes are as bright as Randolph's; he has had rather too much wine. "Profit from recklessness?" I ask, wrenching my fingers from his fist. Alison has looked away from her nephew and watches us now, expressionless. I hear murmurs around us; a young courtier in purple satin and green hose raises an eyebrow.

"This is my castle," Gregory says. "My halls and land, my musicians, my servants and clerics and nobles; my wife. No one can hurt you here, Juliana."

"No one save you, my lord. Kindly retain your good sense – "

"My invitation." His voice holds little kindness now. "My invitation allowed you entrance, as it has many other times; I provide you with splendor, and fine nourishment, and a training ground for the girl, and I am glad to do so. I am no slave of Alison's priests, Juliana; I know full well that you are not evil."

"Kindly be more quiet and discreet, my lord!" The courtier is carefully ignoring us now, evidently fascinated with a bunch of grapes. Caitlin and Randolph, transfixed by each other, sway in the last steps of the minuet.

Gregory continues in the same tone: "Of late you have paid far more attention to Caitlin than to me. Even noblemen are human, and can be hurt. Let the young have their pleasures tonight, and let me have mine."

I lower my own voice, since he refuses to lower his. "What, in the middle of the ballroom? That would be a fine entertainment for your guests! I will come to you tomorrow – "

"Tonight," he says, into the sudden silence of the dance's end. "Come to me tonight, in the usual chamber – "

"It is a poor lord who leaves his guests untended," I tell him sharply, "and a poor teacher who abandons her student. You will excuse me."

He reaches for me again, but I slip past his hands and go to find Caitlin, wending my way around gaudily-dressed lords and ladies and squires, catching snippets of gossip and conversation.

"Did you see them dancing – "

"So the venison disagreed with me, but thank goodness it was only a trifling ailment – "

"Penelope's violet silk! I said, my dear, I simply must have the pattern and wherever did you find that seamstress – "

"Gregory's brother in failing health, and the young heir staying here? No uncle can be trusted that far. The boy had best have a quick dagger and watch his back, is what I say."

That comment hurries my steps. Gregory's brother is an obscure duke, but he is a duke nonetheless, and Gregory is next in the line of succession after Randolph. If Randolph is in danger, and Caitlin with him –

I have been a fool. We should not have come here, and we must leave. I scan the colorful crowd more anxiously than ever for Caitlin, but my fears are groundless; she has found me first, and rushes towards me, radiant.

"Oh, Godmother – "

"Caitlin! My dear, listen: you must stay by me – "

But she hasn't heard me. "Godmother, he's so sweet and kind, so sad with his father ill and yet trying to be merry – did you see how he danced? Why does it have to be a prince I love? I don't care if he's not a prince, truly I don't, and just five days ago I scorned that other gawky fellow for not having a title, but he wasn't nearly as nice – "

"Caitlin!" Yes, we most assuredly must leave. I lower my voice and take her by the elbow. "Listen to me: many men are nice. If you want a nice man you may marry a blacksmith. I am not training you to be a mere duchess."

She grows haughty now. "Duchess sounds quite well enough to me. Lord Gregory is no king."

Were we in private I would slap her for that. "No, he isn't, but he is a grown man and come into his limited power, and so he is still more useful to us than Randolph. Caitlin, we must leave now – "

"No! We can't leave; it's nowhere near midnight. I don't want to leave. You can't make me."

"I can strip you of your finery right here."

"Randolph wouldn't care."

"Everyone else would, and he is outnumbered."

"Randolph picks his own companions — "

"Randolph," I say, losing all patience, "still picks his pimples. He is a fine young man, Caitlin, but he is young nonetheless. My dear, many more things are happening here tonight than your little romance. I am your magic godmother, and on some subjects you must trust me. We are leaving."

"I won't leave," she says, raising her chin. "I'll stay here until after midnight. I don't care if you turn me into a toad; Randolph will save me, and make me a duchess."

"Princesses are safer," I tell her grimly, not at all sure it's even true. On the far side of the room I see the courtier in the green hose talking intently to Lady Alison, and a chill cuts through me. Well, he cannot have heard much which isn't general rumor, and soon we will be in the carriage, and away from all this.

"Caitlin!" Randolph hurries up to as, as welcoming and guileless as some friendly dog. "Why did you leave me? I didn't know where you'd gone. Will you dance with me again? Here, some wine if you don't mind sharing, I thought you'd be thirsty — "

She takes the goblet and sips, laughing. "Of course I'll dance with you."

I frown at Caitlin and clear my throat. "I regret that she cannot, my lord — "

"This is my godmother Juliana," Caitlin cuts in, taking another sip of wine and giving Randolph a dazzling smile, "who worries overmuch about propriety and thinks people will gossip if I dance with you too often."

"And so they shall," he says, bowing and kissing my hand, "because everyone gossips about beauty." He straightens and smiles down at me, still holding my hand. His cheeks are flushed and his fingers very warm; I can feel the faint, steady throb of his pulse against my skin. What could Caitlin do but melt, in such heat?

"Randolph!" Two voices, one cry; Alison and Gregory approach us from opposite directions, the sea of guests parting before them.

Alison, breathless, reaches us a moment before her husband does. "Randolph, my love – the players are going to give us another slow tune, at my request. You'll dance with your crippled old aunt, won't you?"

He bows; he can hardly refuse her. Gregory, standing next to Caitlin, says smoothly, "And I will have the honor of dancing with the young lady, with her kind godmother's assent."

It isn't a petition. I briefly consider feigning illness, but such a ruse would shake Caitlin's faith in my power and give Gregory the excuse to protest that I must stay here, spend the night and be made comfortable in his household's care.

Instead I station myself next to a pillar to watch the dancers. Alison's lips move as Randolph guides her carefully around the floor. I see her press a small pouch into his hand; he smiles indulgently and puts it in a pocket.

She is warning him away from Caitlin, then. This dance is maddeningly slow, and far too long; I crane my neck to find Caitlin and Gregory, only to realize that they are about to sweep past me. "Yes, I prefer roses to all other blooms," Caitlin says lightly. (That too is artifice; she preferred forget-me-nots until I taught her otherwise.)

So at least one of these conversations is insignificant, and Caitlin safe. Alison and Randolph, meanwhile, glare at each other; she is trying to give him something on a chain, and he is refusing it. They pass me, but say nothing; Caitlin and Gregory go by again a moment later. "Left left right, left left right," he tells her, before they are past my hearing, "it is a pleasing pattern and very fashionable; you must try it."

A new court dance, no doubt. This old one ends at last, and I dart for Caitlin, only to be halted by a group of rowdy acrobats who have just burst into the hall. "Your pleasure!" they cry, doing flips and twists in front of me as the crowd laughs and gathers to watch them. "Your entertainment, your dancing hearts!" I try to go around them, but find myself blocked by a motley-clad clown juggling pewter goblets. "Hey! We'll make you merry, at the generous lord's invitation we'll woo you, we'll win you – "

You'll distract us, I think – but from what? I manage to circle the juggler, but there is no sign of Caitlin or Randolph. Gregory seems likewise to have disappeared.

Alison is all too evident, however. "Where are they? What have you done with them?" She stands in front of me, her hands clenched on the fine silk of her skirt. "I turned away from Randolph for a mere moment to answer a servant's question, and when I looked back he was gone – "

"My lady, I was standing on the side. You no doubt saw me. I am honestly eager to honor your wishes and be gone, and I dislike this confusion as much as you do."

"I know you," she says, trembling, her voice very low. "I know you for what you are. I told Randolph, but he would not believe me, and Gregory fairly revels in dissolution. I would unmask you in this hall and send town criers to spread the truth about you, save that my good lord would be set upon by decent Christian folk were it known he had trafficked with such a creature."

And your household destroyed and all your riches plundered, I think; yes, the poor welcome such pretexts. You do well to maintain silence, Alison, since it buys your own safety.

But I dare not admit to what she knows. "I am but a woman as yourself, my lady, and I share your concern for Randolph and the girl – "

"Nonsense, they are both charming young people who dance superbly." Gregory has reappeared, affable and urbane; he seems more relaxed than he has all evening, and I trust him less.

So does Alison, by the look of her. "And where have you hidden our two paragons of sprightliness, my lord?"

"I? I have not hidden them anywhere. Doubtless they have stolen away and found some quiet corner to themselves. The young will do such things. Alison, my sweet, you look fatigued – "

"And the old, when they get a chance. No: I am not going to retire conveniently and leave you alone with this creature. I value your soul far more than that."

"Although not my body," Gregory says, raising an eyebrow. "Well, then, shall we dance, all three? With linked hands in a circle, like children? Shall we sit and discuss the crops, or have a hand of cards? What would you, my lovelies?"

Alison takes his hand. "Let us go find your nephew."

He sighs heavily and rolls his eyes, but he allows himself to be led away. I am glad to be rid of them; now I can search on my own and make a hasty exit. The conversation with Alison worries me. She is too cautious to destroy us here, but she may well try to have us followed into the countryside.

So I make my way through corridors, through courtyards, peering into corners and behind pillars, climbing winding staircases and descending them, until I am lost and can no longer hear the music from the great hall. I meet other furtive lovers, dim shapes embracing in shadows, but none are Randolph and Caitlin. When I have exhausted every passageway I can find I remember Caitlin and Gregory's discussion of roses and hurry outside, through a doorway I have never seen before, but the moonlit gardens yield nothing. The sky tells me that it is midnight: Caitlin will be rejoicing at having eluded me.

Wherever she is. These halls and grounds are too vast; I could wander all night and still not find her by dawn. Gregory knows where she is: I am convinced be does, convinced he arranged the couple's disappearance. He may have done so to force me into keeping the tryst with him. That would be very like him; he would be thrilled by my seeking him out while his guests gossip and dance in the great ball. Gregory delights in private indiscretions at public events.

So I will play his game this once, although it angers me, and lie with him, and, be artful and cajoling. I go back inside and follow hallways I know to Gregory's chambers, glancing behind me to be sure I am not seen.

The small chapel where Lady Alison takes her devotions lies along the same path, and as I pass it I hear moans of pain. I stop, listening, wary of a trap – but the noise comes again, and the agony sounds genuine; a thin, childish whimpering clearly made by a woman.

*Caitlin?* I remember Alison's threats, and my vision blackens for a moment. I slip into the room, hiding in shadows, tensed to leap. If Alison led the girl here –

Alison is indeed here, but Caitlin is not with her. Doubled over in front of the altar, Gregory's wife gasps for breath and clutches her side; her face is sweaty, gray, the pupils dilated. She sees me and recoils, making her habitual sign of the cross; her hand is trembling, but her voice remains steady. "So. Didn't you find them, either?"

"My lady Alison, what – "

"He called it a quick poison," she says, her face contorting with pain, "but I am stronger than he thinks, or the potion weaker. I was tired – my leg…we came here; it was close. I asked him to pray with me, and he repented very prettily. 'I will bring some wine,' he said, 'and we will both drink to my salvation.' Two cups he brought, and I took the one he gave me… I thought him saved, and relief dulled my wits. 'Mulled wine,' he said, 'I ground the spices for you myself,' and so he did, no doubt. Pray none other taste them."

So much speech has visibly drained her; shaken, I help her into a chair. What motive could Gregory have for killing his wife? Her powers of observation were an asset to him, though he rarely heeded them, and he couldn't have felt constrained by his marriage vows; he never honored them while she was alive.

"It is well I believe in the justice of God," she says. "No one will punish him here in the world. They will pretend I ate bad meat, or had an attack of bile."

"Be silent and save your strength," I tell her, but she talks anyway, crying now, fumbling to wipe her face through spasms.

"He tired of me because I am old. He grew tired of a wife who said her prayers, and loved other people's children although she could have none of her own. No doubt he will install you by his side now, since you are made of darkness and steal the daughters of simple folk."

Gregory knows far better than to make me his formal consort, whatever Alison thinks. "We choose daughters only when one of us has been killed, Lady Alison. We wish no more than anyone does – to continue, and to be safe."

"I will continue in heaven," she says, and then cries out, a thin keening which whistles between her teeth. She no longer sounds human.

I kneel beside her, uncertain she will be able to understand my words. This does not look like a quick-acting potion, whatever Gregory said; it will possibly take her hours to die, and she will likely be mad before then. "I cannot save you, my lady, but I can make your end swift and painless."

"I need no mercy from such as you!"

"You must take mercy where you can get it. Who else will help you?"

She moans and then subsides, trembling. "I have not been shriven. He could have allowed me that."

"But he did not. Perhaps you will be called a saint someday, and this declared your martyrdom; for now, the only last rites you will be offered are mine."

She crosses herself again, but this time it is clearly an effort for her to lift her hand. "A true death?"

"A true death," I say gently. "We do not perpetuate pain."

Her lips draw back from her teeth. "Be merciful, then; and when you go to your assignation, tell Gregory he harms himself far worse than he has harmed me."

It is quick and painless, as I promised, but I am shaking when I finish, and the thought of seeing Gregory fills me with dread. I will have to pretend not to know that he has murdered his wife; I will have to be charming, and seductive, and disguise my concern for my own safety and Caitlin's so I can trick her whereabouts out of him.

I knock on his door and hear the soft "Enter." Even here I need an invitation, to enter this chamber where Gregory will be sprawled on the bed, peeling an apple or trimming his fingernails, his clothing already unfastened.

Tonight the room is unlit. I see someone sitting next to the window, silhouetted in moonlight; only as my eyes adjust to the dimness do I realize that Gregory has not kept our appointment. A priest waits in his place, surrounded by crucifixes and bottles of holy water and plaster statues of saints. On the bed where I have lain so often is something long and sharp which I force myself not to look at too closely.

"Hello," he says, as the door thuds shut behind me. I should have turned and run, but it is too late now; I have frozen at the sight of the priest, as they say animals do in unexpected light. In the hallway I hear heavy footsteps – the corridor is guarded, then.

The priest holds an open Bible; he glances down at it, and then, with a grimace of distaste, sideways at the bed. "No, lady, it won't come to that. You needn't look so frightened."

I say nothing. I tell myself I must think clearly, and be very quick, but I cannot think at all. We are warned about these small rooms, these implements. All the warnings I have heard have done me no good.

"There's the window," he explains. "You could get out that way if you had to. That is how I shall tell them you escaped, when they question me." He gestures at his cheek, and I see a thin, cruel scar running from forehead to jaw. "When I was still a child, my father took me poaching for boar on our lord's estate. It was my first hunt. It taught me not to corner frightened beasts, especially when they have young. Sit down, lady. Don't be afraid."

I sit, cautiously and without hope, and he closes the book with a soft sound of sighing parchment. "You are afraid, of course; well you should be. Lord Gregory has trapped you, for reasons he says involve piety but doubtless have more to do with politics; Lady Alison has been weaving her own schemes to destroy you, and the Church has declared you incapable of redemption. You have been quite unanimously consigned to the stake. Which is – " he smiles " – why I am here. Do you believe in God, my dear? Do your kind believe in miracles?"

When I don't answer he smiles again and goes on easily, as if we were chatting downstairs at the dance. "You should. It is a kind of miracle that has brought you to me. I have prayed for this since I was very young, and now I am old, and my prayer has been answered. I was scarcely more than a boy when I entered the religious life, and for many years I was miserable, but now I see that this is why it happened."

He laughs, quite kindly. His kindness terrifies me. I fear he is mad. "I came from a poor family," he says. "I was the youngest son, and so, naturally, I became a priest. The Church cannot get sons the normal way, so it takes other people's and leaves the best young men to breed more souls. You and I are not, you see, so very different."

He leans back in his chair. "There were ten other children in my family. Four died. The littlest and weakest was my youngest sister, who was visited one day by a very beautiful woman who made her lovely, and took her to parties, and then took her away. I never got to say goodbye to my sister – her name was Sofia – and I never got to tell her that, although I knew what she had become, I still loved her. I thought she would be coming back, you see."

He leans forward earnestly, and his chair makes a scraping sound. "I have always prayed for a way to reach her. The Church tells me to destroy you, but I do not believe God wants you destroyed – because He has sent you to me, who thinks of you only with pity and gratitude and love. I am glad my little sister was made beautiful. If you know her, Sofia with green eyes and yellow hair, tell her Thomas loves her, eh? Tell her I am doubtless a heretic, for forgiving her what she is. Tell her I think of her every day when I take the Holy Communion. Will you do that for me?"

I stare at him, wondering if the watchers in the hallway can distinguish words through the thick wooden door.

He sighs. "So suspicious! Yes, of course you will. You will deliver my message, and I'll say you confounded me by magic and escaped through the window. Eh?"

"They'll kill you," I tell him. The calmness of my voice shocks me.

I am angry now: not at Lord Gregory, who betrayed me, not at Lady Alison, who was likewise betrayed and died believing me about to lie with her husband, but with this meandering holy man who prattles of miracles and ignores his own safety. "The ones set to guard the door. They'll say you must have been possessed by demons, to let me escape."

He nods and pats his book. "We will quite probably both be killed. Lady Alison means to set watchers on the roads."

So he doesn't know. "Lady Alison is dead. Gregory poisoned her."

He pales and bows his head for a moment. "Ah. It is certainly political, then, and no one is safe tonight. I have bought you only a very little time; you had best use it. Now go: gather your charge and flee, and God be with you both. I shall chant exorcisms and hold them off, eh? Go on: use the window."

I use the window. I dislike changing shape and do so only in moments of extreme danger; it requires too much energy, and the consequent hunger can make one reckless.

I have made myself an owl, not the normal choice but a good one; I need acute vision, and a form that won't arouse suspicion in alert watchers. From this height I can see the entire estate: the castle, the surrounding land, gardens and pathways and fountains – and something else I never knew about, and could not have recognized from the ground.

The high hedges lining the road to the castle form, in one section, the side of a maze, one of those ornate topiary follies which pass in and out of botanical fashion. In the center of it is a small rose garden with a white fountain; on the edge of the fountain sit two foreshortened figures, very close to one another. Just outside the center enclosure, in a cul-de-sac which anyone exiting the maze must pass, another figure stands hidden.

*Left left right.* Gregory wasn't explaining a new dance at all: he was telling Caitlin how to reach the rose garden, the secret place where she and Randolph hid while Alison and I searched so frantically. Doubtless he went with his wife to keep her from the spot; with Alison's bad leg, and the maze this far from the castle, it wouldn't have been difficult.

I land a few feet behind him and return to myself again. Hunger and hatred enhance my strength, already greater than his. He isn't expecting an approach from behind; I knock him flat, his weapons and charms scattering in darkness, and have his arms pinned behind his back before he can cry out. "I am not dead," I say very quietly into his ear, "but your wife is, and soon you will be."

He whimpers and struggles, but I give his arm an extra twist and he subsides, panting. "Why, Gregory? What was all of this for? So you could spy on them murmuring poetry to one another? Surely not that. Tell me!"

"So I can be a duke."

"By your wife's death?"

"By the boy's."

"How?" I answer sharply, thinking of Randolph and Caitlin sharing the same goblet. "How did you mean to kill him? More poison?"

"She will kill him," he says softly, "because she is aroused, and does not yet know her own appetites or how to control them. Is it not so, my lady?"

My own hunger is a red throbbing behind my eyes. "No, my lord. Caitlin is no murder weapon: she does not yet know what she is or where her hungers come from. She can no more feed on her own than a kitten can, who depends on the mother cat to bring food and teach it how to eat."

"You shall teach her with my puling nephew, I warrant."

"No, my lord Gregory. I shall not. I shall not teach her with you either, more's the pity; we mangle as we learn, just as kittens do – and as kittens do, she will practice on little animals as long as they will sustain her. I should like to see you mangled, my lord."

Instead I break his neck, cleanly, as I broke Alison's. Afterwards, the body still warm, I feed fully; it would be more satisfying were he still alive, but he shall have no more pleasure. Feeding me aroused him as coupling seldom did; he begged to do it more often, and now I am glad I refused. As terrible as he was, he would have been worse as one of us. When I am finished I lick my fingers clean, wipe my face as best I can, and drag the body back into the cul-de-sac, where it will not be immediately visible. Shaking, I hide the most obvious and dangerous of Gregory's weapons and step into the rose garden.

Caitlin, glowing in moonlight, sits on the edge of the fountain, as I saw her from the air. Randolph is handing her a white rose, which he has evidently just picked: there is blood on his hands where the thorns have scratched him. She takes the rose from him and bends to kiss his fingers, the tip of her tongue flicking towards the wounds.

"Caitlin!" She turns, startled, and lets go of Randolph's hands. "Caitlin, we must leave now."

"No," she says, her eyes very bright. "No. It is already after midnight and you see — nothing horrid has happened."

"We must leave," I tell her firmly. "Come along."

"But I can come back?" she says, laughing, and then to Randolph, "I'll come back. Soon, I promise you. The next dance, or before that even. Godmother, promise I can come back — "

"Come along, Caitlin! Randolph, we bid you goodnight — "

"May I see you out of the maze, my ladies?"

I think of the watchers on the road, the watchers who may have been set on the maze by now. I wish I could warn him, teach him of the world in an instant. Disguise yourself, Randolph; leave this place as quickly as you can, and steal down swift and secret roads to your father's bedside.

But I cannot yet speak freely in front of Caitlin, and we have time only to save ourselves. Perhaps the maze will protect him, for a little while. "Thank you, my lord, but we know the way. Pray you stay here and think kindly of us; my magic is aided by good wishes."

"Then you shall have them in abundance, whatever my aunt says."

Caitlin comes at last, dragging and prattling. On my own I would escape with shape-changing, but Caitlin doesn't have those skills yet, and were I to tell her of our danger now she would panic and become unmanageable. So I lead her, right right left, right right left, through interminable turns.

But we meet no one else in the maze, and when at last we step into open air there are no priests waiting in ambush. Music still sounds faintly from the castle; the host and hostess have not yet been missed, and the good father must still be muttering incantations in his chamber.

And so we reach the carriage safely; I deposit Caitlin inside and instruct the driver to take us to one of the spots I have prepared for such emergencies. We should be there well before sunup. I can only hope Lady Alison's watchers have grown tired or afraid, and left off their vigil; there is no way to be sure. I listen for hoofbeats on the road behind us and hear nothing. Perhaps, this time, we have been lucky.

Caitlin doesn't know what I saw, there in the rose garden. She babbles about it in the carriage. "We went into the garden, in the moonlight – he kissed me and held my hands, because he said they were cold. His were so warm! He told me I was beautiful; he said he loved me. And he picked roses for me, and he bled where the thorns had pricked him. He bled for me, Godmother – oh, this is the one! This is my prince. How could I not love him?"

I remain silent. She doesn't yet know what she loves. At length she says, "Why aren't we home yet? It's taking so long. I'm hungry. I never had any dinner."

"We aren't going home," I tell her, lighting my lantern and pulling down the shades which cover the carriage's windows. "We have been discovered, Caitlin. It is quite possible we are being followed. I am taking you somewhere safe. There will be food there."

"Discovered?" She laughs. "What have they discovered? That I am poor? That I love Randolph? What could they do to me? He will protect me; he said so. He will marry me."

This is the moment I must tell her. For all the times I have done this, it never hurts any less. "Caitlin, listen to me. You shall never marry Randolph, or anyone else. It was never meant that you should. I am sorry you have to hear this now. I had wanted you to learn some gentler way." She stares at me, bewildered, and, sadly, I smile at her — that expression she has teased me about, asked me for, wondered why I withhold; and when she sees it she understands. The pale eyes go wide, the beautiful hands go to her throat; she backs away from me, crossing herself as if in imitation of Lady Alison.

"Away," she tells me, trembling. "I exorcise thee, demon. In vain dost thou boast of this deed — "

I think of kind Thomas, chanting valiantly in an empty stone chamber as men at arms wait outside the door. "Keep your charms, Caitlin. They'll do you no good. Don't you understand, child? Why do you think everyone has begun to look at you so oddly; why do you think I wouldn't give you a mirror? What do you think was in the soup I gave you?"

The hands go to her mouth now, to the small sharp teeth. She cries out, understanding everything at once — her odd lassitude after the first few balls, the blood I took from her to cure it, her changing hours and changing thirsts — and, as always, this moment of birth rends whatever I have left of a heart. Because for a moment the young creature sitting in front of me is not the apprentice hunter I have made her, but the innocent young girl who stood holding that first invitation to the ball, her heart in her eyes. *I? I have been invited?* I force myself not to turn away as Caitlin cries out, "You tricked me! The story wasn't true!"

She tears at her face with shapely nails, and ribbons of flesh follow her fingers. "You can't weep anymore," I tell her. I would weep for her, if I could. "You can't bleed, either. You're past that. Don't disfigure yourself."

"The story was a lie! None of it was true, ever — "

I make my voice as cold as iron. "The story was perfectly true, Caitlin. You were simply never told all of it before."

"It wasn't supposed to end like this!" All the tears she can't shed are in her voice. "In the story the girl falls in love and marries the prince and — everyone knows that! You lied to me! This isn't the right ending!"

"It's the only ending! The only one there is – Caitlin, surely you see that. Living women have no more protection than we do here. They feed off their men, as we do, and they require permission to enter houses and go to dances, as we do, and they depend on spells of seeming. There is only one difference: you will never, ever look like Lady Alison. You will never look like your mother. You have escaped that."

She stares at me and shrinks against the side of the carriage, holding her hands in front of her – her precious hands which Randolph held, kissed, warmed with his own life. "I love him," she says defiantly. "I love him, and he loves me. That part of it is true – "

"You loved his bleeding hands, Caitlin. If I hadn't interrupted, you would have fed from them, and known then, and hated him for it. And he would have hated you, for allowing him to speak of love when all along you had been precisely what his aunt warned him against."

Her mouth quivers. She hates me for having seen, and for telling her the truth. She doesn't understand our danger; she doesn't know how the woman she has scorned all these weeks died, or how close she came to dying herself.

Gregory was a clever man; the plot was a clean one. To sacrifice Randolph to Caitlin, and kill Caitlin as she tried to escape the maze; Gregory would have mourned his nephew in the proper public manner, and been declared a hero for murdering one fiend in person as the other was destroyed in the castle. Any gossip about his own soul would have been effectively stilled; perhaps he had been seduced, but surely he was pure again, to summon the righteousness to kill the beasts?

Oh yes, clever. Alison would have known the truth, and would never have accepted a title won by Randolph's murder. Alison could have ruined the entire plan, but it is easy enough to silence wives.

"Can I pray?" Caitlin demands of me, as we rattle towards daybreak. "If I can't shed tears or blood, if I can't love, can I still pray?"

"We can pray," I tell her gently, thinking again of Thomas who spared me, of those tenuous bonds between the living and the dead. "We must pray, foremost, that someone hear us. Caitlin, it's the same.

The same story, with that one difference."

She trembles, huddling against the side of the carriage, her eyes closed. When at last she speaks, her voice is stunned. "I'll never see my mother again."

"I am your mother now. What are mothers and daughters, if not women who share blood?"

She whimpers in her throat then, and I stroke her hair. At last she says, "I'll never grow old."

"You will grow as old as the hills," I tell her, putting my arm around her as one comforts a child who has woken from a nightmare, "but you will never be ugly. You will always be as beautiful as you are now, as beautiful as I am. Your hair and nails will grow and I will trim them for you, to keep them lovely, and you will go to every dance, and wear different gowns to all of them."

She blinks and plucks aimlessly at the poor fabric of her dress, once again a kitchen smock. "I'll never be ugly?"

"Never," I say. "You'll never change." We cannot cry or bleed or age; there are so many things we cannot do. But for her, now, it is a comfort.

She hugs herself, shivering, and I sit beside her and hold her, rocking her towards the certain sleep that will come with dawn. It would be better if Randolph were here, with his human warmth, but at least she doesn't have to be alone. I remember my own shock and despair, although they happened longer ago than anyone who is not one of us can remember; I too tried to pray, and afterwards was thankful that my own godmother had stayed with me.

After a while Caitlin's breathing evens, and I am grateful that she hasn't said, as so many of them do, *Now I will never die.*

We shelter our young, as the mortal mothers shelter theirs – those human women who of necessity are as predatory as we, and as dependent on the invitation to feed – and so there are some truths I have not told her. She will learn them soon enough.

She is more beautiful than Lady Alison or her mother, but no less vulnerable. Her very beauty contains the certainty of her destruction.

There is no law protecting women in this kingdom, where wives can be poisoned in their own halls and their murderers never punished. Still less are there laws protecting us.

I have told her she will not grow ugly, but I have not said what a curse beauty can be, how time after time she will be forced to flee the rumors of her perpetual loveliness and all that it implies. Men will arrive to feed her and kiss her and bring her roses; but for all the centuries of gentle princes swearing love, there will inevitably be someone – jealous wife or jaded lord, peasant or priest – who has heard the whispers and believed, and who will come to her resting place, in the light hours when she cannot move, bearing a hammer and a wooden stake.

# Stormdusk

Every year, my mother vanished on the evening of the first snowfall. She left the house without cloak or bonnet, wearing only the thin woolen shift, blue or green or gray, which was her constant winter outfit. Her feet would be clad in thin slippers, because she could not bear the boots that the rest of us wore to keep our toes from freezing. She always left at dusk, when my brothers and father and I huddled most closely around the fire; and always she headed west, towards the mountains, vanishing quickly – if we cared to watch her – into the thick forests that furred the lower slopes.

We did not often care to watch her, for our father had told us that these journeys into the forest healed the sickness that plagued her the rest of the year. And indeed, she would always return to us the next morning with a new lightness in her step and a new brightness in her eyes; and if she also spent her first few days back home staring yearningly towards the mountains and crying over the stove, tears she thought we failed to notice dripping into our roasts and stews, the sadness left her soon enough. "You mustn't ask her any questions," our father told us once. "They'd only make her feel worse about her illness. It is a great grief to your mother that she does not have more energy to spend on loving us."

For she was always distracted, in all seasons. In the days after the first snowfall, her hunger for the mountains was palpable, and when it wore off, a dull indifference replaced it. My mother was beautiful: tall and pale, thin and white as an alder tree and every bit as graceful, with long glimmering hair that swayed with her movements. Everything she did looked like dancing. I spent my childhood trying to learn to move like that, and I always failed. Perhaps I failed because she took no more notice of me than she did of my father or my brothers, although I was the oldest and the only girl. The other girls I knew, the girls who lived in the village ten miles distant, and with whom I studied on the scattered days when school convened, had mothers who spoiled them, mothers who gave them ribbons and sewed pretty frocks for them. We lived in a hard place, rocky land pinched between steep slopes, the soil nearly as miserly as the rocks themselves, but other mothers still managed to concoct treats for their girl-children. That mine did not was a constant pain to me.

She was dutiful enough, certainly. She cooked and cleaned, made simple clothing for us neatly and well, cared tenderly for the animals and just as tenderly for all of us, especially when we were ill. Sometimes at night as we sat by the fire, sewing or mending or listening to father's impossible stories about magical animals and plotting wizards and frost giants, she seemed almost content. I scorned my father's tales as nonsense, silliness for my rapt brothers, for I had the serious business of my mother's illness to occupy me, and it left no room for fancy. But on those evenings, after my father and brothers had gone to bed, I would sometimes hear her humming snatches of eerie tunes, utterly unlike the hearty ballads I learned from my friends at school. I could never remember my mother's songs afterwards: they faded out of memory like snowflakes on warm glass, leaving only an ache of loss.

Only once did I ask her to teach me the song I had heard her singing the night before. "There was no song," she answered gently. "You were dreaming." But tears filled her eyes as she spoke, and there was such sorrow in her voice that I felt as desolate as if I had struck her.

"I'm sorry, Mama. I didn't mean to make you sad."

"You never make me sad," she told me, but I knew she was lying.

Summer was the only generous time in the country where we lived, the time when berries grew for the picking and flowers sprung up in crannies and fields, the time when birdsong filled our ears, instead of howling wind. Everyone else loved summer, but I could not, because summer was when my mother grew sickest. She hid indoors from the sun, which burned her beet red if she ventured out only for a moment, and she wilted in the heat, stooping and sweating. She wept almost unceasingly, as if she were melting. Her breath came in shallow gasps. Every day I stayed inside as long as I could, to fan her and bring her cool water and help her with the chores she was too weak to do herself, and every day when at last I fled outside, into the glorious sunshine and welcome breeze, I felt as if I had been released from a cage. And so I came to hate both the house, where I felt trapped, and the outdoors, where I felt guilty.

The summer I turned ten, I begged my father to fetch a healer, but he only sighed and shook his head. "No, Marja, healers have seen her, scores of healers, and there is nothing they can do. We must be grateful that she can manage as much as she does."

"I don't remember any healers coming here."

"No, you don't remember. You were too young then."

The summer I turned eleven, I begged my father to move the family further north, where my mother would surely be happier; her energy always began to return in the fall, peaking with her overnight journey into the first snowfall. She needed a land even bleaker than ours, clearly. But my father only sighed and shook his head. "No, Marja, for the rest of us would suffer too much from the cold and the wind, and we could not grow enough to feed ourselves and the livestock there; why, we can barely make do where we are."

"I don't care about the cold. I'll wear my warmest clothing! And I'll make warmer clothing for you and the boys, Father. I can sew almost as well as Mama can."

"Ah, but Marja, we don't have the money to buy even a scrap of all the wool we would need to make that much clothing; and we don't have enough sheep to grow that much wool ourselves, nor enough money to buy more sheep."

The summer I turned twelve, I begged my mother to run away

with me to the north. If Father refused to move the entire family, then he and the boys could stay here. Mama and I would live in the cold places, where she would once again grow bright-eyed and light-footed. Father and the boys would simply have to learn to cook and sew for themselves. But my mother only sighed and shook her head. "No, Marja, I must stay here. This is my home, and it would kill me to leave it."

"It's killing you to stay! Every summer, I think you're going to die. How can you love this place when it makes you so sick?"

"Marja," she said, the sorrow thick as smoke in her voice, "oh, Marja, this place doesn't make me sick. It's all that keeps me alive. You must never ask me to go anywhere else."

"But you do go somewhere else!" I was crying then, torn between rage and utter despair. "Every year you go somewhere else, when the first snow falls! You set out for the mountains at sundown, without even a cloak, and you don't come back again until morning!"

"What?" My mother looked at me as if one of us were speaking in a dream, a smile curling her lips. "What are you talking about? How could I stay outside in the snow all night without a cloak? I'd freeze to death."

"But you don't freeze! You come back happier and stronger! Mama, take me with you. Let me go too, the next time you go there. I want to go."

"Marja," she said, and now she was frowning, "I never go any-where. You've been telling yourself tales."

I gasped and then gulped, telling myself I must not cry anymore, I could not cry anymore, I would not. That would only convince her that I was still a child, when I was almost old enough to marry and have children of my own. She'd lied when she said that I never made her sad, but she'd told that lie to protect me. This one hurt: this one shut me out and made a fool of me.

I was tired of being shut out.

And so the next autumn, the fall before I turned thirteen, I waited and watched, and on the evening of the first snowfall, I was ready. I had told lies of my own, to match my mother's. Minding the herds that summer, I had kept one lamb aside, fed it and hidden it. I told Father a wolf must have gotten it, and he cursed the loss, Father who scarcely seemed to care that Mama was dying, although he stroked her hair so softly when she lay ill in bed. On one of the hottest days, when Father and the boys were in the fields and Mama lay useless in the house, I told them I was going to town to find medicine; and I put the ewe lamb over my pony's saddle and rode the ten miles to the village and sold the lamb, and took the money to the healer's house. There I bought a strengthening powder I knew would do nothing for Mama – for by then I had tried any number of the healer's remedies – but also other powders, darker and more costly.

My heart pounded the whole way home, for surely my deception would be discovered. Someone would say something to Father the next time he went to town; he would learn that I had been there selling a lamb, or that I had bought extra potions at the healer's house.

But evidently my doings meant even less in the village than they did to my mother, for Father never learned what I had done. The heat of summer wore into autumn, and on the evening of the first snowfall, my father and brothers huddled around the fire even more insensibly than usual, because I had put sleeping powder in their supper.

My pony was already saddled in the barn: I had dressed in my warmest things, but I knew I must ride after Mama rather than walk, because I could never move as quickly in my heavy clothing as she could in her shift and slippers. I was afraid to carry a lantern, but luck was with me, for the moon was full, and gave light even through the swirling snow. And so at last I followed my mother into the forest at the foot of the mountains.

The way grew darker and harder when we entered the shelter of the trees, for although the branches protected us from the snow, they also kept out the moonlight, and my pony was too wide to follow Mama between and around the tree trunks. Desperate to keep up with her, at last I dismounted and tethered the pony to a tree. Floundering on foot, Mama a dim shadow ahead, I quickly grew tired and very cold, and then I was glad she had not agreed to run away with me to the north, for what gave her health would surely have killed me.

We went on like that for an hour, maybe, or maybe three; often I thought I had lost her, but always I caught sight of her again. If she knew I was there, she gave no sign, for she never slowed or looked back. And at last, just when I thought I could go no further, I saw more light ahead, and stumbled to the edge of a clearing, a circle of moonlight. My mother was dancing there, whirling with her arms outstretched and her shift clinging to the lively, lovely lines of her body – and she was not alone.

I realized then, with a shock of dread, that my father's stories had never been nonsense, for my mother danced in the clearing with shimmering columns of snow, luminous creatures with swirling faces and massive, graceful limbs: the frost giants of my father's tales. And I remembered the story about the snow-maiden kept captive by the cruel giants, the maiden rescued by a kindly woodcutter, who loved her and bound her in human form that he might marry her, and that she might live all year round and revel in flowers and sunshine, rather than taking shape only in the hardest winter weather. But every year, at midnight of the winter solstice, it was her doom to return to the giants' den until dawn, there to be tormented by them: her pain their price for not destroying the gentle woodcutter and every human habitation within reach.

Of course it was the same story. Why had I not recognized it? Why had I not been able to see what was right in front of my nose, what indeed obsessed me?

Because the maiden in the story loved her human form, loved to revel in flowers and sunshine, when Mama so clearly did not.

Because the woodcutter loved the snow-maiden so dearly and risked all for her, when my father seemed to pay no attention at all to Mama's plight.

Because the giants in my father's story wanted the maiden only to torture her, and she always went to them with dread and loathing, when this one evening – I knew now – was the only time Mama was truly happy.

For I was not watching torture: I was watching utter joy, an enraptured reunion. Mama and the frost giants twirled and bowed and glided, flowing and reaching, every movement they made so beautiful that it brought tears to my eyes, until my cheeks were covered with ice. I crouched there, throat aching and skin burning, in the trees at the edge of the clearing, knowing that Mama would never love me as much as she loved her dancing partners, even though the enchantment that held her would not allow her to remember the dance clearly tomorrow morning. I knew that she had told the truth when she told me that she could never move farther north, for the frost giants were creatures of place, and she could only be reunited with them here. And I knew that my father was not the kindly woodcutter of his own telling, but rather the plotting wizard who had somehow entrapped and enslaved her.

I watched that beautiful dance until I was stupefied with cold. Part of me wanted to die there, I think, to lie down in the snow and simply sleep. I have never known how or why I managed to rouse myself: perhaps only because witnessing my mother's joyous movement, and being unable to join it, grew too painful. Whatever the reason, at last I stood on numb feet and stumbled back the way I had come. Surely it was miracle or magic that guided me back through the maze of the trees to my pony, to the poor beast half dead with cold herself, and surely nothing else that led us limping home.

Soon enough we had a beacon, the amber glow of flames flickering against the sky; and then life returned to my limbs and I fairly flew, dragging the exhausted pony with me, for I knew what had happened. I had left my father and brothers snoring around a fire they could not tend. I had thought only of my mother, not of them.

I ran back home, blinded by shame and grief. Trying to save my mother, I had killed the others, who were more kin to me than she was, for all that I was indeed her child.

But by miracle or magic, they were safe. Perhaps I had drugged them more lightly than I had thought. The house was ruined, but I found my father putting out the fire with armfuls of snow, having settled the three boys safely in the barn. I helped him, carrying armful after armful, knowing that it was Mama's body I used to quench the flames. Again and again we ran back into the searing heat, into smoke that scorched our nostrils and sucked the breath out of our bodies, bearing burdens that burned our arms with cold.

He never asked me where I had been; indeed, we did not speak at all. When we had put out the fire, he carried me to the barn – for I had collapsed at last at his feet – and when I woke, feverish and aching, it was daylight, and Mama was bending over me, wiping the sweat from my brow and murmuring a lullaby. Bright-eyed and light-footed, lovely as starlight, she nursed me through that illness; and I told myself that maybe she was healed for good this time, that maybe she would not sicken with summer.

But she did, of course. It has been five years since then: the house is rebuilt, and my brothers are on the verge of manhood, and still I have found no one to marry. None of us have ever spoken of the fire. I do not think I can, for whenever I think of it, my throat fills with choking ash. Nearly every night I dream of my mother dancing with the frost giants in the moonlit grove; and nearly every morning – especially in the heat of summer, when she suffers so – I vow that I will confront my father. I will learn how he ensnared her, and I will set her free: I will release her from this house and this family. I will be brave. I will let her return to the ones she truly loves.

Nearly every morning, especially in the heat of summer, I promise myself that I will do this. But I never have.

# Sorrel's Heart

He found the girl crouched in a ditch by the side of the deserted road, using a jagged rock to try to sever the muscled cords that connected her heart to her body. She was bleeding, of course, and she was weeping, too: her hair a brown tangled mass, yellowish-green snot running down her face, her hands slimy with dirt and gore. She might have been eight or ten, half his own age, or older than that but starved, her thin ribs showing through a tear in her shirt. The tear, he guessed, had once been a hole she'd made for her heart to go through, but had widened with wear and weather; it now showed so much of her scrawny chest that he wondered why she wore a shirt at all. The shirt might have been pink once. She tried to cut the pulsing cords, sawing at them, and when that didn't work, she began to bash them with the rock, crying out in pain with each impact.

"Don't do that," he said, and she looked up, quivering, flinching away as if from a blow. He himself had just walked ten miles or so, fleeing the fire he had set, and was pleasantly tired from the exercise. The stink of charred fur still clung to him, heady incense. "Can't live without a heart."

She squinted at him. "Hurts too much."

He inclined his head politely. "You born that way?" There were all kinds of stories: people born with their skeletons outside their bodies, people born with two heads or none. He'd seen a lot of other freaks, but this was the first that truly interested him. When she bent her head in a shy nod, he said, "Where your people?"

"Don't want me. I'm a freak. Where yours?"

He shrugged. "Never had none. Gave me to the North Wind when I was but a baby. Been wandering ever since. You hungry?" He reached out his hand to her: she didn't take it, but clung to the rock. Her heart pulsed, throbbing.

"You smell," she said.

"Yeah. I know. No chance to wash."

"What's that smell from?"

"Kittens. In a barn. I burned them. They screamed, but only for a second." One hand came up from the rock, now, to cover her mouth, and her eyes brimmed over again. Her heart writhed for a moment before it resumed its steady beat, and he smiled for the first time since he'd seen her. "That hurt you, huh? You'd save them if you could."

"You're a monster. They'll get you. The freak patrol."

"They'll try to get me. They'll try to get you, too."

She raised her chin. "Nobody out here anyway, is there? All the normals went away."

"For now. They'll be back. They never go away for good." He knelt down next to her, mind racing. He made his voice as gentle as he could. "Listen. We can help each other."

She shrank away again. "Won't help you burn cats."

"No no no. I know you won't. You'll help me not burn them."

She squinted. "How?"

"You'll listen to me." He'd always been smart, always been able to think quickly; it was how he'd lived this long. "You'll listen to what I want to do. And it'll hurt you, but not as much as it would hurt them, the animals and whatnot, and then I won't have to do it. Because hurting you will be enough. And I'll help you hide from the normals, get you food and that. You wouldn't last on your own. Me neither. We'll both last longer this way."

She pulled her knees up, as if to protect the heart now nestled between them and her chest. "Don't want to hurt. Told you that. Want to stop hurting. Gotten hurt already."

"How?" She had her own stories; of course she did. She could feed him that way, too.

She looked away. "Poking it with sticks. My heart. Throwing rocks at it. Calling me names. Trying to hurt me, like you want to do."

He couldn't see her heart now, but he knew it was writhing again. He smiled. "That pain ever save anything? Save kittens? Save, oh, baby birds? Let me tell you what I did one time – "

"Stop it!" Her voice was a thin howl.

He went on, implacable. "Let me tell you what I want to do next. Let me tell you this idea I have about horses. An old horse, an old mare just up the road here. A sorrel mare. I want to take red-hot irons and poke out her eyes and then stick a red-hot iron up – "

She was lying on the ground now, sideways, her heart still hidden: but all of her was writhing, hands clenched over her ears, tears streaming down her face. "Stop it! Stop it!"

"All right," he said, as lightheaded as if he'd been drinking wine. "You just did. You stopped it. Look at me." He reached out a tender hand to touch her knee, just barely brush it; she flinched away, but he reached out again, and this time she let his hand stay there, although she whimpered. "Look at me," he said again, and she did, finally. Her eyes were a muddy brown, red with crying. "You saved that sorrel mare. Just now. By listening. By letting me hurt you, by letting me see how it hurt you. You saved her. I won't touch her now. I promise. I don't need to anymore. It's done. You did that."

"You're a monster."

"I am. But I always tell the truth. Everything hurts you: everything hurts your heart, because it's out there where everything can touch it. Right?" She nodded, as he had known she would, and he removed his hand from her knee. "I'll never touch you again, not unless you want it. All I'll use is words. Listen: you cut your heart away, you die. You don't hurt anymore, but things die, because I kill them. You walk away from me and live, you still hurt, and things still die, because I kill them. You stay with me, you still hurt, but those things don't die.

You save them. And maybe you save me too, from the freak patrol."

She was listening, although she hadn't said anything. Her eyes were fixed on his. She had lowered her knees a little, and he could see her heart, beating more calmly now. He reached into his pocket and pulled out a translucent stone he'd found weeks ago, a rock the color of the sea; he hadn't known until now why he'd been carrying it with him. When she saw it her eyes widened and she smiled, startled, and he said, "See? There's beauty too, in the world. Good things, not just hurtful ones. Reasons to stay. Your heart is beautiful."

The smile faded. "No it ain't."

"I say it is, Sorrel. That's what I'm going to call you. Your heart is beautiful to me. Your heart is a reason to stay in the world. Come on now: get up, and we'll go get food."

She couldn't get up: she was after all too weak, from lying in the ditch and trying to hurt herself. She'd been there for hours, maybe days. At last he asked permission to pick her up, and she gave it, and he lifted her in his arms and carried her, his own heart filled with unaccustomed peace. She weighed hardly anything. He looked down at her, her head cradled on his shoulder in sleep, and he wanted to kiss her forehead. But he didn't, because he hadn't asked her leave.

They were together for years after that. He called her Sorrel, and she called him Quartz. He grew into a quiet man, a man neither thick nor thin, with hair the color of wheat and eyes that gazed into far distances and sometimes went dead and blank, and at those times he would tell her what he wanted to do, tell her his yearning dreams, tell her about torn skin and roasted flesh and organs torn from their bony cradles, and she would weep and moan and clutch herself until he was done. When he was done, he would dry her tears and tell her he loved her, and if indeed he was capable of love, then it was true. He was true to his promise, certainly: he never performed the deeds he described to her in such vivid detail. And certainly he found her beautiful, and not just her heart: for if he had grown into a man few people noticed, she had grown tall and lovely, her hair a reddish-brown cascade of curls and her body as graceful as autumn aspens.

And yet he kept his own promise not to touch her, until the night when she crept into his bed and asked him to. Then he did his clumsy best to give her pleasure, and she did her best to teach him, although pain came far more naturally to him, and fear to her. He had been used to meeting his own needs with his own hands, and he found the rhythms of another's flesh unnerving, as unnatural as walking on some other creature's legs. When Sorrel cried out beneath him and then began to weep, he thought that he had broken his promise, that he had hurt her with something other than words; he could feel her heart, crushed between them, beating frantically, and he feared that she would die. But at last she opened her eyes and laughed up at him, and he kissed her on the forehead then, as he had wanted to so many years before.

They were in a barn that night, much like the one where he had burned the cats so long ago. The farmhouse was deserted, and Quartz and Sorrel had raided it for quilts to wrap around themselves and books to use as fuel. They would not destroy the house itself, which might give needed shelter to other freaks some other day. The normals were long gone, the place bereft of food and livestock; this family might not be coming back. It was dangerous to linger in places known abandoned, because that was where the freak patrols hunted, knowing anything left alive would be twisted and diseased. Sometimes there were tales of bands of freaks, groups who had ganged together for protection, but they were hunted and slaughtered, always: no safety in numbers, and even if the stories were invented to prevent such bands from forming, Quartz and Sorrel put their trust in speed and secrecy. They kept always on the move, stopping in normal towns when they had no other choice. At such times they would wrap Sorrel's heart in a shawl and pretend that it was a nursing infant, and when townsfolk asked to see the child, or commented with narrowed eyes on how it never cried, Quartz would bully and bluster, cursing them for daring to disturb his wife, showing them his scarred fists. Did they want to fight? Did they? Dared they suggest that he, so clearly normal, would wed some filthy freak, or father one?

The challengers backed down, always: not from Quartz' words, which meant little – for there were those who would rape any freak, male or female, left unprotected, and countless freaks had been born to normal parents – but from his fierce body, and from his eyes. He would let himself go stone-cold then, let the cruelty come out, and they could see it plain enough. Sometimes he almost wished for a fight, but always when the attackers backed off, he and Sorrel fled. There had been close calls, too many to remember. Always he marveled that no one followed them. And sometimes they would near a town, or enter one, and hear reports of what had just occurred: a shopkeeper saying, *That tinker with horns and a tail, we hung him sure enough*; or children laughing about last night's sport, *The lady who crowed like a rooster, we chased her through the streets until the dogs got her*; or women gossiping idly in the market, *Oh, of course they had to kill the devil-child, born with a fish's tail, and killed the mother, too, it was only a mercy, who knows what else she might have birthed*. And sometimes they heard nothing, but saw instead: gutted three-legged corpses by the side of the road, heads with no mouths rotting on fenceposts, misshapen bodies dragged behind carts.

All such towns they skirted, or left as quickly as their legs would carry them. And soon enough Sorrel told him, "If that's normal, you must be normal too, Quartz, freak only that you've found a way not to do it." They were curled in a ditch, then, not so different from the one where he had found her, save that it was night, and warm, and stars and a round moon shone overhead.

"No. They hurt freaks. It's the normal I want to hurt, what's whole and healthy."

She shook her head. "No different. You could – you could live normal. Give me up, give up the danger. Cut my heart from my body and leave me, live in some town, take joy in their hunts and hatreds."

"None," he answered, stubborn. "I'd have no joy in that: only in hurting what they love. Kittens and horses, baby birds, their own children, maybe."

"They don't love me." Her voice was quiet. "Hurting me is what saves the kittens and babies, the things they love that you hunger to hurt instead. That's how you said it worked, all those years ago. But they don't love me. They'd kill me if they saw me uncovered."

That stopped him. He raised himself on one elbow and peered down at her in the moonlight. He could feel himself frowning. What did she mean? "You don't want me to hurt you anymore? You're tired of saving those other creatures, when you can't save freaks from the normals? You want to die again. You want me to go live in some town where – "

"No. No, Quartz. None of that. None of it. All I mean – " and then she stopped, for so long that he thought she'd fallen asleep, or forgotten what she meant. "All I mean," she said at last, and suddenly he found that he could breathe again, "is that when you found me, you said I'd protect you. But you don't need me for that. You don't need me to stop you from being what you are. You could be what you are; you could live among them, and they'd never know no difference."

She looked up at him, and he saw tears shining in her eyes. "Quartz, when you found me, you said as how you needed me. But you don't, not now. If you're with me, you're with me because you want me. I'm a choice then, after all. Not a cage or a burden. You see?"

He saw. He sat up, and took her heart in both his hands, and kissed it, feeling it pulse against his lips. "I told you it was beautiful," he said.

Not long after that – and later they thought perhaps it had happened that very night – she told him she was with child. She could tell, she said, although her belly was still flat. She knew. And she was afraid. Afraid that he'd hurt their child, Quartz thought she meant at first, when she told him about the fear; but no, her fear was different.

"My mama died giving birth to me," she said softly. They were sitting under a rare tree off the road, sitting in the shade: sometimes a cart passed by, and then they'd nuzzle each other and pretend to be young lovers, which was true enough. "She died because I wasn't shaped right, because I tore her up inside, and I almost died too, because my heart got trapped inside her. The midwife had to reach in to pull it out, and then my mama died, and my daddy and my aunt had to pay the midwife all the money they had not to kill me too, not to tell anyone what had happened. They had to run. And finally they were tired of running, tired of having to hide me, and they left me behind, abandoned me so they could live as normals."

"We won't leave our baby, Sorrel."

"What if I die? What if the baby dies? Having babies is hard work. No midwife will help me, Quartz. We don't have money to pay anybody, to buy silence."

"We'll figure something out. Hush now. Hush, Sorrel." But fear rose in him, too. They couldn't always be moving, with a child. They'd have to settle somewhere, and where was safe? "We'll go to the mountains, the high places. We'll find our way there before you're too big."

"That's where the worst freaks are," she said. "The ones who eat people, the monsters who'd eat us too, oh Quartz, you've heard the tales – "

"Tales. That's all they are. Tales told by normals, and how much truth can those hold? Who's been to the mountains and come back to tell the tales?"

"Nobody! Because they get eaten!" Her heart fluttered wildly, and he put out a hand to soothe it.

"Sorrel, hush. They don't come back to say, so we don't know. Maybe they don't come back because it's so beautiful, because they're happy. Maybe they don't come back because – because the freaks welcome them. Maybe all the freaks there are the ones who've gone to have their babies in peace, like we'll do, Sorrel."

She shuddered, her heart still racing. "And maybe there's no freak settlement in the mountains at all. Maybe the normals put that story out so they can trap and kill any freaks who try to go there, jump them on the road."

He'd thought that, too, more than once. It was why he had never suggested going there until now. He closed his eyes. "We have months. We have months to get there. We'll find a side road, a secret way. A cave. We'll be careful."

And so they began to walk towards the mountains, visible only as a faint blue line in the distance, and then only in the clearest weather. They walked as quickly as they could, and yet they found the going slow. Sorrel was sick and grew weak; she craved foods Quartz could only get in towns, butter and cheeses and cured meats, and he had to take to thieving to meet her appetites. Her ankles swelled as her stomach did, and sometimes, when she cried out in pain, Quartz found himself cursing the child, wishing that this baby would either lose itself or come more easily. He himself was afraid, afraid. He had never wished to nurture any small thing, only to harm it, and he found himself craving release, longing to torture rabbits he startled in the fields or the piglets they passed being driven to market, hungering for the feel of blood flowing through his fingers, for the stench of burned flesh and the agonized screams of the slaughtered.

He shared one such fantasy with Sorrel, but her grimaces were so dreadful, her heart so reckless in its pounding, that he stopped, knowing his own face ashen. She could not protect him anymore. Her world was all the child within her belly, and so must his be. And so he tried to content himself with hunting game she did not wish to eat, with skinning fowl whose smell, as they roasted, made her retch.

And yet the baby clung, and her belly grew, and the mountains grew nearer. They walked uphill now, more and more slowly, and their choices of road narrowed. Quartz scouted other paths as Sorrel slept, but found only wildernesses of brambles, pathless forests, sheer rocky slopes: places that would be difficult for him to travel, impossible for her. There was one road only, now. And he thought of the tales, the tales of how no one survived in the mountains, and dread settled in his gut, as heavy as if he, too, bore a child.

There was one road only, and it led to a small village they must pass to reach the heights. They arrived there at dusk, Sorrel exhausted and dragging. They stood in a square surrounded by houses and barns: Quartz could hear bleating and neighing, and had to close his eyes to fight his lust for torn flesh, for pain and blood. He opened them only when he heard panting next to him: Sorrel, fighting for breath. He put his hand on the cloth covering her heart; it beat alarmingly, very very fast and then too slow. "The baby," she said. "I think — "

"Too early," he said. "It's too early, Sorrel, it can't be coming yet." Only seven months had passed, and they weren't in the mountains. They weren't safe yet.

"Babies come when they will," someone said, and Quartz looked up to find a woman in front of them, staring at them in the fading light. She was wearing a red kerchief, and immediately the color made him yearn for blood. "What's that your wife's holding in her arms?"

Quartz swallowed. "An infant, we — "

"She's so big with one child, and has another so small?"

"Wet-nurse," Sorrel said, her voice somewhere between a whisper and a moan. "My sister's child. I had a baby died, and my sister died and I took hers, and then we made this one who's coming, see. Goodwife, I need to lie down now."

Quartz had no idea if the woman in red had been convinced by Sorrel's explanation or not, although it was far cleverer than anything he'd have been able to invent, quick brain or no. "I can work," he said, his voice tight. "To pay for any help you give us. I'm good with my hands. I can thatch roofs, slaughter animals."

No one was listening to him. The woman in red had taken Sorrel's arm, with a clucking sound, and was leading her towards one of the houses. Quartz followed numbly. How many people lived here? All he had seen so far was the one woman, whose kerchief looked so much like blood, and he could kill her sure, could wring her scrawny neck as if she were only a chicken. He let himself picture that for a moment, imagine how her spine would feel snapping under his hands. He let the lust for pain fill him. And then Sorrel screamed.

Sorrel screamed, and he ran to follow the sound, found himself standing in one corner of a lamplit room as the woman carried in towels and basins of water and Sorrel thrashed on the bed, moaning, and now the woman was doing something between Sorrel's legs and now Sorrel was screaming again and now the woman was pulling her wrap away, trying to give her more freedom of movement maybe, pulling away her clothing to reveal her heart beating there, her heart pounding on her chest, just as Quartz had seen it that day so many years ago when Sorrel had sat in the ditch, battering herself with the jagged rock.

He had to protect her. He had promised. He had promised, and he had never failed in that promise, whatever else he had done or not done. He had promised that only he would hurt her, no one else. The woman with the red kerchief was reaching for Sorrel's heart as Sorrel screamed, and Quartz leaped forward, tears choking him, and a rush of blood and something else poured out of Sorrel – blood, too much blood – and the woman grabbed Sorrel's heart and Quartz tackled her, made her let go of Sorrel, dragged her as far away from the birthing bed as he could to protect the beating heart there. And then he strangled the woman in the red kerchief, killed her as he had wished to do since the moment he first saw her; he dug his fingers into her throat and felt her own heart stop beating. This wasn't even cruelty. It was justified. She had reached for Sorrel's heart before ever he reached for hers.

The lamp had gone out, kicked over or snuffed by the wind of the fight. Quartz smelled blood and shit, heard only a thin wailing cry. "Sorrel?" he said. He could not hear her heart. "Sorrel!" He began crawling towards the bed on all fours, afraid that he would trip and fall on her, hurt her, if he tried to walk in this crowded, wet darkness. "Sorrel, can you hear me?"

And then he saw flickering light outside, heard voices and footsteps, and here were more lamps now, held by a group of men who pressed in through the door, who had cudgels and knives – Quartz could see the metal shining in the lamplight – and they were surrounding him and surrounding the bodies, and he heard someone say, "The baby's alive. Little girl. Looks normal, but who can tell? The mother wasn't."

"We heard the screaming," one of the men said to Quartz, and Quartz did not know why his voice was so kind. "We came to help you. You got them, didn't you? Nobody right's lived in this place for years, so when we heard voices, we knew it must be freaks."

"What?" Quartz said. The man who had spoken to him was holding up the red kerchief; someone else kicked the dead body, and through the gaps between people's legs, Quartz saw now that there had been no hair or skull under that kerchief, but only brain, a gray wrinkled thing that maybe had pulsed once like Sorrel's heart, but now was still. A foot came down and ground the brain into slimy mush.

"Freak," someone said, and Quartz closed his eyes. The woman in the red kerchief had been reaching for Sorrel's heart in love or joy or anyway knowledge, not hatred. She had been reaching out to claim one of her own. He had understood nothing he had seen.

"Must've holed up here to have the whelp," someone grunted. "Some sicko raped her maybe, or she got knocked up by one of her own who didn't want her, and this one came too, to help her." They hadn't connected Quartz to the women yet. Of course not; he looked normal.

Now someone was talking to him. "You found them here and took care of them, right? Good man. Wish we'd gotten here in time to help."

"Give me the baby," Quartz said. He forced himself to stand up. "Give me the baby, if she's normal." How was he going to feed her? "Give me the baby. She's mine. My spoil for what I've done, for killing those two." The words caught in his throat. "Give me the baby and bring me some milk. There are animals here. Find one I can milk."

"You want to raise a freak-whelp? Be a while before you can use her." Laughter.

But they brought her, the tiny, mewling, naked thing: someone had cut the cord that had bound her to her mother, as Sorrel had so long ago wanted to cut the cord that held her to her own heart. The baby was howling, and Quartz took off his shirt and wrapped her in it and looked down at her, knowing that he was truly a freak now too, because now he held his own heart in his hands. He cradled in his arms what was most precious and fragile, what could most easily be taken from him: what, if it was hurt, would cause him the deepest and most unending pain. He must not weep, because the men around him would not understand. He bent and kissed the baby's forehead; and when they snickered, felt the old blood-fury seize him.

# GI Jesus

I don't know if it was a miracle or not, what happened at the hospital. I can't make up my mind about that. I always thought those headlines about "Instant Miracle Cures" in the trashy supermarket newspapers were a crock. You know the ones: THALIDOMIDE BOY GROWS ARMS TO PROTECT MOM FROM RAPIST! "I had to save her, and was the only way!" BARNEY PERFORMS CPR ON SEARS SANTA CLAUS! "I was walking through the TV department and all of a sudden I couldn't breathe, and this little purple guy jumps straight out of the set and starts pounding on my chest!" SIAMESE TWINS SEPARATE WHEN THE MEN THEY LOVE MOVE TO OPPOSITE COASTS! "The doctors said it could never be done because we shared a brain, but love conquers all!"

I never believed any of that stuff, but what happened at the hospital would sound just like that, if I let it. So I don't know anymore. Maybe my story's a crock too, or maybe those trashy ones are truer than anybody ever thought. One thing I can tell you, though: if there are miracles, they don't happen in an instant. Whatever a miracle is, it takes its own sweet time growing. When I see those newspapers now, I wonder what stories those people would tell if they had more than two square inches of the *Weekly World News* to do it in. Because if anything real happened to them they do have stories, trust me on that, and probably long ones, too.

Mine started months ago, the day I went to church with Mandy. I'm not religious, never have been — nobody in my family ever has been,

189

so far as I know — but Mandy's been my best friend for thirty years, and when your best friend calls you up crying and asks you to go to church with her, you do it, even if you've never been too sure you even believe in God, even if you're very sure that you don't believe in anything the priest in that church has to say. The last time I'd been in that church was when Mandy and Bill got married. I was their maid of honor, and I shouldn't have been. Cindy should have been. So I guess the story really started back then, twenty years ago, because when Mandy asked me to be maid of honor I said, "Now wait a minute, how come you aren't asking your sister that? That's a sister's job."

We were sitting in Sam's Soda Shop, where we always went to have important conversations. Mandy had called me and told me to meet her there, and I figured she needed to tell me about some fight she'd had with Bill, or fret about how his mother still didn't like her. We'd ordered what we always did, a root beer float for me and a vanilla shake for her, and then she came out with the maid of honor thing and I choked and started spurting root beer out my nose. There are certain ways of doing things, in a little town like this. I don't know how it works other places, but if you get married in Innocence, Indiana, and you don't ask your sister to hold the bouquet, that has to mean you don't love her. What's worse, it means you want everybody to know you don't love her, because even sisters who can't stand each other do what's right at weddings. And I knew Mandy loved Cindy. She was the only person in her family who did. "You have to ask Cindy," I said. "She's your *sister*."

Mandy hadn't touched her shake. She hadn't even taken the paper wrapper off the straw. "I can't ask her. My parents would kill me."

"Your parents?" I'd never liked Mandy's parents, and I wasn't very good at hiding it. I knew they must be mad at Cindy about something, but they were always mad at Cindy about something: smoking or drinking or having too many boyfriends or having the wrong boyfriends or having boyfriends at all. Plenty of other girls in town did all the same things Cindy did, but they lied about it, and Cindy never would. Mr. and Mrs. Mincing were ashamed of her: not because of what she did, but because everybody knew about it. They cared about their reputation more than they cared about Cindy, and Mandy knew that as well as I did, and she hated it too. So I shook my head at her and said, "Mandy, your parents are *already* married, aren't they? What business is it of theirs? Whose wedding is this, anyway?"

"They're paying for it," Mandy said, in this tiny voice she gets when she's really upset, and then, all in a rush, "She's pregnant. She's starting to show: that's how we found out. And she won't say who the father is and she won't say she's sorry and I'm not supposed to tell anybody, Cece, not even you, so you have to *promise* to keep it a secret."

"Oh," I said, thinking a lot of things even I knew better than to say, like if she's showing already it's not going to be a secret for long, like if your mother's so happy about the lovely grandchildren you and Bill are going to give her, why can't she love this grandchild too? But I saw right away that Mandy's parents would never let Cindy be in the wedding, and I knew Mandy would do whatever they wanted, because she always did. She never could talk back to them. That's why she was the favorite daughter.

Mandy was my best friend, but sometimes I got just plain disgusted with her. She never stuck up for herself at all, and somehow she got everything she wanted. Here she was marrying Bill and planning this big wedding while Hank Heywood, who made me dizzier than anybody I'd ever met, hadn't even kissed me yet. And if I ever did get married my dad couldn't afford to pay for a fancy wedding, and my mother had died when I was a baby, so there wouldn't even be anybody to fuss over the dress and stand there crying during the ceremony. It wasn't fair.

I wanted to say something really mean to Mandy, right then, but I knew I was just feeling sorry for myself when I should have been feeling sorry for Cindy. So I took a swig of root beer float to calm myself down and tried to say something useful instead. "What does Bill say about this?"

"Bill's staying out of it."

Bill stayed out of a lot of things, mainly debt and drugs and trouble, which was why Mandy's parents liked him so much. A fine upstanding young man, they said. I could have told them a few things about what he got into, and what stood up when he did it. I'd had a scare myself, about a year before Mandy and Bill started going together, but nobody knew about that except Bill, and I wasn't about to tell a soul, and neither was he. I'll say this much for Bill: he knew how to keep a secret. He knew how to keep promises too, mostly. Turned out I was just late, but we had a few nervous weeks there, and the whole time he said, "Now don't you worry about anything, Cece. I'll get the money for a good doctor if that's what has to happen, I promise." He'd have done it, too. Funny, I never doubted that, even though I knew full well I didn't love him and he didn't love me. I don't doubt it now. He was a better man when he was seventeen and scared than when he was thirty-five and broke his big promise, the one he'd made to Mandy at the altar, in front of the priest and all those people and God, if you believe in God.

But I'm getting way ahead of myself. So I said to Mandy, "Well now, look, if I'm not your maid of honor, who will be?" Because I still didn't like the idea, not one bit. A bridesmaid, fine, but maid of honor? Standing at the altar next to Mandy and Bill, knowing that Cindy should have been the one up there and that I wasn't any better than her, just luckier? Knowing that Bill knew all this too, and that Mandy didn't know any of it and now I'd never be able to tell her? Even back then I watched enough soap operas to know that once you get into a tangle like that, you don't get out. You're in it for life. Your kids are in it, probably, and their kids too. It doesn't end.

"I guess I'd have to ask my cousin Sandra," Mandy said, looking at me like I'd just drowned the last puppy in the world. She still hadn't touched her shake, and I gave up. First of all, Sandra was the snootiest bitch in the county; I didn't know anybody who liked her, not even Mandy, and Mandy liked everybody. Secondly, there was the cousin thing. If you don't ask your sister to be your maid of honor and ask your best friend instead, maybe you can get away with it. "We're so close." "We're just like sisters." Something like that. But not to ask your own sister, and then to ask *another* relative, some cousin you don't even like? That's ten times more of an insult all around, and there's no way of hiding it.

"Okay," I said. "I'll do it." I guess I didn't sound very honored, but I've never been good at lying about things like that. Mandy smiled at me and let out a big sigh of relief, and finally reached for her shake.

So I was the maid of honor, and Sandra and our friends Christy and Diane were the bridesmaids. We carried pink sweetheart roses and white carnations, and wore pink satin dresses with big bunches of tulle at the shoulders. I still have that dress hanging in my closet, not that I'll ever be able to fit into it again, not that I've been able to for years now. I always thought I'd give it to my daughter, when I had one. That's never going to happen now, I guess, even if I ever do get married. You hear stories on the news about women having babies after forty, but that always smacks of Instant Miracle Cure to me. And going through the Change is enough work, without having to chase a toddler around while you're doing it. I guess I could give the dress to one of Mandy's girls, but what would I say? "This is the dress I wore when your mother married the man who ran off with his secretary fifteen years later"? The girls are real bitter about Bill. The oldest was only thirteen when it happened, and when you're that age everything's easy: black and white, right and wrong. And the other three believed whatever their big sister told them.

So no one will ever get to wear that dress again, which is too bad, really. It's still the fanciest dress I've ever owned, and I was excited about wearing it in the wedding, even if it should have been Cindy's dress. I squared my conscience about that by promising myself that if I had to be maid of honor I was going to do it my way: I was going to be real nice to Cindy, so that maybe Mandy would be brave enough to be nice to her too, and then when Mr. and Mrs. Mincing saw the two of us being nice their hearts would soften and they'd take Cindy back into the family. I was going to fix everything, oh yes I was. I had it all planned out.

That's the kind of plan you can only come up with when you're nineteen and don't know how anything works yet. I'd never been in a wedding before: I didn't know how scared I'd be, in front of all those people. I didn't know that Cindy would sneak into the church late and sit in the very back pew, rows and rows behind the rest of the family, cowering there trying to hide. Cindy'd always been so bold about everything that I thought she'd be bold about the wedding too — especially since by then everybody in town knew she was expecting, it wasn't like it was a secret at all — but maybe the church made her lose her nerve. Who could blame her? The priest had been saying something boring but pretty nice, and then all of a sudden he gets going on how we're there to bless the joining of two souls, to make a marriage that will last until death, longer than youth and longer than beauty, longer than the sinful desires of the body. He wasn't looking at Mandy and Bill anymore by the time he said that; he was glaring over their heads, practically yelling at the back of the church. And then all three of us knew what must have happened, even though we hadn't seen Cindy come in. You could feel everybody else in the church fighting not to turn around and stare at that back pew. Some of them did, mostly kids, before their parents yanked them back around again. I couldn't see that from where I was, but Hank told me about it after the ceremony. That was only about a week before he got shipped out to Vietnam: he was one of the last ones to get sent over. He never did kiss me before he left — he was so shy, Hank — but he wrote me letters until he disappeared. He just vanished into the jungle; nobody ever found out what happened to him. I wore one of those silver POW/MIA bracelets for a while, you know, back when everybody was wearing them. After a while it stopped being the thing to do; people would give you funny looks when they saw it, ask what it was. Some people thought it was a MedicAlert bracelet, thought I was diabetic or something. And it was ugly, to tell you the truth, so finally I took it off. But

I've never stopped wondering what happened to Hank. A lot of my nightmares are about jungles, even now.

So. Anyway. I'm standing up there at Mandy's wedding, I can't see anything but the altar and the priest – he was young then, handsome, like that guy in *The Exorcist* – and he's thundering along about the transience of youth and beauty and the body like we're not at a wedding at all, more like we're at a funeral, and Mandy's making little choking noises and Bill's clutching her hand and all three of us are glaring at that guy. Shut up, shut up, *shut up*. Well, he didn't. Never so much as looked at us. I should have said something. Maybe I would, now, but I was too scared then, especially since it wasn't my church and who was I to challenge somebody else's priest? I tried to catch his eye, I did, I'll say that much for myself, but he wouldn't look at me, so I was left staring at the statue on the wall behind him, the one of Jesus nailed to the cross. If you want to feel lousy about having a body, all you have to do is look at that thing. Ouch. Every nail. Every drop of blood, I swear, and that poor man in so much pain he must have been out of his mind with it, just praying to die soon so it would be over. You can tell all that, from that statue. I guess that makes it good art. I tried to talk to Mandy about it once, but Mrs. Mincing was there and she gave me a lecture about how Jesus wasn't suffering on the cross, he was at peace, he was happy to be doing the Lord's will, and if I'd been a godly person I would have known that. Well, religious or not, you'd never know it from looking at that statue. Even now, whenever I think about what might have happened to Hank in the jungle, I wonder if he wound up looking like that. It's what my father looked like, when he was dying of cancer.

So I'm standing there looking at that statue, figuring that's what Cindy feels like too – like she's nailed to a piece of wood with everybody staring at her and nobody doing a thing to help – and I'm thinking, well, I'll talk to her at the reception, I *will*, even if the whole town cuts me dead for it. I'll go up to her and say something friendly. Better yet, I'll go up and give her a big hug. Except that I never got my chance, because Cindy didn't go to the reception. Of course she didn't: I should have known she wouldn't. She walked out of that church and she disappeared. For years. Like Hank.

Well, it ate at Mandy like you wouldn't believe. She thought it was her fault, because if she'd included Cindy in the wedding maybe everything would have happened differently. "You were right," she kept saying. "You were right all along. I should have asked her." Which made me feel like dirt, of course. I kept telling her I hadn't been right, I'd just been self-righteous, and that's not the same thing. Her parents paid for that wedding and it was their show all along, not hers and Bill's, and they sure didn't want any spotlights on Cindy. Mandy couldn't have done anything.

"Blame the priest," I kept telling her. "Blame your parents, if you have to blame somebody." Mr. and Mrs. Mincing didn't even look for Cindy: just said good riddance, as if you can wash a daughter off your hands as easily as a speck of dust. Mandy and Bill looked, got the police to put out a missing-person report, checked with bus stations and lying-in homes and hospitals, everyplace they could think of. They printed up fliers with Cindy's picture, and every year on Cindy's birthday they put ads in papers all over the country: "Happy Birthday Cindy, We Love and Miss You, Please Call Your Sister Mandy Collect." They did all that stuff for six or seven years, I don't even remember how long it went on, and they couldn't find a clue. It wasn't cheap, either, taking out all those ads. Bill was a prince about it, he really was, and it can't have been easy on him. I used to wonder if maybe he was the father of Cindy's baby, especially after what had happened to me, but I decided that no, he couldn't be, because Cindy had to have gotten pregnant while Bill and Mandy were a steady couple – practically engaged already – and I just couldn't believe that Bill would do such a thing. I still can't, even with what he did later. And there were plenty of other guys who could have been the father. So I think he was so good about the search because he was a decent man, not because he felt guilty.

But finally, after years of not finding anything, Bill told Mandy that

their marriage was haunted and that she had to choose between looking for Cindy and living with him. She and I had a long talk at Sam's
Sodas over that one, believe me. She didn't touch her vanilla shake at
all that time, and we talked and talked and finally I told her I thought
Bill was right. "You've done everything you can," I told her. "You'd
have found her by now if she wanted to be found. Wherever she is,
she wants you to be happy, Mandy." I don't know if I believed that
even while I was saying it, but Mandy did, and she said it made her
feel better, and she prayed for Cindy every night and settled down to
loving Bill and her kids the rest of the time.

You can't forget a lost sister, though. Mandy and I still talked about
Cindy, how she'd probably gone to some big city – Chicago, Houston
– and gotten a good office job, because Cindy could type like nobody's
business. We decided Cindy was happy. We knew it. We had her life
all planned out for her. Except that we didn't know anything, of
course, and we knew *that*, even though we never admitted it. We told
each other that she'd probably had her baby and then gotten married
to some nice young lawyer or doctor who wanted kids, in a church
with a *nice* priest this time. Mandy always insisted on that, that this
new priest would be kind, he'd forgive Cindy her past the way her
husband forgave her, her past, the way priests are supposed to forgive, because that's what Christ did. That's what Mandy said; I didn't
know, not being religious. The only priest I'd ever met was the one
who married Mandy and Bill, and I'd heard so many different things
about Christ from so many different people that I didn't know what to
think. Seems to me you can make anything you want to out of Christ;
he's like a politician that way.

After Mandy and Bill stopped looking for Cindy they seemed happy
for a long time. Bill was going great guns with his CPA business – even
in a little town like Innocence, everybody needs their taxes done –
and Mandy kept busy taking care of the kids, which would have been
a full-time job for anybody. They looked like the perfect family, and I
was jealous again. Thinking back on it, I guess I should have known
better. There was plenty of tension there, like the way Bill always

talked about how his girls were going to go to college, not just get married right out of high school and have babies like all the other women in town. The girls were smart enough to know that every time he talked that way he was putting down their mother, and they didn't like it. Mandy didn't mind that so much – she wished she'd been able to go to college too – but whenever Bill talked about teenagers having babies she remembered Cindy, and the old wound opened all over again. So really, that family was in an awful mess even before Bill fell for his secretary.

That was the first time Mandy ever called me crying, when she found out about Bill and Genevieve. That was the girl's name, a movie-star kind of a name, the sort of name most wives around here wouldn't trust even if she hadn't been twenty-two and blond, with the kind of figure you usually only see on swimsuit calendars. She said the whole thing, too, Genn-eh-vee-ehve, didn't shorten it to Jean or Jenny, so everybody thought she gave herself airs. God only knows what she thought she was doing in a little town like this, aside from making trouble. Somebody said she came here after college – of *course* Bill would fall for a college girl, even if she only majored in phys-ed – to work and save enough money to go to California and be an actress. Seems to me like if she'd really wanted to be an actress she wouldn't have settled down in Muncie with Bill after the divorce, but what do I know? Maybe she really loved him. He was handsome, Bill was, even then. He'd kept himself fit all those years when Mandy and I were getting bigger and bigger, Mandy from having four kids and me from sitting around Yodel's Yarns, eating candy bars and dreaming about the day when Hank would come home from 'Nam and walk through the door and ask me to help him pick out a nice wool blend for a cable sweater because it's cold back here, away from the jungle, and what are you doing tonight, Cece? Want to help me stay warm?

I'd been dreaming about Hank all those years, and Mandy had been dreaming about Cindy, and Bill, it turned out, had been dreaming about platinum-blond secretaries with 38C cups and twenty-four-inch waists who took *Penthouse* letters in the nude at the hot sheets hotel on the highway. The kid who worked the front desk told his girlfriend, who told her cousin, whose hairdresser gave Mandy's godmother her monthly perm. It made it a lot harder on Mandy, that all those people had known before she did, and of course she was beside herself. Who wouldn't be? But when she called me crying and started ranting about Genevieve, calling her a slut and a bitch and a little whore, I still thought, *This isn't the Mandy I know.* Because she never used words like that, and they were the kinds of words her parents had used about Cindy, the words that priest would have used if he hadn't been in a church. "I hope she rots and dies," Mandy hissed at me. "I hope she gets hit by a truck. I hope she burns in hell."

Mandy wanted me to be angry too, to keep her company, and of course I felt sick about the whole thing. But mostly I was sad, listening to her, because I felt like everyone I knew had died somehow, changed into other people when I wasn't looking, people I didn't like very much. The Mandy who'd cared about people even when they got into trouble had turned into her mean mother and into that horrible priest both, and the Bill who made promises turned into the Bill who broke them, and the Cece who was smart and pretty and deadset on marrying Hank turned into — well, what I am now. Not pretty, except maybe in the face, and not married, and not much of anything, really, except somebody who runs on at the mouth and runs a yarn store, helping people who still know how to knit pick out patterns for baby blankets. I'd turned into Aunt Cece — that's what Mandy's four girls always called me — just like I really was Mandy's sister, just like Cindy really had never existed.

I couldn't spend a lot of time being sad, though, because there was too much else to do. First of all, I was mad myself, mainly at Bill. Mandy wanted Genevieve to rot and die and I wanted Bill to rot and die — or part of him, anyway, the upstanding part. And I knew I had to stop hating Bill and concentrate on loving Mandy and the girls instead, because that's what they needed now. That's what Bill had taken away from them: knowing that they were loved, the way you know the sun will always come up, the way you know there will always be air to breathe whether you've done anything to deserve it or not. And right then, I had to keep Mandy from doing anything that would make her hate herself later on. So I said, "Mandy, honey, I know you want that woman to die right now, but when you calm down you won't feel so good about saying so, I know you won't, and you have to think about that. You have to be careful now, because you're so upset. You have enough to feel bad about, without adding anything that doesn't have to be there. I don't care a fig about that woman, or Bill either. All I care about is you and the kids. You just sit tight, Mandy. I'll be there in ten minutes."

So I went over and stayed there, shut down Yodel's Yarns for a solid week and did what Mandy needed me to do: cooked, did laundry, answered the phone and the door. News got around fast, the way it always does about something like that. I kept the people Mandy didn't want to see away from her and made coffee for the ones who were welcome. I looked after the kids and tried to help them make some kind of sense out of what had happened. I helped Mandy find a lawyer and went with her to talk to him, because I knew I'd hear more of what he was saying than she could. I did the same kinds of things that Mandy had done for me when my father died. But that makes sense, because when a marriage dies it's pretty much like a person has, anyway.

Mandy's parents had moved to Albuquerque for their arthritis years before that – and good riddance, if you ask me – so I was really the only person around who could do all those things for her. I did whatever I could to help, but the whole time I felt like I didn't know Mandy at all anymore, like there was this new person where my best friend had been and I just had to keep pretending she was the person she was supposed to be, because otherwise what would I do? There I was, in this house I knew as well as I knew my own, better maybe – it was the house where Mandy'd grown up; she and Bill had taken it when her folks left – doing all the things I'd known how to do my whole life, like making sandwiches and telling the kids stories, and I felt completely lost.

So now maybe you can understand a little bit how I felt the second time Mandy called me crying. That was four months ago, about five years after Bill left, and I'd gotten used to the new Mandy by then but sometimes I still missed the old one, the one who loved everybody and never cursed anybody out, even the people who'd hurt her. The new one was a lot tougher, I've got to give her credit for that, but she was colder too, more selfish, less able to be nice to people just for the sake of being nice. I guess she had to be that way. Maybe she missed that earlier part of herself too. People who didn't like Mandy, before Bill left, always said that she'd never grown up, that she was just a little girl inside, and that's what they meant, I guess: that she was so sweet to everybody, that she always tried to think the best of people. Mandy grew up fast, after Bill and Genevieve, and the people who hadn't liked her before started to like her better. They said she'd finally found her backbone. Seemed to me she'd lost her heart, or thrown it away because it hurt her too much, and I wasn't sure she'd made such a good trade.

So I was almost glad, when she called me crying again, because it meant she'd gotten her heart back, whatever else had happened. Oh, I was scared too, and guilty about that first flash of gladness. All three of those feelings went through my head in the minute between the time when I picked up the phone and the time when I could understand what she was saying. Because she was crying so hard I couldn't, at first. I thought something must have happened to one of the kids, or Bill had come back — I didn't know what. It was 9:45 on a Sunday morning, and I'd just started a donut and my first cup of coffee. I was standing in the kitchen in my robe, holding the phone in one hand and my coffee mug in the other, saying, "Mandy, what's wrong? Mandy, you have to slow down, I can't understand you, what happened?"

"Cindy's come home," she said finally, in a great gasp, and my knees went weak and the coffee mug shattered on the floor — my favorite mug, too, it was the one my father always used, all the way from Hawaii. It had bright fish and flowers all over it. I don't know where Dad got it; he'd never been to Hawaii. I always meant to ask him, and a few months after he died I was drinking coffee out of that mug and I realized that I never had asked, that I'd forgotten to ask, and that now I never could. And I started bawling like a baby, just like I was bawling now, with the mug in a zillion pieces on the floor and hot coffee everywhere.

"Oh, Mandy," I said. "Oh Mandy. I'll be right there. Just let me get dressed. Is she – is she – "

Is she happy, I wanted to know, does she have the life we made up for her? But Mandy said, "No, no, don't come here, meet me at the church."

"*What?*" I said. Mandy hadn't been in that church since her wedding, because of the priest. She said she never could believe that Father Anselm knew any more about God than the tomatoes in her garden did, probably less. She said she'd go back when the church got a new priest, but the last I'd heard Father Antsy was still there, even though Catholics usually rotate priests every five years. Bill always made it into a joke and said the Church had forgotten about Innocence, but Mandy thought we were stuck with Antsy because the bishop couldn't find anybody else who wanted him. So it seemed to me that church was the last place she'd want to go.

"There?" I said. "Why? I don't – "

"Ten o'clock Mass," Mandy said, still crying. "Hurry."

Then she hung up. I looked at the clock; it was 9:50. "Oh, Lord," I said, and ran to get ready.

Well, you can imagine how fast I drove to get there. If I was ever going to get a speeding ticket in my life, it would have been then, and I don't know what I would have said if I'd been stopped. "I'm late for church, Officer." But nobody stopped me, even though I was zooming along at about seventy miles an hour. I thought Cindy would be at the church too. I kept wondering what she'd look like, after all this time.

I got there after the service started, of course, and had to sneak in those big doors, feeling like some kind of thief, thinking about Cindy sneaking into the wedding so long ago. It was dark inside, except for the stained glass and the candles. I didn't think it was pretty, today. The place stank of incense, and the organ howled and rumbled and wheezed like something out of some old movie, probably one with Vincent Price. There weren't many people there: two or three families, some old ladies, and Mandy. I saw her right away, sitting in the third pew.

By herself. I hustled up and slid in beside her. "Mandy! Where – "

"Shhhh," she said, and reached out and grabbed my hand and squeezed, hard. "She wants us to pray for her."

"Us?" I said. "Who, us?" Mandy knows I'm not religious. "Where *is* she?"

People were glaring at us, by then. "Home," Mandy whispered. In the candlelight I could see that she was crying again. "Hush, Cece. Just pray. Pray for her to be well."

Which meant she wasn't, which meant, as far as I was concerned, that we had no business sitting there in that stink, that we should have been with Cindy, taking care of her or taking her to a doctor or doing something that would do some good. I couldn't see how this was going to do any good, sitting in this cave listening to Father Antsy droning about the temptations of television. When he got going on Teenage Mutant Ninja Turtles as the four reptiles of the Apocalypse I whispered to Mandy, "Look, I can't stand this, I'm leaving, I'll go to your house – "

"No," she whispered back, and grabbed my hand again. "She asked for you to be here. Because I told her – how we used to talk. How we used to tell ourselves she was happy. It meant a lot to her, that you did that. She wants you here, Cece. She asked us to come to Mass because she couldn't. Please."

Well, I didn't feel I could leave, after that, but I sure couldn't pray, either. I just sat there, fuming, wondering what was wrong with Cindy, trying not to listen to Antsy – he'd started in on soap operas – staring at that horrible cross up front, with that Jesus looking like he was going to open his mouth and scream in agony any second. Which was pretty much how I felt, just then. I heard Antsy saying something about body and blood and thought, *Well, now he's talking about TV movies*, and then everybody stood up and filed out into the aisle and I did too, I just followed Mandy, I was so distracted I couldn't think straight, and I took the stale biscuit and the sip of wine and then I remembered, when we sat back down again, that I wasn't supposed to do that, that at Mandy's wedding she'd said you were only supposed to take the communion if you were Catholic. I couldn't see that it mattered. Father Antsy wouldn't know the difference – I hadn't been in that church for twenty years and he wasn't exactly a big yarn buyer, so for all he knew I was a Catholic cousin visiting from another state – and anyhow I hadn't had much breakfast, not that a tiny little stale biscuit helped much. Mandy had said the wine and biscuit were supposed to be Christ's body and blood, I remembered that now, and the whole thing made me a little sick to my stomach, and even angrier. This priest lectures about the sinfulness of the body and then he makes people eat stale biscuits that are supposed to be pieces of a body – what kind of sense does that make? It's no better than those mountain climbers who eat each other when they run out of food, in my opinion. I don't see how anybody can believe that about Jesus' body anyway. The biscuit's just a cracker; it's not even meat. If they fed you hamburger, well, maybe that would be different, but they don't, and thank goodness too.

So anyway, finally the Mass was over and we drove back to Mandy's house, with me shooting questions at her the whole way. Cindy'd shown up at five in the morning, just knocked on the door and there she was, standing on the porch, said she'd taken Greyhound from New York, said she didn't know where her baby was, it had been a boy and she'd left it in a train station where somebody would be sure to find it, said she'd done a bunch of things since then, in New York and Florida, wouldn't say what they'd been, but from the sound of it they hadn't been anything good. She hadn't been doing anything like what we'd imagined for her, that much was sure. "She's very thin," Mandy said, trying not to cry, "and she looks very tired, and she has a terrible cough. She wanted to know if I thought I could still love her. I told her, of *course*, Cindy, do you have any idea how much time I spent looking for you? And she said, but you didn't know I'd look like this, and then she asked me if I thought God could still love her."

God's too busy watching television, I thought, but I didn't say that. Antsy was the one watching television, and if there was a God, he probably didn't like Antsy any better than I did. So I just said, "She's home. She's home now. She's come home to get better. It's going to be all right, Mandy."

But when I saw her – lying in bed upstairs, with Mandy's oldest girl feeding her soup and the younger ones standing there looking scared – I knew it wasn't going to be all right, and that getting better wasn't what Cindy had come home for. She looked like the Christ hanging in that church, the same way I always pictured Hank looking in the jungle, the way my father had looked at the end: like somebody who's dying by inches and can't even think of what to hope for anymore, except for the pain to be over.

That was the beginning of the darkest time I've ever known. Mandy kept saying that Cindy was going to get better, she was, of course she was, she had to, and even when Cindy got worse instead, Mandy wouldn't take her to a doctor. I think she knew the truth, deep down, and was afraid to hear it from someone else. I was over there as much as I could, helping to take care of Cindy, but most of the time I'm not sure she knew where she was or who we were, or who she was herself. And finally even Mandy had to see that, and she took Cindy to the doctor and the doctor said Cindy should go into the hospital right away, right now, and Mandy said nonsense and took Cindy home again. And she screamed at me when I said the doctor was right. And in the meantime the girls had gotten more and more sullen and angry and confused, and the oldest one's boyfriend had gotten killed on his motorcycle, and the youngest one had started staying out way too late and getting bad grades in school. And it seemed to me like Mandy'd gotten her heart back only to have it broken again, for good this time, and maybe her mind too. I was afraid for her.

I was afraid for myself. A few days after Cindy came back I'd started having belly pains and the runs, and I told myself it was just the excitement, just worry and stress, it would get better in a little while. It didn't, though. It got a little worse each day, and each day I got a little more scared, because intestinal cancer was what had killed my father, and this was how it had started. I was afraid to go to the doctor and I was afraid not to go to the doctor, and I was too embarrassed to talk to anybody except Mandy about it. Too many times when I've been sick, even with a cold, people have blamed me for it, because I'm overweight. I don't know if those extra fifty pounds are my fault or not, but being sick isn't. Mandy knows that.

But I couldn't talk to Mandy, because she had too many problems of her own, and I knew she was counting on having me there, and how could I tell her I was afraid I might be going away too? Half the time she was so distracted she couldn't understand what you were saying even if it was about something simple, like buying milk. How could I tell her I was afraid I had cancer?

I couldn't. And if I couldn't talk to her I couldn't talk to anybody, and that hurt almost as much as my belly did. I lay awake for hours at night, worrying, and I looked worse and worse all the time, more and more exhausted, and nobody at Mandy's house even noticed. All of them were looking more and more exhausted too, and I guess it was silly of me to feel like they didn't care about me anymore, but that's how I felt anyway.

The morning after Mandy refused to put Cindy in the hospital, I woke up and thought, I'd better go to the doctor today. Don't ask why I decided to do it then: because Mandy's pig-headedness made me see my own, maybe, or because the pain had woken me up in the middle of the night – that had never happened before – or because there was so little hope left that what did it matter? I'd already decided I had cancer. What could the doctor say that would be any worse than that? He'd just be telling me what I already knew.

So I called the doctor's office and told them what was going on and made an emergency appointment – they were mad at me for making them find a space that day, you could tell – and I closed the store for a few hours and went over there. It was Dr. Gallingway, the same one who'd treated my father. I'd never much liked him, but he was the best doctor around for that kind of thing. The nurse came and asked me a bunch of questions and took a bunch of blood and had me get undressed and get into one of those ridiculous paper gowns, and then Dr. G. came in.

"You've let yourself go," he said, looking at me. "You used to be an attractive woman, Cece."

You see what I mean? No "hello, Cece, how are you, what are you doing these days?" Just an insult, and then he starts lecturing me on how I have to watch my diet, I'm ruining my health the way I live – as if he has any idea how I live when he hasn't even seen me for ten years – and I'm already at risk for cancer because of my family history. As if I didn't know that.

I just sat there and looked at him. Later I thought of lots of things I should have said – "You've let yourself go, Dr. Gallingway. You used to have manners. You used to have hair." – but naturally none of that occurred to me when it would have been useful. I just sat there feeling ashamed, and when he finally wound down I said, "Well, I guess the question's whether you want to make any money off my unhealthy lifestyle or not. Because if you don't stop talking to me that way I'm walking out of here."

Dr. Gallingway shut up, goggling at me like his stethoscope had just demanded a raise, and I swallowed hard and told him why I was there. When I was done he shook his head and said, "You shouldn't have waited so long to come in. First thing tomorrow morning I want you to go over to the hospital for an upper GI."

"Sounds like a soldier," I said. It was supposed to be a joke, even though when I said it I thought of Hank, dying in the jungle somewhere.

He didn't laugh. He looked at me and said, "It stands for *gastrointestinal*," a little more slowly than he'd been talking before.

"I know," I told him. You pronounce that very well, Dr. Gallingway.

How many years of medical school did it take for you to learn such a long word? I thought about saying that, I swear, but I'm glad I didn't. It was like Mandy's saying she wanted Genevieve to die: one of those mean things you'll probably regret later, when it's too late.

I remembered when my father had his upper GI. He'd called it Upper Guts, Inner, because he couldn't remember all those syllables. I teased him about it, on the way to the test. I think that was the last time Dad and I laughed about anything, because when they did the test they saw something growing in there, and they told me they had to keep him in the hospital and then they told me they had to operate and then they told me it was cancer. I drove home from Dr. Gallingway's office wishing I could just die in my sleep.

The upper GI was at eight in the morning in a room that looked like the inside of a rocketship, all metal and huge machines. I'm not a morning person, especially when I'm not allowed to have my coffee and donut, especially when I haven't gotten any sleep because I spent all night crying, and I never much liked science fiction movies. The last one I saw was *Alien*, and I didn't exactly want to think about that right now, with my own gut feeling just like something was about to come busting out of my belly. I sat there in another smock – cotton, this time, and at least they'd let me keep my underwear on – hoping the doctor who did the test wouldn't have too many tentacles and wouldn't look at me he like he thought I did. At least I'd never met him before, so he couldn't tell me I used to be an attractive woman.

When he came in I saw that he was real young and handsome, and wearing, I swear, a collar that made him look just like a priest. Later he told me that it was a lead shield to protect his neck from radiation, but when I first saw him it didn't incline me to be friendly. I hadn't been too impressed with doctors and priests lately, and here was somebody who looked like both.

He smiled at me and held out his hand and said, "Good morning, Ms. Yodel. I'm Dr. Stephenson," and I thought, well, at least he has manners. He asked me how I was feeling and I told him, and I told him about Dad, and I thought, well, here comes the lecture.

He didn't lecture me, though. He just looked serious and said, "I'm sorry. You must be very frightened," which made me feel better right away, because I hadn't been able to tell anybody about being scared, not even Mandy, and you'd think Dr. Gallingway could have said something nice like that, with all the money I was paying him, but of course he didn't. Then Dr. Stephenson said, "Your symptoms could be caused by a lot of other things, you know."

Well, I didn't know that. Dr. Gallingway sure hadn't bothered to say anything like that. So I decided I liked Dr. Stephenson, even if he did look like a priest. He knew his job was to make people feel better, not worse. You'd think every doctor would know that – and every priest, for that matter – but as far as I could tell, not too many of them had figured it out. It made the entire world seem a little bit friendlier, meeting someone like that. The way I felt then, it was almost worth having to have the upper GI.

"So what we're going to do," he said, "is have you drink a glass of this barium" – he held up this big paper cup of white stuff, looked like one of Mandy's vanilla milk shakes, with a big plastic straw in it – "and I'm going to watch it on the fluoroscope, this screen over here, as it travels down your esophagus into your stomach and your small intestines. The barium tastes chalky, kind of like Mylanta, and the test doesn't hurt. It's boring, more than anything, because it takes a long time. Sometimes I'll have you roll over onto your sides and onto your stomach, so I can see things more clearly on the screen, and during part of the test I'll have to press on your abdomen with that balloon paddle over there." He pointed at this weird plastic and rubber thing hanging on the wall, looked like a plastic tennis racket with a rubber middle, had a bulb dangling from it, like one of the ones they use to inflate blood pressure cuffs. "That's to make the barium move around to the places I want to look at. Do you have any questions, before we start?"

"Yes," I said. "Barium's radioactive, right? How do I get it out of me?" I was worried that even if the barium didn't find any cancer, it could cause cancer if it stayed in there.

He nodded and said, "It comes out the way anything else you eat comes out, and the barium's not all that radioactive, actually. After you leave here, make sure to drink a lot of fluids for the rest of the day, to flush the barium out of your system. Prune juice is good; it moves things along."

"How about coffee?" I said.

He laughed. "That's fine. That moves things along too."

The test wasn't bad, really. It was interesting even at the beginning, because I could look at the screen, so I could watch the barium traveling down my throat and into my stomach. It looked just like those pictures of the inside of the body you see in books, only in black and white. The barium was white in the cup, but on the screen the barium was black and my innards were white, like a negative.

Dr. Stephenson said my throat looked fine and my stomach looked fine, and we'd have to wait awhile for the barium to move through the small intestine. I should move around, he said. I'd have wanted to move around anyway, because it was cold in there. So he went away for a while and I walked around and read the labels on the machines and wondered how my father had felt, pacing in a little room like this, in the last minutes when he didn't know yet that something was growing in his gut.

So I'd gotten myself pretty scared again by the time Dr. Stephenson came back, especially since the pain was acting up. He took the balloon paddle off the wall and had me lie down again, and I craned my head back so I could see the screen, and he turned on the machine. And the face of Jesus stared out at me from the fluoroscope, just the same way he looked on that cross in Mandy's church, like *he* was in so much pain he could hardly stand it.

"Oh my God," I said. "Look at that!"

"What's wrong?" said Dr. Stephenson. He didn't act like he'd noticed anything, and I thought maybe I was crazy. When I looked at the screen again I could see that Jesus' face was made up of all the curls and folds of my gut, but it still looked like Jesus' face, with the thorny crown and everything. It was just like one of those pictures you see on the cover of the *National Enquirer*: Jesus in somebody's fingerprints, the Devil in somebody's cornflakes, Elvis everyplace. I always thought all that stuff was nonsense, even worse than Instant Miracle Cures, and here it was happening to me.

"Doesn't that," I said, "doesn't it look to you like, well, like a face?" I didn't want to say whose face. Dr. Stephenson would think I was a religious fanatic.

He cocked his head sideways and squinted at it and said, "Why, so it does. I see what you mean. Isn't that interesting. I'm going to press on your stomach with the balloon now, Ms. Yodel." And he did, and I watched Jesus' face kind of roll around on the screen. He must have been seasick in there. He looked about as green as I felt. And Dr. Stephenson worked away with his balloon and told me about how fluoroscope images are like Rorschach blots – you can see anything in them if you look hard enough. Once he did an upper GI on a little boy who swore he saw Big Bird.

The place where Dr. Stephenson was pressing now made Jesus' mouth open and close, like he was trying to say something. "Get me out of here," probably. And I wondered how he'd gotten in there to begin with and then I realized, of course: it was that stupid biscuit, the one I'd eaten by mistake when I went to church with Mandy. The pain had started right after that, come to think of it. So there must have been something to its being Christ's body, although if that was true I didn't see how Catholics walked around without bellyaches all the time. Maybe it didn't hurt, if you were Catholic. Maybe that's why you weren't supposed to eat the biscuit unless you were. I mean, you'd think they'd *tell* people something like that, honestly, there should be a Surgeon General's warning. Here I was, I'd been in pain for months, I'd thought I was dying, I was paying all this money for this upper GI – which wasn't cheap, believe me – and the whole time the problem was nothing but a piece of stale biscuit.

Well, I got pretty mad when I started thinking like that, let me tell you. I was fuming, by the time the test was over. Dr. Stephenson squeezed my hand and grinned at me and said, "I have good news for you, Ms. Yodel, I see no evidence of a Mass," and I just looked at him like he'd lost his mind.

"A mass," he said gently after a minute, "a lump, that means I don't see anything that could be cancer."

You're damn right there's no cancer, I thought, furious, and then I thought I'd had to drink this stuff that could cause cancer, maybe, to find out I didn't have any, and I got even madder. But none of that was Dr. Stephenson's fault and he'd been real nice to me, so I had to try to be polite. "Thank you," I said, "I'm very glad to hear that." And then I realized that must sound very cold to him, so I said, "You're a very nice man. Most doctors don't explain things as well as you did. Thank you," and that made him look happy and I felt a little better, about him, anyhow.

Not that I felt better about anything else. How was I going to get Jesus out of there? With prune juice? He'd been in there for months and plenty of other things had come out, but he hadn't. Who do you talk to about something like that? Any doctor would think I was crazy, and I couldn't see myself going to Father Antsy. He'd just tell me everyone should have Jesus inside them, and that's fine if you're a believer, but I didn't feel much more religious than I had before I ate the biscuit. Jesus hurt, and that's the truth, and I wanted my intestines back to myself. If it had been the Devil inside me, maybe a priest would have been some help. I wondered if Jesus could make your head turn all the way around, like Linda Blair's.

I thought about all of this when I was getting dressed and I walked through the hospital lobby still thinking about it, so mad I wasn't even looking where I was going, and I practically walked straight into Mandy.

"Cece!" she said, and grabbed me and started crying. She didn't even ask me what I was doing there, which shows you how upset she was. "Cece, I finally decided the doctor was right, Cindy's upstairs now, I brought her here two hours ago and went home to get her toothbrush because I'd forgotten it and I was just heading out the door again when they called me to say she's dying, she'll only last another few hours, and she knows it, too. She's asked for Father Anselm."

"She asked for *him*?" I said. We were already heading for the elevators. "Why in the world would she do that? He's the one who drove her away from here in the first place!"

"She wants last rites," Mandy said. "He's the only Catholic priest in town. It has to be him. Last rites are a formula: How badly can he do? She's dying and she wants forgiveness, Cece."

"She won't get it from him," I said. A wedding's a formula too, and we both knew what Antsy had done with that. "That man wouldn't forgive his own grandmother if she took too long crossing the street. He'd blame it on her sinful body." It's a good thing Mr. and Mrs. Mincing were in New Mexico, baking their joints, or Cindy probably would have wanted them there too. All three of those people should have been asking Cindy's forgiveness, as far as I was concerned, but I guess Cindy was too sick to see it that way. Or maybe if she'd been able to see it that way she wouldn't have wound up where she was in the first place.

It seemed like that elevator took forever to come, and when we finally got upstairs we found Cindy pretty much looking like a corpse already, lying there just barely able to blink with about five tubes in each arm, and old Antsy standing next to her bed, holding his Bible and yammering away. I don't know if he'd done the rites yet or not; he was halfway into a rip-roaring sermon, from what I could tell. "Cynthia Marie, let us pray that the Lord will see fit to wash clean your heinous sins," that kind of thing, as if the Lord might think about it and decide not to after all, with that poor woman dying and wanting just this one thing before she went. It made me crazy, and I guess the Jesus in my belly must have felt the same way, because my stomach started hurting something awful. I could just picture the little guy squirming around down there, just wishing he could set this idiot straight, and I decided I'd help him out.

"Oh, *shut up*," I said – exactly what I'd been wanting to say to that man for twenty years now, ever since the wedding – and Mandy actually giggled and Father Antsy glared at me like I'd just committed a really world-class sin. But my belly quieted down, so I figured Jesus approved. "You want to talk about heinous sins?" I asked Antsy. "Before you start in on Cindy's, why don't you think about your own?" He glared even harder when I said that, but I kept talking anyway. The Jesus in my belly must have given me confidence, or maybe I was a little loopy with being so tired. "Listen to yourself," I said. "When's the last time you said anything nice to anybody? I know all the things you hate, Father Anselm. You hate bodies and you hate TV and you hate people who make mistakes. Why don't you talk about what you love, for a change? Isn't that part of your job?"

"I love God," he said, looking down his long skinny nose at me, and my belly panged and I thought, *GI Jesus doesn't think so.*

"If you love God," I said – as if I was some kind of authority on God, what a joke! – "it seems to me you've got to love people too, since God's supposed to love them. I don't think you've gotten that part down yet. Why don't you practice? Tell Cindy something you love about her. Go on."

He looked down at her, down at the bed, and wrinkled that nose like Cindy was some piece of meat that had fallen behind the refrigerator and stayed there way too long, and he said in the coldest voice I've ever heard, a voice that would turn antifreeze into icicles, a voice that would give the Grinch nightmares, "God loves you, my daughter."

"And you don't?" Mandy said. She was shaking. "No, of course you don't. How could you? Get out of this room, Father Anselm."

Antsy got, in a hurry, and I gaped like an idiot. I'd never heard Mandy talk that way to anybody. Even when she wanted Genevieve to die, she never sounded like that. She practically had sparks coming out of her ears, she was so mad. At first I couldn't believe it and then I thought, well, why not? Here's the old Mandy who cares about people joining forces with the new Mandy, the one who sticks up for herself, and they make a pretty good pair after all, don't they? "Good for you," I said softly. I'd never been so proud of her.

She didn't answer, just went over to the bed and took one of Cindy's hands in hers and started rubbing it, and I went over too. Cindy just stared up at the ceiling. There was no way to tell if she'd even heard anything that had just happened, or if she'd hear anything we said now, but I knew I had to say something to her, because I'd never have another chance. And it occurred to me that I'd said a lot of things to Cindy, all those months she'd been at Mandy's house, but they'd always been about the present, not the past. "How are you feeling today, Cindy? Can I get you some water? Do you want another blanket?" I'd never said anything about how we'd all gotten to where we were, and I'd never told her anything about how I felt.

"I'm so sad you're so sick," I told her, and then, all in a rush, "it isn't fair, you know, it isn't, not one little bit. I know you think you're being punished for something, but what happened to you could have happened to just about any girl in this town, Cindy. It could have happened to me. I had a pregnancy scare when I was seventeen years old, I never even told Mandy that, and when she and Bill got married and I was standing up in front of the altar I felt just awful, because I wasn't any better than you were and by rights you should have been the one up there, if your mother and daddy hadn't been so mean about what had happened to you. I know Mandy thought so too, she did. I wanted to tell you all of that, but you left before I could. I don't blame you for leaving; I'd have done the same thing in your place. And whatever else you did, after you left, well, I'm not in any position to judge. All I can say is I wish you hadn't suffered so much, Cindy." We still didn't know much about what had happened to her, or where, but we'd seen things when we were taking care of her. Scars, from needles it looked like – and from other things too, things I didn't want to think about. It looked like people had hurt her, and not by accident either, and it looked like she'd tried to hurt herself. "You were just a little girl, Cindy, no worse than anybody else, and more than I wish anything I wish you hadn't had to go through your life thinking you were bad."

It was the truth, that's all. She hadn't so much as twitched the whole time I was talking, and I still couldn't tell if she'd heard a word I'd said. I bent and I kissed her forehead and I said, "God bless you, Cindy," because I knew she believed in God, even if I wasn't sure I did, and I knew she'd wanted some kind of blessing from Father Antsy and she hadn't gotten one. Mine probably wouldn't do her much good, but at least I'd tried. And when I straightened up from kissing her I realized that the pain in my belly was gone, completely gone, for the first time in months, and I thought, well, GI Jesus must have liked it, whether Cindy did or not.

Mandy hadn't said anything. She just stood there, holding Cindy's hand and looking at me, and I could see she was about to start crying again and I didn't think I could take it. "I'm going home now," I said, "so you can say your goodbyes in private. Call me – later. All right?"

She nodded, and I left. It wasn't even that I wanted to give her privacy, because I knew Mandy wouldn't have minded if I stayed, but it was just too sad in that room. Whenever I looked at Cindy I thought about my father, and Hank in the jungle, and that poor wooden Christ on his cross, and I just couldn't stand it, not after a sleepless night and no breakfast. I wouldn't have been any good to Mandy if I'd stayed, and I had things I had to do for myself. On my way home I bought a gallon of prune juice, and as soon as I got home I started drinking it. I didn't like the idea of that barium spending one more second sloshing around my insides than it absolutely had to.

I drank prune juice for the next two hours, and then I drank water for two hours after that, and nothing was happening except that I had to pee every two seconds. All that liquid was coming out, but the barium wasn't. I was starting to get pretty worried about it when the phone rang, and I thought, Oh, Lord, that'll be Mandy, crying her head off, and it was and she was. I kept saying over and over, "I'm so sorry, Mandy," and finally I realized that she was trying to say something herself.

"Cece, listen to me, it's not what you think, she's not dead, she's better."

"She can't be better," I said, as gently as I could, and I thought, well, it's over. Cindy's dead and Mandy's gone clean out of her mind, and now I'm going to have to bring up those four girls all by myself. And then I remembered that Mandy was religious, and I thought, maybe this is just church talk. Maybe she's trying to comfort herself. "You mean — she's in heaven now, Mandy?" It felt weird even saying the word, but if it helped her that was what counted. "With the — angels?" Like I said, I was really tired.

"*Angels?*" Mandy said. "I don't believe in angels any more than you do, Cece Yodel! I mean she's better, right here in the hospital, every bit as alive as I am!"

I nearly groaned. If Cindy was still alive that meant they'd put her on some kind of machine, and people could keep breathing for years on those things, sucking money into the hospital faster than a drowning man gulps seawater. "Mandy, I really truly don't think she'll ever be better — "

"But she *is*," Mandy said, babbling. "It's a miracle, that's all, that's the only word for it, she's so much better the doctors can't believe it, *they* say it's a miracle even, her fever's gone and she knows who I am and they did some blood tests and they're *normal* now, Cece, they were all haywire before and they've just gone back to plumb normal, Cece, I swear to God I'm not crazy and I'm not making this up — "

"I know you aren't," I said. All of a sudden I knew what had happened. "Mandy, honey, I can't tell you how happy I am and I'll be there just as soon as I can, but I have to go now, all right?"

I did, too. The prune juice was finally working. I rushed into the bathroom and got there just in time, and sat there, just being happy, while the prune juice did what it was supposed to do. So there, Father Antsy. Even Jesus needs a body to work miracles with, and he picked mine, how do you like that? I know religious people think pride is a sin and most of the time I agree with them, but this time I felt like I hadn't had anything to feel proud of in so long that maybe I deserved it, and anyway I was mainly happy for Mandy and Cindy. And I sat there thinking about miracles, and I thought, Well, GI Jesus, how about one more miracle, how about letting us know where Hank is?

How about bringing him home, happy and healthy?

I figured Jesus wouldn't have enough time for that, though, because he was probably on his way out of my body, now that Cindy was better. I wondered what he'd look like when he left, if maybe he'd look happy too, finally. When the juice had finished its work I looked down wondering if I'd see a tiny cross in there, or a little guy in a beard and loincloth, or what.

Well, that was just silliness, of course. What came out was white, whiter even than the barium had been when I drank it, white as freshly bleached sheets or new snow or any of the other things people talk about when they're trying to describe whiteness – so white it looked almost like it glowed, but maybe that's because it was radioactive, I don't know. It didn't look like anything to do with Jesus, though. It looked like a big fish, and then when I flushed and it was whirling around it changed shape and looked like a bird, and then it was gone. Which just goes to show you that Dr. Stephenson was right: if you look at a shape that isn't much like anything in particular, you can see anything you want.

So I had to laugh at myself, the way I'd given myself all those airs about pulling off a miracle. Oh, Cindy's been getting a little stronger every day since then: the next day she drank some Sprite and the day after that she sat up in bed and then she started going to the bathroom by herself and watching game shows and asking for cheeseburgers. She's coming home from the hospital tomorrow. So it sure looks like an Instant Miracle Cure, but even if it is, it probably has nothing to do with me or my intestines. Cindy just decided she wasn't ready to die, that's all – you hear stories about that all the time – or the blood tests were all wrong to begin with. You hear stories about that, too. So I'm still not going to say I'm religious. But I have been putting in a few prayers for Hank, just in case there's a God after all.